T0033278

Headland

Headland

JOHN BYRNES

ALLEN&UNWIN

SYDNEY · MELBOURNE · AUCKLAND · LONDON

First published in 2023

Copyright © John Byrnes 2023

All rights reserved. No part of this book may be reproduced or transmitted in any form or by any means, electronic or mechanical, including photocopying, recording or by any information storage and retrieval system, without prior permission in writing from the publisher. The Australian *Copyright Act 1968* (the Act) allows a maximum of one chapter or 10 per cent of this book, whichever is the greater, to be photocopied by any educational institution for its educational purposes provided that the educational institution (or body that administers it) has given a remuneration notice to the Copyright Agency (Australia) under the Act.

Allen & Unwin
Cammeraygal Country
83 Alexander Street
Crows Nest NSW 2065
Australia
Phone: (61 2) 8425 0100
Email: info@allenandunwin.com
Web: www.allenandunwin.com

Allen & Unwin acknowledges the Traditional Owners of the Country on which we live and work. We pay our respects to all Aboriginal and Torres Strait Islander Elders, past and present.

A catalogue record for this book is available from the National Library of Australia

ISBN 978 1 76106 761 7

Set in 13/18 pt Granjon by Midland Typesetters
Printed in Australia by McPherson's Printing Group

10 9 8 7 6 5 4 3 2 1

The paper in this book is FSC® certified. FSC® promotes environmentally responsible, socially beneficial and economically viable management of the world's forests.

For Nanny and Poppy

1

A cold, fat drop of rain slapped onto the back of Craig Watson's neck and rolled down his spine. He shivered, hunched his shoulders, and tried to soak the icy rivulet into his shirt before it made its way any further down. He clenched his cheeks just in case.

'Miserable' was how the weatherman had summed it up. Cold and wet, raining for a week.

He'd only just arrived: tired, anxious, and absolutely gagging for the sweet relief of a toilet after three hours behind the wheel and four foul service station coffees. The rain was coming down hard and had done for the last two hours of the trip. His eyes were stinging, and his back was aching. The town looked worse than he'd expected—and he hadn't been expecting much.

Gloster was the end of the road, where a sluggish inland river met the sea. One bridge in and one road out, a towering headland looming over one main street, tired, cracked and weedy, shut up shops and peeling paint. The few locals he'd seen out braving the rain looked like survivors from a shipwreck.

The car park at the rear of the Gloster police station was a muddy, potholed wrecker's yard. Half-a-dozen smashed-up hulks lined a sagging, gap-toothed fence, old yellow police tape streaming in the wind. A mud-spattered police vehicle was pulled up hard against the back door, a large, land-locked boat taking up most of the other parking spaces.

Watson had chosen a spot as close to the rear door as possible—next to a sporty little hatchback with a My Family sticker on the rear windshield showing two netballers and a cat. The sign over the parking space read: VISITORS ONLY.

Wishful thinking.

He dodged a couple of big puddles and knocked hard on the rear door of the station, checking the handle with his other hand. To his surprise the door was unlocked. He shouldered it open and stood steaming in a dimly lit kitchen. Watching his entry, wide-eyed with surprise, was the most overweight copper Watson had ever laid eyes on. He was wearing sergeant's stripes and polishing off the remains of what appeared to be a leftover butter chicken by running a thick, margarine-soaked piece of white bread through a takeaway container.

The sergeant nodded at Watson, both cheeks ballooning, too full to speak. When he'd got most of the mouthful down, he muttered something incoherent, stuffed the rest of the bread into his mouth, binned the container and motioned for Watson to follow him.

'Sergeant Thomas Philby,' he said as he slumped into a well-worn seat. He was grey-haired, late fifties, had the flushed cheeks of a heavy drinker, maybe diabetes. The small, disorganised office smelt of BO, dirty socks and quiet desperation—or maybe that was just the sergeant. He wiped his right hand on his pants then offered it to Watson.

'Detective Senior Constable Craig Watson,' Watson said, shaking it. 'Look, Sarge, if you don't mind, I've really got to go.'

'Oh yeah, of course,' Philby said. 'Just across the hall.'

The station was fifty years old. The toilets were the originals, chipped tiles, bloody freezing. Watson zipped up and exhaled a long foggy breath, his back teeth swimming.

The mirror had a corner missing and was covered in dark spots. Watson moved his face around, making sure he hadn't contracted measles on the trip. His black-brown eyes were red-ringed and surrounded by tiny broken capillaries. He hadn't bothered shaving. He looked every single day of his twenty-four years.

Not too bad. Considering.

He splashed some icy tap water onto his face, dried himself with a paper towel, and combed his wet, black hair with his fingers. Then he took a packet of pills from his inside suit jacket pocket, dropped one onto his palm and swallowed it.

He stood there for a minute, staring down at the sink, avoiding his own eyes, until he felt the warm opiate glow snake its way out of his belly.

———

As he re-entered the sergeant's office, Philby spun around in his chair, grabbed a file from a chaotic pile stacked on a metal cabinet and slapped it down on his desk. Movement of the file disturbed the computer mouse sitting on his desk. Watson caught a flash of pink flesh reflected on the window behind the sergeant. Philby grabbed at the mouse and quickly switched screens.

'So, all squared away?' he asked. 'You must have had an early start.'

'Yeah, all good,' Watson said, cruising now, comfortably numb. 'Got away just after five.'

He caught a quick flicker in the other man's eyes at this and realised what he must be thinking: it was a three-hour drive, and it was just after nine thirty now.

Watson had spent the night before leaving for Gloster alone in his Sydney apartment. Sitting in the dark, streaming videos and mixing things he shouldn't be mixing. His phone didn't ring; there were no messages on his pathetic attempt at an Instagram account. When the alarm sounded at 5 a.m., he'd switched it off and stayed in bed for another hour, trying to summon the impetus to move.

'Ah. Well, there's been plenty of weather, hasn't there?' Philby said, unsure.

'Yep.' Watson stifled a yawn.

Philby turned his attention to the file, shuffling pages till he found the one he wanted. He tapped it with a pen. 'Says here you'll be joining us for six months, while Alan Bishop is, er, convalescing.' He seemed to struggle with the word.

'Yep, that's the situation,' Watson agreed, without enthusiasm.

Philby blinked. 'He's a good man, Alan. Well respected. Big pair of shoes to fill.'

Watson wondered who he was trying to convince. If Bishop was any good, what the hell was he doing here?

'Yeah, so I've heard. Very highly regarded.'

'Yes, and it's left us short-staffed here, as you've probably heard.'

Watson had heard nothing. 'Be there Monday' was the start and the end of his parting brief.

'But we've managed to keep on top of most of Alan's cases. You'll find Arthur and Martha know what they're doing, if you keep on the right side of them.' He went for what Watson presumed was a conspiratorial smile—either that or the man had developed a nervous tic.

Watson was doing his best to stay upright in his chair.

Philby glanced down at the file again, flicked a couple of pages, and then slowly closed the cover. When he looked up his jowly cheeks had taken on a rosy glow. His expression said that Watson might hold the last piece to a particularly vexing jigsaw puzzle he had been labouring over for the past twenty years.

'Look, I know it's not much of a posting here,' he said, consoling. 'It's a quiet little town. We get the odd domestic, a punch-up at the pub on Saturday night, and some of the kids are ratbags, but it's nice and quiet, and we like to keep it that way. Are you hearing me?'

'Loud and clear, Sarge,' Watson said, doing his best.

Philby frowned. 'Right. Well, come with me and I'll introduce you to the boys.'

Watson followed a gasping and heaving Philby up a creaking internal staircase.

'You'll be in here,' Philby wheezed.

The second floor was one large open-plan room. Dirty yellow neon and dark carpet gave the place a depressing sheen. The room was separated into individual cubicles by moveable partitions. A bank of windows on the far wall let in what there was of the grey, drizzling, natural light.

Muffled conversation and soft music came from the cubicles at the far end of the room. Philby cleared his throat, and the murmuring ceased. Philby stopped short and stood with arms folded while Watson continued the extra two steps to the open-ended workstations at the back of the room.

'The boys'? What a fuckhead!

'Senior Constable Ellie Cameron, this is Detective Senior Constable Craig Watson,' Philby announced formally from his position two metres to the rear.

Watson held out his hand to a smallish, triathlete-fit young woman who stood and took the proffered hand in a firm, cool grip. Her auburn hair was tied back, regulation perfect, and she wore no make-up. Her features were handsome rather than feminine, which, Watson guessed, was exactly the effect she was going for.

'How are you?' Ellie asked, her voice cool.

'Yeah, not bad,' Watson replied. He switched his attention to the other constable, who had risen to stand beside Ellie.

'Constable Larissa Brookes,' Philby announced. If he was going to add to the introduction, he was stopped short by a glare from Ellie.

'Ah, your shifts and the casework will be on the usual drives. Senior Constable Cameron here will help you get set up. Let me know if you need anything,' Philby said as he walked backwards to the door, turned and exited.

'Larissa,' Brookes said, smiling as she held out her hand. She was taller than Ellie, and it didn't look like she had ironed that morning. Long dark hair piled up on the back of her head, brown eyes, a smooth olive complexion. She could easily pass for a relative of mine, Watson realised, and wondered randomly whether she thought the same.

'Craig,' he said, pasting on a smile.

They all took a moment.

'So, how long are you here?' Ellie asked, before it became uncomfortable. She was still glaring towards the doorway, as if Philby had left something distasteful in the air.

'Six months,' Watson replied, distracted by Larissa's still-smiling face.

Ellie took a proprietary step closer to the other woman then said, 'You'll be over here.' She motioned for Watson to follow her to the end cubicle, opposite hers, on the other side of the room.

Ellie spent a good twenty minutes running him through passwords, logins, files and the other administrative complexities of operating out of a new environment. She was patient, friendly and thorough. Watson started to relax.

'Did he tell you about the flood watch?' Ellie asked, gesturing towards the door through which Philby had exited.

She can't even say his name.

'Not a word.'

'Typical,' she said, shaking her head. 'We've had six days of continuous rain here and up in the hills out to the west. The council and the SES have implemented a flood watch. There's a monitoring station down at the main bridge. He really hasn't told you any of this?'

'Nope.'

'We take it in turns, one day each: us, the council rangers and the SES guys. Whoever's turn it is has to go and check the river gauge every four hours and report it to Emergency Services headquarters.'

Larissa, listening in from her workstation on the other side of the room added, 'It's such a pain.'

'So up till now it's just been the two of us,' Ellie said, looking across at Larissa. 'Every third day, one of us has had to be checking the gauge every four hours.' Her gaze shifted to the centre of Watson's forehead. 'So, you will be expected to pull your weight.'

They were of equal rank, but as a detective he could easily have begged off, claiming that his time would be taken up with more important duties, but if Ellie Cameron was expecting a pissing contest, she had picked the wrong man.

'Whatever,' he said. 'You organise the roster and I'll be there.'

Ellie and Larissa exchanged a covert glance. Before Ellie could continue, the internal line began to ring. Larissa answered it, listened, hung up.

'You're wanted down at the front desk,' she called to Watson. 'A Mrs Howard. Apparently, her daughter has gone missing.' She smiled at him. 'Welcome to Gloster,' she said.

2

He took his time.

Fuck me, I've only been here five minutes.

He made himself a cup of coffee down in the kitchen, and carried it out to the front reception. There he politely introduced himself to the middle-aged civilian receptionist, who in turn introduced him to Jenny Howard and her son, Shaun.

The former was clearly a nervous wreck, fidgeting, her eyes raw and red. Her thin, mousy-brown hair pulled back tight behind her ears. The son was a poster child for sullen youth. Fourteen or fifteen, a festering spread of acne, and an attitude as dour as his mop of greasy hair.

Watson guided the pair into an interview room off to the side of reception. It was cold and dim, the low wattage, cost-effective bulb doing little to cut through the gloom. Mother and son both reeked of stale cigarettes and damp carpet.

Watson started with the formalities required for a standard missing person's report.

'Your daughter's name?'

'It's Tayla. Tayla Louise Howard. She's only just turned sixteen,' Jenny said, barely holding it together.

'Describe her for me.'

'About my height, maybe a little taller now, brown hair, just down below her shoulders, brown eyes, pretty, slim.'

Watson wrote directly onto the form. Didn't look up.

'And you haven't seen her since last night?'

'Tayla's never stayed out all night,' Jenny insisted. 'Never.'

'But it wasn't unusual for her to be out late on a Sunday evening?'

'Well, no,' Jenny said. 'She goes around to friends' places; they've always got something on, you know?'

'Not unusual,' Watson murmured aloud as he wrote it on the form. Stifling a yawn, he moved to the next question. 'Have there been any obvious changes to Tayla's demeanour, or any traumatic events in her life recently?' he asked, going down the list.

'Oh, for God's sake,' Jenny said, folding her arms.

Shaun's first input was to roll his eyes and shake his head at Watson's cluelessness.

'The accident,' Jenny snapped. 'Where have you been? The moon?'

Shaun snorted.

'I only got into town'—Watson checked his watch—'an hour ago. What accident?'

'Tayla's best friend, Laura—Laura Sweeney—and her father, out on the highway, two weeks ago. Surely, you've heard?'

He had heard about a double fatality on some no-name country road, hard not to really, but he had no idea where it had occurred.

'The accident. Yes. So that was Tayla's best friend and her friend's father?' He was writing it down as he spoke.

'We were all shattered by it, the whole town.' Jenny had gone back to fidgeting. Shaun was picking his nose.

'Well, it's not uncommon for people—young people, especially—to need some time alone after a tragedy like that,' Watson said, 'and she's been gone less than twenty-four hours. So, what we'll do for now is issue a description to all our local patrols and the Local Area Command to keep an eye out for Tayla.' He turned to address the boy. 'Shaun, can you speak to your friends, and Tayla's friends at school, and ask if they've seen her?'

Shaun looked at Watson as if he were speaking a foreign language. Jenny nudged her son in the ribs with her elbow.

'Yeah,' Shaun mumbled.

Watson kept his gaze trained on the teenager. 'Shaun, is there anything you know about your sister that might help us to locate her? Any preferred hiding places or places she likes to go to be by herself?'

Shaun scowled. 'No idea.'

Watson looked hard at the boy. There was something not quite right. Maybe he should spend some time establishing rapport, building trust with the kid.

But it's his sister and he doesn't seem to give a shit.

'Look, Mrs Howard—Jenny—like I said, it's not uncommon for young people, teenage girls especially, to take off for a few days. They might be punishing you for something, or it might be a cry for help—there's a thousand different reasons—but nine times out of ten they're back within a couple of days, so try not to worry yourself too much, okay?'

Watson walked them to the door with a reassuring word, a hand on the shoulder. Astounded at his own capacity for bullshit.

3

Watson was a city boy through and through, used to round-the-clock conveniences. Thai takeaway at 2 a.m. A twenty-four-hour gym membership that he never used. Dealers on tap. Standing outside the Gloster Galleria on Tuesday morning, after a night staring at the blank walls of the fibro shack that was to be his home for the next six months, he thought: *What the fuck is this place?*

The Galleria was a good ten years past its use-by date. Peeling white paint, fly-specked cobwebs in every damp corner, cigarette butts and chewing gum underfoot—even the graffiti looked second-rate. Like the rest of Gloster, it looked tired; sick of the effort required to keep its head above the river rising slowly just on the edge of town.

The automated entry doors stood defiantly shut, daring him to keep coming, and Watson was just at the point of shortening his stride when, with a shudder and an asthmatic wheeze, they begrudgingly allowed him entry.

Eighties elevator music and the tang of cheap disinfectant welcomed him inside. He strolled quickly past a bank, a building society, a discount shoe shop and a newsagent. All quiet, all bereft of customers. At the end of the arcade he looked both ways. Right would take him to a sad-looking food court, left to a dozen or so retail stores heading inexorably towards liquidation. He turned left.

His eyes scanned slowly left, then right, observing the score of witty closing-down-sale signs—SORRY FOR THE INCONTINENCE and END OF THE WORLD—without a hint of amusement.

Near the end of the arcade stood Madeleine's Crystal Emporium. *A New Age Romance* was the underwhelming marketing pitch. Watson removed his police notebook from his inside jacket pocket, and followed the distinctive odour of patchouli oil and incense into the store. It was crowded to overflowing with trinkets, cheap silver jewellery, rocks and crystals, and posters of wizards, and wolves howling under a full moon.

There was a hard-faced, prematurely greying woman behind a long glass-topped counter to the right of the entrance. If looks could kill, Watson would have bled out before he got through the door.

Oh, here we go.

Her lips were puckered with the creases of a long-term smoker. They were bloodless, angry and ready for action.

'Took ya bloody time, didn't ya,' the woman barked, crossing her skinny, heavily bangled arms.

'Dawn Russell?' Watson enquired blankly, stopping short of the counter and checking his notebook for the quickly scribbled details.

'Two bloody days ago. Two bloody days I've been waiting for you lot.'

14

Watson remained calm, looking down at his pad for an extra second or two, fighting the urge to turn around and walk out again. Finally, he raised his tired eyes to meet hers, then shifted his gaze deeper into the shop, before looking over his shoulder. Not a customer in sight.

'Yeah, I can see you've been busy,' he said. 'And it's been one day. One.'

Dawn's nostrils flared, but before she could argue Watson continued, 'I'm Detective Senior Constable Watson. This is my second day here. There's been a lot to catch up on. Why don't you tell me what I can do for you?'

Her eyes flashed brilliant, just for a moment, before she slumped, deflated, defeated.

'Kids: bloody schoolkids,' she managed. 'Good-for-nothing, rotten little bastards.'

'Shoplifting,' Watson prompted, searching for a pen in his shirt pocket, flicking to the page in his notebook with the relevant facts. 'Crystals?' he read aloud.

'Amethyst, like I told the girl at the station when I reported it. Amethyst earrings and necklaces. I've only had 'em in a week, and the little bastards have almost cleaned me out. The most expensive things in the bloody shop. It's hard enough –'

'Show me,' Watson interrupted, looking up from his pad.

Dawn leaned over to retrieve a felt-lined display board from the glass cabinet doubling as the shop's counter, and slapped it down in front of Watson. There were six, sharp-edged, purplish-coloured stones attached to a selection of silver and gold chains. There was space for another half-dozen.

'There. Six of them. Gone, just like that. Do you know how much that's gonna cost me?' She pointed to the price tag on the top of the board; it read $69.95.

Watson didn't for a second consider doing the maths.

'And you said you know who is responsible for the theft?' he asked, going back to his notes.

'Of course I bloody well know. It's not like I get mown down in the rush here all day, is it? The little mongrels come in yesterday afternoon. A pack of 'em. Two of them ask to look at the earrings in the display at the back while the others helped themselves up here.'

'Right,' Watson said, his pen poised. 'So you didn't actually see them take anything?'

She bristled. 'It's not half fucking obvious, is it? Christ, I leave the counter for five minutes and they've cleaned me out. Who else –'

'So, you know them?' Watson interjected.

'Of course I bloody well know them. I'll give you their bloody names.'

'Yeah, that'd be handy.'

'It was Jenny Howard's useless bloody kids that did it: Shaun and what's her name.'

'The Howards? Are you sure?'

'Yeah, of course I'm sure. I've known their mother all me life, haven't I?'

'Shaun and Tayla Howard were here? What time was that?'

'Just after lunch, about one.' She looked a bit nervous now, a bit unsure of herself.

'About one?'

'Yeah, nah, about one thirty. I remember I closed up for a little while. My show finishes at one, so I was open again at quarter past, and they came in just after that.'

Watson took a moment, tapping his pen on his pad.

16

'Look, it's unlikely we'll be able to take any action unless we actually find them in possession of the merchandise. I'll just take a couple of quick photos of these ones.' He replaced his notebook in his pocket and pulled out his phone.

As he snapped some photos of the remaining necklaces his phone buzzed with an incoming text message. He checked the quality of the photographs then clicked on his messages.

You can run but you can't hide ya maggot.

He didn't hear a word Dawn said as he turned and walked out of the shop.

———

Watson drove straight past the station, heading for the McDonald's drive-through, the only piece of landscaped garden in the entire town, and the one place he could get a hot coffee without getting soaked to the skin. His second day in Gloster, and he was already actively avoiding the workplace.

When he reached for his wallet to pay for his coffee, he felt his phone lying heavy in his pocket. *You can run but you can't hide ya maggot.* It wasn't the first one he had received.

What the fuck?

He drove on to the station, parking in the visitor's spot again. Philby's door was closed when he hurried inside out of the rain. Unbelievably, it seemed to be raining even harder than it had been the day before. He ran his fingers through his wet hair as he bounded up the stairs two at a time, careful not to let his McCappuccino spurt out the little hole in the lid.

When he entered the squad room, Ellie eyed the hot coffee pointedly. 'No, we're right, thanks, Craig—we'll just stick with the instant,' she said without a trace of sarcasm.

He frowned. 'What? Oh, the coffee. Sorry. Didn't think. Listen, the Howard kid, Shaun, he lied to me.'

As Larissa joined them in Ellie's cubicle, he described his meeting at Madeleine's Crystal Emporium. Jenny Howard had reported Tayla missing at 10.30 on Monday morning and Shaun had been adamant that he had no idea where she was, only to be busily shoplifting with her at the Galleria three hours later.

'Well Jenny Howard rang first thing this morning for an update,' Ellie said. 'Tayla still hasn't been seen.'

'Have you got a contact at the school?' he asked. 'I need to speak to that little prick Shaun again.'

'Yeah, we've got one,' Larissa said. He thought he caught a look pass between the two women. 'Why don't I give her a call then take you over there?' she suggested. 'I wouldn't mind getting out of here for a while.'

———

Caroline Harper was one of the youngest senior school principals in the state, Larissa explained in the car on the way to Gloster High. She had put a bad marriage behind her and focused hard on her career, leaving most of her peers and a lot of professional jealousy in her wake. At thirty-eight, she exuded an air of sophistication and unbridled determination that would have earned her universal respect as a man but being a woman it only earned her a reputation as a ball-breaking bitch.

'What's she really like?' Watson asked.

'She's different,' Larissa said, giving him a long sideways look. 'I'll let you work her out for yourself.'

After two days of working with her, Watson had determined that the happy look on Larissa's face was simply her natural expression. Intentional or not, you couldn't help but respond with a smile. It had that effect on Watson, anyway, and it seemed to have the same effect on Caroline Harper, who, Watson sensed immediately, didn't smile much at all.

'So, the new man in town, huh?' Caroline said after the formal introductions were made.

'He's covering for Alan Bishop,' Larissa added helpfully, glancing at Watson.

Caroline unselfconsciously tucked the side of her highlighted bob behind her left ear, exposing a heavy golden teardrop earring.

Watson's breath caught involuntarily.

He was eighteen again. Saw her watching them from the shadows of the corridor outside Alison's bedroom door. Alison Fuller's mother.

He met Alison at the local pub on his first leave home from the police academy. On their second night together, she invited him back to her place and led him straight to her room. They were lying on her bed, the door still open, taking things nice and slow. Touching, caressing, kissing. Talking occasionally, fizzing with excitement and anticipation. Alison helped him pull his shirt over his head. He was super fit back then, toned and tanned. He caught a flicker of movement outside the door and was about to say something, but Alison was insistent, holding him with her eyes, her hands on the back of his neck. Then he saw her in the doorway—a woman who could only be Alison's mother. Her eyes flashing. A crooked smile. A finger raised to her lips and then slowly sliding down, into the darkness below.

'I've sent a message down to Shaun Howard's classroom,' Caroline said. 'He should be with us shortly. I understand this is in relation to Shaun's sister, Tayla—is that correct?'

'Ah . . . yes. Yes, it is.'

Caroline cocked an eyebrow.

Focus, man. Focus.

'I spoke to him yesterday about Tayla's whereabouts,' Watson explained, 'and I don't think he was as forthcoming as he could have been.'

There was a knock at the door and Caroline stood to open it. Shaun Howard took a step forward, and then froze when he saw Watson and Larissa seated inside.

'Come in, Shaun,' Caroline ordered. 'These police officers are here to talk with you about your sister.'

Shaun's eyes darted from Larissa to Watson to Caroline and back to Larissa before he cautiously entered with his arms crossed.

'Sit there,' Caroline said, indicating a vacant chair in front of her desk. 'I am going to leave you here with Senior Constable Watson and Constable Brookes, but you can come and get me if you think you need me, okay?'

Shaun slumped into the chair without speaking or making eye contact.

Caroline closed the door softly on her way out.

Watson started in on the questions immediately before the atmosphere had a chance to thicken.

'Now, Shaun, you will recall we had a chat yesterday morning, around ten thirty, when you and your mother reported your sister, Tayla, missing?'

Shaun grunted.

Watson leaned in. 'You need to answer me, Shaun. I'm not playing games here.'

Shaun met his gaze for a millisecond then he glanced away, his lip curled.

'Yes,' he said, petulantly.

'And when we spoke you said you hadn't seen your sister and you didn't know where she was.'

'Yeah, so?'

'Well, I've just been speaking to the owner of the crystal shop in the Galleria, and she tells me that you and Tayla were in there yesterday afternoon.'

Shaun unfolded his arms, and placed his hands on the arms of his chair as if he was about to get up to leave.

'Sit the fuck down,' Watson whispered, inches from the boy's face. He felt Larissa's hand brush the back of his shirt.

Shaun chanced another quick glimpse into Watson's eyes and what he saw there immediately brought tears.

'So, what's going on Shaun?' Watson said, sitting back in his seat.

Shaun sniffed and wiped away a tear with his shirtsleeve. 'I was there, but I didn't fucking steal anything, all right?'

'Tayla, Shaun,' Watson said impatiently. 'What's going on with Tayla?'

'I dunno.' He shrugged. 'She just said she needed money and it's easy to get stuff from the crystal shop. She's done it before— nicked jewellery from there and then sold it.'

'Why did she need money?'

He shrugged again. 'To get out of here. Can you blame her?'

———

'I don't like what you did back there with Shaun,' Larissa said.

Watson glanced over at her in the passenger seat. For the first time since they had met, Larissa's habitual happy expression had darkened.

'Yeah, well, sometimes you just gotta do what you gotta do,' he said.

She shook her head and mumbled something that could have been 'Fuckhead.'

'Coffee?' he said.

She didn't respond.

'Coffee?' he said again.

She shook her head, resigned. 'Yeah, why not. Better get Ellie one as well.'

He detoured via the drive-through on the way back to the station.

'So, what was going on with you and Caroline?' Larissa asked when she had her coffee in her hand. 'You looked like you'd seen a ghost.'

'Oh yeah, she just reminded me of someone, that's all.'

'Oh yeah?' She cracked a faint smile, her demeanour softening for the first time since they'd left the school. 'Someone?' She rolled the word around in her mouth like she was tasting it.

Lying on the bed in Alison's room, he had closed his eyes. Deliberately didn't look. Indulged himself in Alison's skin, her flesh, her tongue, her hot breath in his mouth. He was growing hotter, harder. He felt it building, creeping closer, sensation peaking. He chanced a look. The hallway was dark. Empty.

'Yeah, a woman I used to know.'

'A strong and powerful woman, was it?' she said, clearly enjoying herself now.

'Oh, you bet,' he said.

4

They spent the afternoon writing up formal statements and records of interview. They inventoried three amethyst necklaces that they had recovered from tearful schoolgirls who admitted to paying Tayla between ten and twenty dollars for them. As for Tayla's current whereabouts, none of them had a clue. As expected, she had definitely seemed to be struggling since she lost her best friend, Laura, in a car accident two weeks earlier.

Shaun, meanwhile, had been considerably more forthcoming. There was a boy on the scene, maybe, who might have been Laura's boyfriend, but he couldn't be sure because Tayla had been secretive about it. Maybe the boy lived in the caravan park; someone had seen Laura and Tayla there late one night. There might have been a shack or an abandoned hut up on the headland, where kids went to smoke and get pissed and have sex. Tayla might be there. Maybe it was all worth checking out. Or not.

But it's all going to have to wait until tomorrow, Watson decided, *because I'm fucked.*

'Tomorrow it's our turn again on the monitoring,' Ellie reminded him when she noticed him packing up. 'I'll do the first one, at four a.m., then you meet Larissa there at eight and she'll show you the routine. The schedules are on your email.'

It was already dark outside; reception was shut and most of the lights were off downstairs. Philby hadn't been in the office since Watson and Larissa returned from the school, but he still knocked and waited a second before he opened the sergeant's door. The wind had picked up and the rain was battering the window behind Philby's desk. The room was lit in a blue neon glow from the screensaver. When Watson dropped the files onto the desk and turned to leave, the room immediately brightened as the monitor came to life and revealed the stark image of a young girl.

She was young, no more than fifteen or sixteen at best. Her petite breasts and shaved crotch were paler than the rest of her thin-hipped torso, the telltale lines of a bikini tan. Her skinny arms and shapeless legs were spread wide and tied to a cheap wooden bed frame with scraps of coloured material. The shadow of the amateur hour photographer had fallen partially over the girl's bound legs, but it was the eyes that caught his attention. Distant, trying for an expression that the young girl had neither the experience nor the maturity to pull off, her attempt at sultry coming off sad, and used, and dirty.

His head pulsed. His nails bit hard into his palms. He held back a dry-heave.

He heard footsteps clumping down the stairs outside the office. Ellie and Larissa rounded the corner into the corridor together just as he shut the office door.

'We usually just leave the summaries in a tray at reception,' Ellie said. 'Never know what you'll catch going in there.'

25

Larissa laughed.

He was glad it was dark.

———

The two women pulled the hoods of their heavy-duty water-proof coats over their heads and ran screaming across the car park together to the little hatchback. He stood at the door of the station waiting for any sign of a temporary easing in the torrent. His clothes were already beginning to take on the sour pong of perpetual damp.

Fuck it. He just went.

The Surfside Hotel had a drive-through bottle shop; he had spotted it the morning before as he passed through town. He had to lean forward and peer hard at the kerb to determine where the driveway into the bottle shop met the road. The gutters were swollen with running water, and the wipers could hardly keep pace with the pelting rain.

'What can I do for you, mate?' the driveway attendant asked as he pulled to a stop.

'Bottle of Jack and a large bottle of Coke.'

He could see into the public bar from his car. Philby was clearly visible, wearing the standard cop's disguise of an old windcheater pulled over his uniform shirt. He appeared to be well oiled.

Watson paid for his drinks and drove back out into the rain.

———

The barracks they called it. Every country station had one. Gloster's version was a two-bedroom fibro shack that pre-dated the 1950s. He pulled into the sagging carport and made a dash for the front door.

He dumped his bottles on the worn Formica table in the kitchen, grabbed a glass that he had left drying by the sink, cracked the Jack Daniels and poured himself a big one. He swallowed and gagged, topped it up and did it again.

The interior of the house was painted a pale green that managed to make it seem colder inside than out. Most of the rooms had patches of mould on the ceiling as the rain and the damp made its way through the old tiles into the roof space. The bathroom walls were cheap painted fibro, and were decorated with dark festering mildew. Watson eyed it with distaste as he stood, fully clothed and shivering, waiting for the hot water to eventually make its way up to the showerhead.

He had left the inadequate two-bar heater on to suck some of the wet chill out of the air, and by the time he hit the lounge chair with his bottles and glass, dressed in as many layers of clothes as he could get on, the room was bearably warm.

He flicked around the TV stations: cop shows, reality TV, nightly news updates. He drank quickly, feeling the edges soften and the cracks crack open. He didn't bother with the Coke after his fifth or sixth strong one. He sat, trembling lightly, and then reached for the pipe sitting on the small coffee table beside him.

It was loaded, ready to go, a small crystalline rock in a glass bowl. He leant forward, shaking with anticipation. Sweating as he held the pipe to his lips and put flame to it. He sucked in the hot, acrid chemical fumes. Once, twice: sucking it back, holding it in.

He had seen Alison every day of that first four-day leave. They were more in lust than in love—at least that's how he saw it then.

They couldn't be alone together more than five minutes before they were literally tearing each other's clothes off. Hungry for each other. Biting, licking, tasting.

He dropped the pipe onto his lap. Euphoric. Majestic. His head back, swimming with sheer ecstasy.

He shook himself alive twenty minutes later and reached for the bottle. He took a long, hot slug, holding it in his mouth before swallowing. Gritted his teeth.

There was a spark in Alison's eyes when she made the introductions. 'This is my mother, Andrea.'

Andrea grinned at him, made him feel guilty. She was thirty-seven but could have passed for younger. Climbing her way up the ladder in the snake pit of local council politics. Doing very well by all accounts. Well-maintained figure, immaculate bobbed hair, expensive tailored suit, tanned, vicious.

He loaded the pipe again and sat back. The walls were closing in, the TV had gone fuzzy. Lightning was flashing through the room. He was sweating. He turned off the heater and pulled off the windcheater and the t-shirts. Sat back again, gasping. Grinding.

The text had come from Alison but she wasn't home when he got there. The door was answered by Andrea, who was dressed for business. Solid gold teardrops hanging from her ears, a cream silk blouse, a tailored skirt that revealed long, tanned legs, gold heels.

'Come in, Craig,' Andrea said. 'Alison has had to step out but I need to have a word with you anyway.' She led him to the large

hard sofa where he and Alison had made furious love the night before. 'Sit,' she commanded.

He sat.

She stood over him, a hand on her hip. 'Just who do you think you are, Craig?'

He just stared at her stunned, speechless.

'I said, who do you think you are Craig?' Louder this time, baring her teeth.

'What?' He gaped at her. 'What are you talking about?'

'Do you really think you are good enough?' Her eyes were ablaze.

'What?'

She slapped him, hard, across the face.

He grabbed at the half-empty bottle and held it to his lips, the liquid spilling down his chin as he swallowed. He lurched to his feet, grunting, and stumbled to the bathroom. He grabbed at his soggy suit pants, still lying discarded on the floor. Pulled his heavy buckled belt out through the loops. Held onto the walls as he staggered back to the lounge. Pulled his track pants off before dropping into the chair. He picked up the pipe. Fired up the lighter. Sucked back another cone of fire. He was hard.

His hand went up to his stinging cheek. 'What the fuck?'

She leant forward. 'I said: Do—you—think—you—are—fucking—good—enough, Craig?' Spittle landed on his cheek with every word.

'I don't know what you mean.' But he said it without conviction; he felt things starting to slip. What did she know?

She grabbed his hair and yanked his head back. 'You heard me,' she growled. 'Do you think you are good enough, Craig?'

It came with a surge of relief like nothing he had ever felt before, like a huge weight was lifted from his shoulders. 'No!' he cried. 'No, I'm not.'

She slapped him again and it felt . . . right.

Then she moved closer, until she was standing only inches from his face, and she lifted her skirt to expose herself to him. She wasn't wearing underwear.

He knew what he needed to do: he needed to please her; to show her he was worth something. He moved forward . . .

He coiled the belt around his fist two, three times. A heavy, black leather strap with the steel buckle dangling at the end. He leant forward, and whipped the belt over his shoulder. He straightened, arched his back. The pain was hot. He whipped it again and again. It was searing, it was burning. He roared and rocked as he came.

5

'Jesus, what happened to you?' Larissa asked when he finally opened the door to her insistent knocking.

'Migraine,' he said. 'Couldn't sleep. Been up most of the night.'

She nodded, dubious.

'Here—I brought you this.' She handed him an umbrella.

The overnight deluge had settled down into a light misty rain but the sketchy lawn in front of the barracks house was covered in wind-rippled puddles. The gutters outside on the street were surging.

'Are you sure you're okay?' Larissa asked, her habitual smile replaced with a frown of concern.

'No, no, all good,' he said. 'Come on—let's go.'

———

The river gauge was a new, high-tech affair attached to the old two-lane bridge that allowed Gloster access to the highway across the other side of the river. They stood off to the side, under their umbrellas, avoiding the splashing waves thrown up by the traffic swishing through the ever-growing puddles building up across the roadway.

'Shit,' Larissa said, 'fourteen-point-eight metres.' She clicked her fingers in front of Watson's face. 'Hello?'

'Ah, sorry, yeah—fourteen-point-eight.' He wrote it down.

'It was eight metres when I last looked three days ago. If it gets up to twenty, we have to start the evacuation protocol. Twenty-two and it's everybody out.'

She stopped and looked down at his pocket. 'Are you going to get that?'

He'd been hoping Larissa wouldn't hear the continuous buzzing in his coat pocket. He switched his umbrella to the other hand and grabbed the phone.

'Craig, it's Ellie. Jenny Howard has just turned up here at the station. You better get back here; it doesn't sound good.'

———

Jenny Howard looked the worse for wear. Her thin hair was hanging in limp strands down to her shoulders and her eyes were wide with fear. When Watson entered the downstairs interview room, followed by Ellie, she jumped to her feet, almost knocking over the steaming mug of coffee on the table in front of her.

'Someone's got her,' she blurted.

Watson took the seat opposite her while Ellie went to the other side of the table, put her arms around Jenny Howard's shoulders and gently urged her back to her seat. 'It's going to be okay,' she said soothingly.

'You've got to help me find her,' Jenny Howard sobbed, head

down, her hands wrapping around the coffee mug, the only real source of warmth in the room.

Ellie stood for a second with her hand on Jenny's back, before she moved away to take her seat across the table at Watson's side. She pressed a button on the in-built recording device and watched to make sure the system was up and running, then nodded at Watson.

'Now, Mrs Howard, I know you've been through this on the phone already but I need you tell me *exactly* what happened this morning,' Watson said.

'It's Tayla—she called me.' Jenny Howard raised a hand as if she were holding a telephone to her ear. 'She said, *You've got to help me, you've got to come and get me, Mum, he's going to kill me.*' Jenny broke into fresh sobs.

'I'm sorry, Mrs Howard, but could you be more precise?' Watson asked with as much delicacy as he could muster. 'What time did Tayla call?'

She took a moment to collect herself, pulling a used tissue from under the cuff of her jumper and drying her eyes. Then she reached down, pulled a mobile phone out of her handbag on the floor and checked the call log.

'Ten to eight,' she said.

Watson glanced at Ellie, motioning towards the phone.

'My phone rang,' Jenny continued, staring down at the screen. 'There was no caller ID, but when I answered it, it was Tayla. She was scared, she was in a hurry, she said: *Mum, you've got to help me.* I said, *Tayla, where are you?* and she screamed, *She's going to kill me!*'

Ellie opened her mouth to speak but Watson placed his hand on her arm.

'I said it again—*Tayla, where are you?*—and she screamed and the phone went dead. Because there was no caller ID, I couldn't call back.' Her faced screwed up in a mask of agony.

'Mrs Howard, did Tayla say *he's* going to kill me or *she's* going to kill me? It's very important that we get this one hundred per cent right.'

She stared straight through Watson, her eyes flicking up and to the right, accessing her memory. 'I . . . I think she said'—a pause—'*he* is going to kill me.'

Ellie shifted, and Watson could sense she wanted to speak again, but he needed to give Mrs Howard more time to process.

'She said *he*.' It was no more confident than the first time.

'Are you sure?' Ellie pressed.

'Yes, I'm sure.'

'Okay, we are going to need your phone, Mrs Howard,' Watson said. 'But first, tell me everything that you can remember about Tayla's behaviour in the last few weeks leading up to Sunday, no matter how insignificant it might seem.'

It was much as expected: since the car accident that had killed her best friend, Tayla had spent days and nights in her room crying, not eating. The funeral was a living hell. Mrs Howard had given Tayla one of her prescription sedatives and even that didn't seem to calm her down. She was hysterical all the day of the funeral, and for two days after. She had only been out a couple of times since—for a walk she'd said, and both times she had come back appearing even more upset than before she left.

'Do you know where she went on these walks?' Watson asked.

'She usually liked to go up along the cliffs, I think, but the weather has been too bad lately; it's dangerous up there.'

Mrs Howard stopped, blinked like she had seen a light. 'I saw her coming out of the caravan park last Friday night.'

————

Philby was waiting for them in the hallway outside his office when they had finished up with Jenny Howard.

'We're going to have to kick this upstairs now,' he said once Watson was seated in his office. Ellie refused a chair, looked at it like it was stained with smallpox.

Watson needed painkillers stat. His back was raw and bruised, his head a thumping pulse.

'Yeah, it makes sense,' Watson said.

'It's a possible kidnapping, a major crime,' Philby went on. 'Local Area Command will want to put their team on it.'

What do you want? An argument?

'So, what are we supposed to do?' Ellie interjected. 'Sit on our hands and wait? She could be out at the caravan park right now.'

Philby was flustered—just what he didn't need with only six months to go before retirement.

'Look, why don't you kick it up to the LAC, boss,' Watson suggested, searching for a compromise, 'and in the meantime we'll go and check out the caravan park, get a head start on things. Okay?'

————

Ellie drove; she didn't like the look of him.

'You look like you're about to throw up,' she said.

'No, I'm good,' Watson lied. He spun her the same story about the migraine. Ellie looked even less convinced than Larissa had.

35

'But I need to drop by the barracks on the way. All my clothes are wet; I need to get them to a laundromat and a dry cleaner before they shut.'

It was true, but it was only half the story. While Ellie waited impatiently in the car, he piled all of his wet clothes into a bag, took his toiletries bag into the bathroom, swallowed an Oxy-Contin for the pain and choofed a fat line of biker-grade speed for the hangover.

When he'd finished hoovering up the line off the bathroom cabinet, he stood and rubbed at the hot chemical burn stinging his nostrils, tasted the chemical slug sliding down the back of his throat, felt strong. In control.

He could see that Alison was beginning to well up, tears forming in the corners of her eyes.

'Hey, hey,' he soothed her. He cupped her face in his hands. 'What's the matter?'

'I don't want you to go,' she managed, and the tears ran silently down her cheeks.

They had been at school together for six years, in the same year, but Craig had hardly noticed her. She was on the outer. Craig and his crew were kings of the world back in high school. Hard to believe it was only twelve months ago.

'Hey, come here,' he said, and he gently pulled her to him across the front seat of his car. He held her tight, and she wiped her tears on the front of his shirt, looking up now, smiling, a little embarrassed.

'I'm sorry,' she said.

'Don't be,' he said, smiling into her face, so close that their noses were touching. He kissed her lightly, and it struck him that maybe

he was going to miss her too. He had another six months to go at the academy. It suddenly seemed an interminable amount of time.

When she got out of the car in her driveway, she stood there silently watching him, trying to smile. He could see Andrea, standing up on their first-floor balcony, looking out at the view. She was smoking a cigarette. She glanced down at him. He felt the burn.

They found the site manager down where the caravan park backed on to the river. It was dark brown, swollen and running swiftly. Large tree trunks, branches, roadside debris and the occasional drowned farm animal swept past on the rising brown current.

'Not gonna be long now,' he said by way of introduction.

'You would have been mailed the evacuation protocol with your last rates notice,' Ellie told him.

He looked at her like she was speaking Greek. 'Yeah. So, come in out of the rain,' he said, and he headed off at a fair clip for a man easily on the high side of seventy.

'I got your message,' he said, when they were seated at a table inside his demountable office home. 'Said you wanted a list of all the permanents.' He had a wrinkled piece of A4 in front of him, printed in red ink, overlaid with coffee rings and dusted with ash.

'And all the overnighters for the past week,' Watson added, taking the paper when the manager offered it to him.

'Jesus, you don't want much, do you?' he grumbled. He got up from the table and had a mumbled conversation with a young Asian woman nursing a small infant in the bedroom of the cabin.

'She'll print it off for you,' he said when he returned, lighting up a cigarette.

Watson could sense Ellie squirming.

'Why don't you show us all of your empty cabins,' she suggested, getting to her feet.

The manager sat and eyed Ellie for a moment, then ashed his cigarette into a coffee cup on the table before slowly getting to his feet. He grumbled something unintelligible to the young woman in the bedroom as he led them out the door.

The park had unsealed roads, potholed and filled with rainwater. The light drizzle persisted, light enough now to dispense with the umbrellas for a short tour of the tired old slum community. There were twenty or so powered caravan sites in the park, the majority of them unoccupied. Grass grew long and haphazard around most of the demountable units; broken-down pipes spewed water out into the public walkways; cracked cement, mould and mildew covered every surface.

'There's three empty,' the manager said, stopping outside of a particularly derelict cabin. It was raised about three feet off the muddy surface, sitting on loose piles of house bricks like most of the cabins in the park. A small set of steps led to a rotting wooden porch and the front door. The manager watched while Ellie and Watson climbed the stairs and had a look through the filthy front window. The roof had mostly caved in and there were plants growing up through the floor.

'Are you fucking serious?' Ellie said, returning to the manager.

'Yeah, well, there's one other cabin,' he said.

It was at the furthest end of the rows of cabins, no more derelict or decrepit than the others but hardly liveable.

'Do you have a key?' Watson asked after he tried the locked front door.

'No—it's not my property,' he said, churlish now.

They wiped holes in the dirt and the grime covering the windows; it was barely furnished but clearly empty. No Tayla.

Standing back down on the roadway, attempting to rub the grime off their hands, Ellie motioned at Watson with her head and eyes at a unit diagonally opposite on the other side of the narrow road. A man was watching, standing behind a screen door inside his cabin, just barely discernible. Ellie led the way over and stood in the doorway. Watson watched over her shoulder as she unfolded a colour photocopy of Tayla's last school photograph, which they had quickly formatted onto a missing persons poster.

'Gloster Police—have you seen this girl?' Ellie held the poster up to the screen door.

The man moved closer into the light. He was thin, drawn, late forties—or more likely a very hard-lived thirties. Goatee, hate oozing from his pores. Jail.

'Never seen her before,' the man spat and shut the door in their faces.

———

Back at the station, they split the lists into three. There were thirty permanents and six overnighters over the last week: twelve names each on which to do background and records checks.

Watson scored an old *obtain funds by deception* count for the sixty-six-year-old female occupant of the first cabin he checked. Two *drink driving* and an *assault police* for her de facto partner.

Fuck me, it's going to be a long haul.

He put the list aside, went to the toilets and split an Oxy capsule in half. He poured half the fine powder onto the side of his fist and snorted it.

Ellie and Larissa watched him closely as he cruised back to his workstation.

There was a large sealed envelope sitting next to his keyboard. He had been avoiding it since he got into the office that morning, shuffling it out of the way as he focused on the tasks in front of him. But when he sat down with his warm Oxy buzz, he felt capable of dealing with some additional work.

The envelope was originally addressed to Alan Bishop, but had been redirected with his name handwritten on it. He tore it open and let the four or five stapled pages fall directly onto his desk. It was an accident report from the Crash Investigations Unit. He went straight to the Actions/Conclusion section on the last page and, sure he must have misread it the first time, read it through again.

In the opinion of the professionals at the CIU, the accident involving Tayla's best friend, Laura, and her father was no accident at all.

6

Paint scrapings, a small dent, skid marks, and the calculated speed of entry. Each an individual bullet point, but together, a powerful and well-reasoned argument that the double fatality rollover that ended with a family car upside down and underwater in the Gloster River had been caused by a deliberate collision rather than a random accident.

The CIU had found a deformation of the left rear panel of Laura Sweeney's father's green Jaguar. The area in and around the deformation of the panel was smeared with a coating of red auto paint for a length of thirty centimetres. Testing of the red paint, standing out obviously against the green panel on attached photographs, showed it to be of a specific type used only on late model Toyotas.

Watson's eyes were burning, his scalp beginning to crawl.

The wreck occurred on a long sweeping left-hand curve that followed a bend of the river, fifty metres away behind a safety rail on the right-hand side of the road. There were no obvious skid marks on the road, which usually was taken as a sign that a

41

driver had fallen asleep at the wheel. But the CIU had revisited the scene after the dent and the fresh paint smears were identified. A more focused investigation located two short rubber burns on the road, twenty centimetres long and ten centimetres apart, signs generally indicating a collision; that a car had been hit from the side, causing it to lift slightly and then hit the road again a short distance away. Enough to send a fast-moving vehicle careering out of control.

Disturbed gravel, deep ruts and skid marks gouged through the long grass at the side of the road showed that the driver had attempted to brake and regain control after the vehicle had left the road, as it speared towards the guard rail. But it was too late. The sideways force of the collision and the momentum of the sweeping left-hand curve had caused the car to flip over and clip the top of the guard rail. Hitting the guard rail had only added to the momentum of the flipping motion of the vehicle. There were signs the car had rebounded off a tree twenty metres further down the embankment, but by then nothing was going to stop the car entering the water. Which it did. On its roof. And it sank almost immediately.

Fuck.

Watson covered his face with his hands. Larissa must have sensed a situation because she made her way over to his workstation, Ellie close behind. He handed the report back over his shoulder without turning around or removing his elbows from the desk. The two women began to read.

He heard one of them gasp as they reached the conclusion.

Watson swivelled around in his chair when he heard the pages being flipped back over. Three sets of eyes met.

'What next?' he said.

———

Ten to four. Watson actually welcomed the chance to get out and check the fucking river gauge. He parked as close to the bridge as he possibly could, in a space reserved for access to a municipal park that ran down to the river. He could tell just by looking that the muddy brown water had risen since he and Larissa had checked the gauge that morning.

He checked the meter and saw the level had hit 15.9 metres. Shit! What had Larissa said? Twenty metres and they had to leave, or was it twenty-two? *Come on down!*

The rain was spattering off his umbrella as he jumped puddles on his way back to the car.

He had just slid behind the wheel when his phone buzzed. He pulled it out of his pocket and read the incoming message.

You will pay maggot.

———

He had been scoring off Jeremy Landers for eighteen months before the shit hit the fan. Jeremy had offered to sell him coke in a city nightclub not long after he had graduated from the academy. They went into the toilets, Watson slipped Jeremy two hundred dollars, and Jeremy slipped him the bag. Watson took his phone number for future reference.

He wasn't sure how Jeremy found out he was a cop; probably through a friend of a friend. Word gets around. It wasn't ever an issue until Jeremy got busted. Just small-time possession. Nothing to worry about, Watson told him. Pay a fine be on your way.

The second time he got arrested Jeremy wanted a helping hand. Demanded it. Started getting heavy. Said he might start dropping names. Do some sort of a deal. Watson couldn't have that. He organised a meeting, brought along a taser.

He put 50,000 volts through Jeremy's sternum while they sat in the front seat of Jeremy's car. When the dealer regained consciousness, Watson shoved his service-issue Glock into Jeremy's mouth and said, 'If you ever threaten me again, I will fucking end you.' Then he dropped just over a trafficable weight of coke under the seat before exiting the car and ringing a mate in the vice squad.

Jeremy got two years. Eighteen months with good behaviour.

———

He dialled Central Records, gave his badge number and his details.

'Jeremy John Landers,' he said. 'Current status?'

'Released from Bathurst Correctional Complex on the twenty-second of June this year, six months' probation continuing,' came the answer.

The twenty-second of June. Eight days ago. The texts had started six days ago.

Doesn't take a rocket scientist.

———

'We've got a good one,' Larissa said when he stalked back into the office. 'Well, Ellie has,' she corrected herself, as Watson approached her workstation.

Ellie came out and joined them in Larissa's cubicle, holding a printout. 'Aaron James Redman.' She said it like she was describing a disease. 'The usual childhood break and enters and car thefts, but then graduating to assaults, assault with a deadly weapon and then rape.' She stopped, looked up at Watson. 'Four counts.'

'I'm guessing we know which one he is?' Watson replied.

'Without a doubt,' Ellie confirmed.

'Well, let's go and pay him a visit.'

'I'll just grab my coat,' she said.

Ellie drove. It seemed to be the way things were done around there.

'I know a short cut,' Ellie said, glancing over at Watson as she turned off onto a potholed dirt track through the trees, just short of the main entrance to the caravan park. It was obviously no short cut, but it took them down close to the far end of the park, down where the empty cabin was positioned across the way from Aaron Redman's cabin. Where they could park the car and not be seen.

She wasn't a tall woman, probably shorter than the average female. There wasn't much to her wiry frame either, but she gave Watson a look before she opened her door that excited him, and very slightly terrified him.

Look out, Aaron.

It was just going on dusk as they negotiated the dripping bush between the track and the back of the caravan park. The wind was back, roaring through the tops of the trees. It was raining heavily. Ellie led the way quickly across to Redman's front porch. She opened the screen door. The door behind it was locked.

Watson looked quickly left and right, up and down the road. There was no one around; the chill wind and the rain was keeping everyone indoors.

Ellie knocked, hard. After a few seconds the door scraped open and Redman stood there. He bristled at the uniform— at the *woman* in the uniform.

Watson held the screen door. Ellie came up and under with an upper cut into Redman's solar plexus. He immediately doubled over, a loud whoosh of air leaving his throat. She straightened him up by grabbing the scabby mullet off the back of his collar. Gave him two short, hard jabs to the middle of his face. Then she threw him inside the cabin.

Watson dragged the screen door closed behind him. Entered and shut the door.

Ellie had Redman down on his stomach, her knee across the back of his neck while she applied the handcuffs. Tight. Then she rolled him over onto his back. Watson knew from experience how painful it was to be lying on top of your own cuffed hands.

They were in the main room of the cabin, a lounge area with a small kitchenette. There was a bedroom and a bathroom off to their left. Every flat surface was covered in dust and dirt, and the threadbare carpet that Redman was now squirming on was filthy and stained. The television was on, and a still-smoking bong sat on the floor in front of a reeking, stained lounge chair.

Ellie stood over Redman, one leg either side of his heaving chest and whipped out her extendable baton. It opened with a loud metallic *clack* in the confines of the small room.

Redman winced; there was no fight left in him.

46

With her free hand, Ellie pulled Tayla's missing persons poster out of her pocket and shook it open.

Watson did a quick scan of the bedroom and the bathroom to ensure that they were alone. He met Ellie's eyes and nodded.

'This girl, you rapist piece of shit—where is she?' She pointed the end of the baton at his face.

Redman stared at the poster, a look of utter terror on his face.

'Yeah, I saw her,' he gasped. 'I saw her a couple of times.'

Watson went through the kitchenette. The bench space was crowded with unwashed plates, pots, pans, cups and cutlery. There were cockroaches and ants feeding on leftovers and dark, furry food in the bottom of opened containers.

'When did you see her?' Ellie demanded. 'Where?'

'Here in the park, the cabin across the road, the empty one.'

There was a plastic Tupperware container on top of a small fridge. The only clean container in the entire house by the look of it.

'When?'

'I dunno. A couple of days ago maybe.'

'How many fucking days ago?'

'I dunno—fucking look at me. I don't know what day it is. I don't even know day from night. It was a couple of days ago.'

Watson opened the Tupperware container. There were six deal bags with solid little rocks of crystal in each of them. He pocketed three.

'Who was she with?'

'I dunno. Some other girls, some woman; I don't know who they were.'

'Describe the woman.'

'Fuck knows. I see them through the window, coming and going. It's in the dark usually.' He was crying now.

Watson looked over at the front window. There was a view of the empty cabin, but the window was filthy and there was a thin lace curtain covering it.

'How do you know it's a woman?'

He hesitated. 'Just . . . I dunno; the way she walks, the hair. Maybe it's a man.'

Ellie looked over at Watson, teeth gritted. 'Anything?'

'Last time you saw her, a couple of days ago, who was she with?'

Redman paused, had to think about it. 'She was on her own.'

'Night or day?'

'Night-time, late.'

'Was she coming or going?'

'She was coming.'

'Was there anyone else there, in the cabin?'

Another pause, more thinking.

'No, the lights were off.'

Watson looked back at Ellie. She kicked Redman over onto his stomach and removed the cuffs. Watson walked to the door and held it open for her. She turned in the doorway, pointed the baton.

'You ever see me on the street, you cross the fucking road.'

———

Watson jumped straight back into the car, shivering, and stuffed his hands together down between his legs. Ellie did not get in immediately. He watched her through the spattered windscreen, standing out in the dark, in the rain, staring back towards the caravan park with the wind blowing the hood of her yellow police-issue rain jacket up around the back of her head.

When she moved, she moved quickly, sliding back behind the wheel of the car. She started the motor to get the heater going but didn't put the car into gear. She pulled two or three moist paper towelettes from a dispenser down by her door and dabbed at her face and neck until she had soaked up most of the rain. Then she turned her head and stared hard at the side of Watson's face.

'Larissa doesn't need to know,' she said flatly.

His hand was in his pocket now, feeling the sharp-edged rocks on the tips of his fingers. He watched the rain splattering against the windscreen and he nodded. Then he turned and met her gaze until she looked away into the darkness.

7

Philby's door was shut when they got back to the station. Reception was dark and empty.

'I've just got to make a quick call,' Watson said, reaching inside his coat pocket for his phone.

He let Ellie go on alone. Back to the squad room to update Larissa however she wanted.

'Yeah, it's me, Robbo,' he said when the phone was answered. 'Remember that dickhead Jeremy Landers who I put you on to a couple of years ago?'

Robbo confirmed that he did.

'Yeah, well I need an address.'

Robbo asked the obvious question. 'Why, mate?'

'Because I need to have a serious word with the fucker.'

Robbo sighed. 'I was just about to leave for the day. Can it wait till tomorrow?'

'Yeah, tomorrow's fine, just text me.'

'Righto. How're things up bush?'

Watson lowered his voice. 'A complete shithole—can't get

out of here quick enough. Listen, mate, I've got to go—thanks.'

He pulled the remaining half of the Oxy capsule out of his pocket, split it, loaded the contents onto the back of his hand and polished it off before heading upstairs.

When he entered the squad room, Larissa was seated in her cubicle and Ellie was standing, leaning on the corner of the divider between their two workstations. They both smiled at him as he sauntered across to his desk.

'Everything okay?' Larissa asked brightly.

What the fuck has Ellie told her?

'Yeah, fine,' he said.

'Look, we were just wondering ...' Larissa glanced up at Ellie. 'Would you like to come around to our place for dinner tonight? Maybe a few drinks?'

If he hadn't just dropped the Oxy the answer would have been a definite, absolute no.

But he'd had the Oxy, so he wavered. 'I'm not sure,' he said.

'Oh, come on,' Ellie said. 'Have you got something else on?'

'No, I haven't, it's just ...' The Oxy had already slowed him down so much he couldn't come up with anything. 'Yeah, okay—why not?'

'Okay then,' Larissa said, 'we'll finish up here and see you at ours at about seven. I'll text you the address; we're just around the corner from you.'

———

The empty cabin where Redman had seen Tayla was listed on the record provided by the park manager as owned by a couple,

John and Eunice McCann, with an address at a farm property not far out of town. Watson made a note to call in first thing the following morning. Checking the map for directions, he could see the property wasn't far from the scene of the fatal car crash.

May as well kill two birds with one stone, he decided. He was curious to see the crash site for himself.

He stopped off at the Surfside bottle shop and grabbed a six pack of beers and a mid-range bottle of red before heading back to the barracks.

There he had a quick shower, and changed into jeans and his warmest shirt before retrieving the rocks from his damp suit pants.

He had dropped down onto the lounge with one of the little bags in his hand when he heard a crash from the kitchen. Something had fallen. He sat absolutely still, facing the door. There was another noise, fainter this time, indistinguishable. He rose slowly to his feet.

My gun—where did I leave it?

He crept silently back through the lounge to the bedroom. There was another loud rustling noise from the kitchen. There was a small gun safe built into the bedroom wall for storage of service weapons. Watson could see his pistol lying on the bedside table where he had tossed it. He took two long steps into the room and picked up the cold, hard piece of black metal.

In the four years since he had graduated from the academy, he had pulled his gun twice, and one of those times had been to threaten Jeremy Landers. He stood frozen to the spot, the pistol pointed towards the bedroom door.

Maybe they will just go away.

The wind was tapping a branch against the side of the house.

A car swished and thumped through the puddles and potholes on the road outside. He heard a screech from the kitchen.

He moved to the bedroom door. Just one step. There was movement in the darkness at the other end of the hall. He got down on one knee and forced out his arms, shaking, aiming at the kitchen door, his pulse thumping in his ears.

Something dropped to the floor at the end of the hall. He heard it scurrying towards the kitchen. Then another. Rats, king-size rats.

He dropped his head, suddenly very cold. A drop of sweat ran off the end of his nose and hit the floor in front of him.

'Fucking rats,' he breathed.

As he approached the kitchen the sound of scratching rat claws increased to a frenzy. Rounding the doorway, the last of half-a-dozen of the filthy vermin, each about the size of a small cat, went leaping and scurrying up through the cupboards, screeching and fighting into a small hole in the wall close to the ceiling.

He had found two boxes of rat poison in the cupboard under the sink when he first arrived. He grabbed both of them, angry now. He found the manhole cover to the roof space in the bathroom ceiling, stood on the edge of the bathtub and pushed up the roughly painted panel into the attic cavity.

Scratching, scurrying, panicked little feet fled into the darkness. The smell was overpowering. He held onto the rim of the opening with one hand while he flicked the open box of pellets out into the roof space. He jumped down grabbed the second box and tossed that up there too for good measure.

When he grabbed the cover, it bumped an object just inside the roof space and he lost his grip. He raised his head slightly to find the corner of the cover snagged against a rotting, rat-chewed hessian sack. He held his breath and pulled the sack down, dropping it straight into the bathtub before sliding the cover back into place.

He stood looking at the reeking, frayed piece of material for a good ten seconds before picking it up with his fingertips. Trying not to gag, he walked quickly to the back door, opened it and tossed the bag out into the knee-high weeds. He slammed the door and then went and stood, fuming, beside the shower while he waited the obligatory five minutes for the hot water, to wash the crawling sensation off his skin.

———

Ellie met him at the front door of their neat little bungalow just two streets away. He shut the door quickly on the wind and chilly rain and followed her through to the kitchen. Like the rest of the house, it was bright, beautifully furnished and warm.

'Take a seat,' Ellie commanded, nominating a particular chair at the kitchen table. He did as he was told while she pulled the bottle of red from its brown paper bag and openly appraised its quality. Seemingly satisfied, she placed it in the middle of the table.

Larissa was busy at the stove, stirring and checking a selection of steaming pots and pans. This was his first time seeing either woman out of uniform but their casual outfits held no real surprises. Ellie was wearing jeans and a checked cotton shirt that could also be a blouse, gender indeterminate, mission accomplished. Larissa was wearing black gym tights with bright pink trainers, and a vintage Nike hoodie over a singlet top. Her long black hair was hanging loose and tousled down her back and over her shoulders. He felt Ellie's lasers on him, and dared not let his eyes linger.

'So, what's the haps?' Larissa asked, resting her hand on his shoulder. She positioned a small plate of baked pastries among the glasses and the cutlery and sat down.

'Rats,' he said, and received knowing nods from both Ellie and Larissa. Obviously, the rat issue in the barracks was a well-known problem.

'Yep, I stayed there for a week myself when I first got here,' Larissa said. 'Luckily Ellie came to the rescue with the offer of her spare room.'

I bet she did.

They each cracked a beer.

'Here's to us,' Larissa said, smiling and holding her stubby out in front of her. They all tapped the glass bottles together. Larissa added, 'It's so good to have you here, Craig.'

Jesus, compared to what?

They sank beers and made small talk about where they had come from and what they were doing before washing up in Gloster.

'Ellie told me how you got that arsehole out at the caravan park to fess up,' Larissa said once they were back to talking shop, onto their third beer each.

'Oh, she did, did she?' he said, poker-faced.

'Yes. You know, you'll end up getting into trouble if you're not careful, Craig. You can't speak to people like that.'

'Yeah, well, like I said yesterday, sometimes you've just got to do what you've got to do.' He glanced at Ellie, who had the slightest trace of a grin creasing the corners of her mouth.

'Dinner should be about ready,' she said, changing the subject like a pro. She stood and moved over to the stove.

Roast chicken and baked vegetables. An all-time classic, and he would have loved it if he hadn't had that pipe before he left the barracks. Very low-quality gear, as he expected; all it did was keep him even and kill his appetite. He was also trying not to neck the beers.

'Now, let's get down to some serious shit,' Larissa said when they had finished eating. They had polished off the bottle of red Watson brought while they ate. Ellie grabbed another bottle of red from a well-stocked wine rack in the next room while Larissa led him into the lounge area. Perfect white paint and fashionable accessories, all pre-warmed to an orange glow by an industrial-strength gas heater.

'So, what's the situation, Craig?' Larissa asked, when they were seated three abreast across a long sofa, each with a freshly topped-up glass.

'What do you mean?' he responded nervously.

Christ. What have they heard?

'Are you'—she struggled for the appropriate word—'attached?'

'What, me?' he scoffed, relieved. 'Have a look at me!'

They both did—Ellie, on the far side of Larissa, even lowering her paperback-sized Android device long enough to inspect him like a lab specimen. His dark hair was too long and a bit of a mess, he needed a shave, and his olive skin was a bit patchy and dry. But he was aware that his strong, square jaw and his tired dark eyes gave him an aura of rugged vulnerability that a lot of women found irresistible.

'Yeah, we are looking at you, Craig. You're full of shit.'

'Well, there was someone,' he admitted, after a moment, 'but, yeah, she's gone. What about you two?' he added, before they could get too deep.

'Us two?' Ellie said, smirking. 'Like the two of us? Together?'

He squirmed. 'No, not like together. You know—you two. What's the . . . situation?'

'The situation?' Ellie twisted the knife a little deeper.

They let him dangle for another awkward moment before Larissa threw him a rope.

'We're both single, Craig. Single, female police officers in a redneck country town. I think you could say our situation is that there is no situation, and there's not likely to be a situation any time soon. Would that be about right, El?'

'Yeah, I think that sums it up,' Ellie agreed. 'Not that there aren't tons of incredibly attractive, eligible bachelors around town.'

'Ooh yeah,' Larissa agreed heartily. 'Like the one we found passed out at the bus stop outside the pub last week.'

'Oh, yes. Pissed himself, hadn't he?'

'And shit his pants.'

Ellie and Larissa laughed. Craig was pleased for the distraction.

His father had left when he was six years old. He'd only seen him a couple of times since. He'd had lots of affairs apparently. A real swordsman. He had played first-grade football, just a few games back in the eighties, but he was a local club legend.

Craig had played the game himself. A natural, they said. Could be as good as his old man one day; maybe even better.

School work had come easy, friends had come easy and, later, the girls had come easy.

Could be anything this kid, they'd say, and when they asked, he'd always give the same answer: 'I'm going to be a copper like the old man.'

'Oh wait, Larissa, you've got to see this.' Ellie scrolled furiously through screens on her Android. 'I saw this today,' she said, slowing down the scrolling, close to her destination image. 'I nearly threw up my lunch.'

Ellie stopped on a photo of a man. She maximised the image on her screen and held it out for Larissa to view. Watson leant forward too, curious. Larissa coughed, held her hand over her mouth, stifled a choking laugh.

The man was bald, looking back over his seriously bulging, tribal-tattooed shoulder, going for smouldering blue steel, coming across as a slightly myopic sex offender.

Larissa grabbed the device and held it in front of Watson, her hand, her whole body, shaking with laughter.

'Craig,' Ellie said, taking a good slurp of red, 'meet Detective Sergeant Alan Bishop. A legend in his own lunch hour.'

'God's gift to women everywhere,' Larissa added. 'You just have to ask him.'

'Fuck me. So that's the bloke I'm replacing?'

'The one and only.'

'Jesus, and Philby told me I had a big pair of shoes to fill.'

The comment seemed to take the wind out of Ellie's and Larissa's sails.

'Yeah, those two were close,' Larissa said.

'A little too close.'

'What? Like . . .'

Ellie smirked. 'No. Not like that.'

'But something wasn't right, was it, El?'

Ellie nodded vigorously, spilling some wine out of her glass. 'Something wasn't right at all.'

Watson felt as if his temples were being gripped by a vice. They were down to the dregs of the second bottle. He was getting edgy. The cosy atmosphere dissipated quickly. The light-hearted banter died a slow, painful death.

'Look, I'm about done for the night,' Ellie said, pouring what was left of the bottle into his glass.

'Yeah, I'd better get going,' Watson said, downing the wine. 'It's getting pretty late.'

'Late schmate,' Larissa slurred.

'I'll see you out,' Ellie said.

After saying goodbye to Larissa, who punched him on the shoulder and then pulled him in for a hug, Ellie walked with him to the front door.

'Hey,' she said, 'about this afternoon . . .'

'Yeah?' He was pulling on his jacket.

'I just wanted to say thanks,' she said, and she moved in close, right up into his personal space, looking hard into his eyes. He couldn't read her expression, couldn't read the situation at all. He stood frozen. Ellie reached a hand up close to his cheek, paused, and then brushed a tiny piece of lint off the collar of his shirt. The contact felt like an electric shock.

'Night, Craig,' she said, with what could have been a smile, but might just as easily have been a sneer.

He stood for a couple of seconds, as awkward and confused as he had ever been in his life, then he turned and walked out the door.

8

The McCann property was forty-five minutes west of town. All the low-lying paddocks were underwater and in places the road was semi-submerged. He took it easy into the corners and eased the car through the deeper puddles lying across the road, still managing to throw up a torrent of muddy water on either side.

His GPS led him up an unsealed side road, thankfully climbing slightly. Five hundred metres further on, amid a strand of wind-whipped eucalypts and carefully tended hedges, stood the McCann residence. There was the obligatory Toyota one-tonne ute and a small Mazda parked in an open-sided shed beside the neat little home. Sparks and thick smoke poured from a chimney on the roof, creating a mist of wood smoke in the trees behind the house.

Watson parked as close to the front door as he could, then made a dash for the cover of the verandah. The wind was howling, blowing twigs and leaves out of the large trees, and the rain continued to hammer down. It was just after 9 a.m. and the house lights were on.

The door opened before he had a chance to knock.

'Come in quickly out of the rain,' Eunice McCann urged, holding the door for him.

'Thanks for that,' he said, almost tripping on a pile of muddy shoes sitting on a stack of old newspapers just inside the door. He slipped his own shoes off without bending down or undoing the laces.

The house was toasty and warm, and Watson watched as a large man added a split log to an already blazing open fireplace on the far side of the room.

'Can't have too much on in weather like this, can we?' the man said, taking long energetic strides over to the door to offer his hand.

'John McCann,' he said, 'and my wife, Eunice.'

John McCann had farmer's hands, big blunt-ended things, rough as sandpaper. What was left of his hair sat thin and grey but neatly barbered around the tops of his ears. He radiated health and robust outdoorsiness. His voice was twice the volume it needed to be inside the house.

'Craig Watson,' Watson replied, shaking McCann's hand. 'Detective Watson,' he added as an afterthought, taking Eunice's hand.

She was a plump little church mouse of a woman. Obviously, the Yin to John McCann's overpowering Yang.

Funny how opposites attract.

'I've just boiled the kettle,' Eunice said, leading the way to a dining table set with plates, cups and saucers. 'Would you like tea or coffee, Detective Watson?'

He cringed a little at the formality but decided to go with it. 'I'd love a coffee, thanks,' he said.

Like John and Eunice, the home was neat and well maintained. The walls of the dining room were covered with single, group and family photographs, all framed and dusted. There was a faded wedding photograph of John, chest puffed up with pride, and a pretty little woman looking for all the world like she had just been sentenced to life without parole. Watson was a little surprised at the number of slightly wilting flower arrangements spread around the lounge, the dining room and the parts of the kitchen he could see from where he sat. Very keen gardeners, he assumed.

Eunice and John both looked a little unsettled, which was not entirely unexpected given they had received an early morning call from the police informing them that a detective would be dropping by to talk to them about a holiday cabin they hadn't set foot in for more than five years.

'So, you want to know about our cabin?' John asked, once the pouring, sugaring and talk of the weather was out of the way.

Over the following ten minutes they confirmed the cabin was theirs, that they'd bought it on a whim from an old mate of John's who had fallen on hard times. They'd spent a few Christmases there in the early years, but other than that they'd hardly ever used it.

'It was mostly our daughter Ellen and her children who used it,' Eunice said.

Watson felt the mood shift. John McCann reached across and placed his hand on top of his wife's. They were both suddenly lost for words.

Watson was lost.

What have I missed?

'Your daughter?' he said tentatively.

'Ellen,' John said. 'Ellen Sweeney.'

Oh, Christ.

'Laura's mother,' John said, now looking at Watson like he had two heads. Eunice was dabbing at her eyes with a tissue.

'I'm sorry,' Watson said. 'I should have known. I've only been in Gloster three days.' He felt ashamed when he said it.

'Is that what this visit is about?' John demanded. 'Something about the accident?'

'No. At least, I don't think so.'

'Well, why are you here then?'

'It's about Tayla Howard, one of Laura's friends. She's gone missing. One of the last places she was seen was your cabin at the caravan park.'

'Something's up,' John said. 'Something stinks.' He pointed a shaking finger at Watson. 'I told you,' he said to his wife. 'I told you something stinks.'

Eunice didn't raise her head.

'Look,' said Watson hastily, 'it's highly unlikely the two matters are connected. It's probably just a coincidence.'

'No. There's something wrong here. That was no accident, you mark my words. He was up to no good. Ellen knows, you –'

'Who was up to no good?' Watson interrupted.

'Anthony bloody Sweeney. Ellen's husband, Laura's bloody father.'

'Oh, John,' Eunice moaned; obviously this was a record she'd heard before.

'No. He should know,' John said, pointing his shaking digit in Watson's direction once more. 'Anthony was up to no good. Why else would Ellen have left him like that, just walked away from her family? Because he was up to no bloody good, and it caught up with him, that's why.'

John's eyes were large, bloodshot and boring into Watson's skull.

'Details,' Watson said. 'What do you mean he was up to no good?' He resisted the urge to rub at his own dried-out eyes.

'We don't know. She won't say. But ask yourself: how does a bloke who works at the Gloster Council afford a brand-new Jag? Hey? Answer me that!' He said it defiantly, like he was slapping down a royal flush.

———

He got to the end of the unsealed road and pulled over before he hit the bitumen. He leant his head against the steering wheel and closed his eyes.

Tayla. Laura. Laura's mother and father. What. The. Fuck?

He banged his head against the steering wheel a couple of times, reached into his pocket and swallowed an Oxy dry.

His GPS told him the accident site was 3.2 kilometres further along the same road. He checked the file notes and found the Sweeneys' address, the home Laura and Anthony Sweeney had been travelling from when the accident occurred. He plugged the home location into his GPS and discovered it was 5.4 kilometres further up the road.

The road heading west followed the course of the river, running fast, fat and brown off to his left. Further to the west, low, heavy, grey clouds hung misty over the ranges in the distance. The wind buffeted the car and yellow police tape streamed wildly among the trees and over the crash barrier at the abandoned accident site. He drove on, comfortably sedated, to the location pulsing on his GPS screen just over two kilometres away.

He could see it from the road. It was impossible to miss, a huge, overblown McMansion sitting on an enormous patch of muddy ground on a windswept hill overlooking the river. The place looked brand-new. In fact, there was still some scaffolding and what looked from a distance like stacks of house bricks and other building materials piled up in front of the massive structure.

There were no signs of life. Access to the property was blocked by large electronically controlled gates across the access road.

He went back to the file notes and located Anthony Sweeney's listed occupation—Manager, Infrastructure Delivery, Gloster Council. Whatever that entailed.

It's not impossible.

He turned back. The road was deserted. He deliberately slowed down and felt the slight lean on the suspension as his car took the long sweeping left-hand curve that was the end of the road for Anthony Sweeney and his daughter Laura. He lined up with the police tape and the obvious damage to the guard rail on the other side of the road and steered off the curve in the line that the Sweeneys' Jaguar would have taken onto the other side of the road, over the guard rail and down into the river.

He pulled up close to the damaged guard rail and got out of the car. He pulled his heavy waterproof jacket close in to his body and held the hood over the top of his head. The ground fell away steeply on the other side of the guard rail. The swirling brown torrent had now reached a level well beyond where the car would have entered the river.

He traced the course of his own vehicle back across the road, searching for the telltale skip marks where the collision had occurred. He searched back and forward for a couple of minutes but the wet slick of the road and the passing of traffic had by now obscured any obvious signs. He kept walking to the soft shoulder on the side of the road where a potential murderer could have sat in his car, waiting for the Sweeneys' green Jaguar to come into sight and then rolling forward, gathering speed, timing it just right to reach the road just as the big Jag cruised past, clipping it, sending it out of control, rolling and flipping into the river with two lives on board.

It's not impossible.

9

He stuck his head in Philby's door when he returned to the station.

'Just checking in, boss.'

Philby was staring vacantly at his desktop home page. On it were a half-dozen icons set up by the IT department and a couple of documents Philby had probably saved there by mistake.

'Ah, Detective Watson,' Philby said, suddenly back with the living, removing a small pair of bifocals from their perch halfway down his nose. 'We need to have a word.'

Shit, thought Watson. *What now?*

As he went to move into the office, Philby stood up. 'No, no, we don't have to talk here. Have you had lunch yet?'

Watson resisted the urge to look at his watch. He knew it was just after eleven.

'No, not yet.'

Philby grabbed the same gravy-stained windcheater Watson had seen him wearing in the bar at the Surfside Hotel two nights before.

'We'll get ourselves a counter feed and a couple of beers, hey?' Philby said, leading Watson out the front door of the station.

———

The main bar of the Surfside Hotel on a miserable Thursday morning was hollow and sad. There was only one other drinker in the place, an elderly man with a pink face and flaking skin, sitting at a window, staring hard out into the rain with a death grip on his half-finished schooner. The tinny cartoon music of the poker machines was bouncing from somewhere deeper in the hotel, obviously the only reason to employ the bored, over made-up, twenty-something-year-old leaning against the drinks fridge.

She had a schooner out of the rack and under the Carlton tap before Philby had even breasted the bar.

'G'day, Phil,' she said. 'What are you having, mate?' she added, eyeing Watson up and down, leaving her mouth slightly ajar when she finished speaking, her lips forming a thick, pink O.

'Yeah, same,' he said, not making eye contact.

'So, you've been absolutely flat chat since you arrived,' Philby said, taking a hungry gulp out of the top of his beer once they had situated themselves at a high-top round table in the centre of the bar area. 'I bet you weren't expecting that when you got here.'

'You can say that again,' Watson said, matching Philby's mouthful. 'They told me I was coming to a quiet little country town.'

Philby looked like he had something on his mind, like he was playing for time.

'So, how are you getting along with those two upstairs?'

He said it like he was referring to an ogre in the attic and he expected Watson to follow suit.

'Yeah, fine. Good workers.'

Fuck him.

'Yeah, good workers,' Philby echoed, rubbing his fingers up and down the side of his condensation-soaked schooner glass.

'Another one, boss?' Watson asked, pouring the bottom half of his schooner down his neck in one go.

'Jesus, a bit thirsty, are we?' Philby answered, clearly impressed. 'Yeah, I can squeeze another one in.'

'So, what I wanted to talk to you about,' Philby said, when Watson arrived back at the table with more drinks, 'is, ah, well I've spoken to Local Area Command, and as you'd expect they're flat out with the flood and what not, so they've, ah, told us to put the missing persons thing on hold—you know, just until things get back to normal.'

Watson stared at him in disbelief.

Bullshit.

'You told them about the phone call? I mean, it's hardly just a missing persons case now, is it? I mean there's evidence of a kidnapping.'

'Oh yeah. I've passed on all the summaries. Well done, by the way.' He necked half his schooner, and Watson followed suit. 'They still believe she's just a runaway—trauma of her friend being killed and all that, you know. No point in jumping to conclusions.'

A couple of old campaigners, all beer guts, varicose veins and form guides, had entered, and were watching Philby and Watson from the bar.

'Just give us a moment,' Philby called out to them.

'So just drop it?' Watson asked, semi-incredulous.

'Yeah. Nah. Just put it on hold. For now.'

'Okay.'

'And there's one other thing . . .'

'Yes?'

'There's some talk about a carry-on down the caravan park yesterday afternoon. Might have involved a uniform. Know anything about that?'

'First I've heard of it, boss.'

Philby looked sceptical but was clearly happy to accept even a half-hearted denial.

'All good then,' he said, smiling. 'Look, I want to introduce you to a couple of good mates of mine. Old coppers—one of them reckons he used to know your old man.'

The sergeant obviously had no intention of going back to work that afternoon. He set a punishing pace with the schooners, but Watson was more than equal to the task, especially after he refreshed himself with a fat line of speed, snorted off the cistern in the pub toilets.

The bullshit flowed with the beers. The old boys talked football, fishing, punting, the good old days. After six schooners Watson had a bit of casual banter going with Bree, the barmaid. After ten schooners she gave him a heads-up that there was some loose powder hanging around under his left nostril. Then she gave him her phone number.

Philby dropped him off at the barracks just after 8 p.m., both of them absolutely blind.

He made it to the lounge chair and collapsed there in the cold and the dark. The rats were rattling in the roof and the rain crackled against the windows. Lightning shot bright lights through his eyelids.

10

Thunder woke him just after 4 a.m. with a searing concussive crack. He was soaking wet, freezing. The rain was spattering in on gusts of wind through the open front door. He climbed off the lounge chair unsteadily. His head was pounding red pulses of pain through his eyeballs.

Stiff, and shivering uncontrollably, he retraced his own wet footprints to the door and slammed it shut. He twisted the hot tap as far and as fast as he could and crouched down beside the shower on his knees, his arms wrapped around himself, praying for the hot water. He was howling in the dark, screaming into his hands, his head exploding in sharp spasms of pain.

When the hot water came, he crawled in under it, hardly adjusting the scorching torrent. He lay there fully clothed and trembling until the water went cold again.

Stumbling to the kitchen, he swallowed an Oxy with icy water sucked straight from the tap. Then he climbed into bed, shaking and shivering until the opiates warmed his belly and slithered out to calm his trembling limbs.

It seemed like no time passed before his alarm woke him at seven thirty. He showered, shaved and dressed in a haze. Motion made him nauseous. He threw up in the sink. Had a pipe before he left for work.

———

Larissa squeaked out a 'thanks' when he dropped the McCafé lattes on their desks, but Ellie just shook her head.

'Out for lunch, were we?' she said to his back as he struggled to his desk.

He nodded, having trouble forming words.

When he switched on his computer, there were twenty-four new emails, most of them admin crap. He deleted them without reading them, then listened to his six phone messages. They were all from Ellie. He felt the women's eyes boring into him as he held his phone to his ear and listened.

The river had broken its banks west of town and there was general localised flooding. As the timing of the messages got later the situation deteriorated. The flooding was just outside of town now and he was needed urgently. The last message was a simple one: 'Fuck you,' and a hang-up.

He put the phone down and reluctantly swivelled his chair around to face his colleagues. Ellie looked furious; Larissa looked disappointed. He needed to throw up again.

'Sorry,' he said.

Ellie rolled her eyes. Larissa looked away.

'I . . .' He was about to make up an excuse but realised he had nothing to say that wouldn't make the situation even worse.

'Well, at least you beat your new best friend in,' said Ellie. 'He's nowhere to be found this morning.'

Watson did his best to look surprised, or like he cared.

'And you need to get over to the council chambers. There was some sort of a disturbance over there yesterday afternoon. We were too busy to deal with it.'

He leapt at the chance to get out of the office. He stood up and started heading for the door.

'You'll need your suit jacket with your phone and your notebook,' Ellie observed.

He had left it hanging over the back of his chair.

'And for fuck's sake, get some Visine or something for your eyes before you bleed to death.'

————

The council chambers was the most modern building in Gloster. A two-storey red-brick edifice built sometime in the late 1970s, it was situated next door to the municipal pool, which was now overflowing. The water running from the pool into the already backed-up stormwater system had the attention of half-a-dozen raincoated council workers whose job, it appeared to Watson, was to stand around looking concerned.

The reception area inside the front door of the chambers was unmanned. A badly patched broken window facing back out onto the street gave the impression the place had been hastily abandoned.

He pressed a button on the front counter marked *Service*, and settled in to wait under the steady gaze of a number of smiling ex-mayors whose portraits hung around the reception area.

He'd got up early to finish a drawing he had started the previous evening. It was a picture of his dad playing footy, like in the stories he'd heard when his dad had other men around to drink beer and smoke cigarettes out on the back verandah. He'd had his breakfast while he waited for his dad to get ready for work. Jam on toast, lashings of it, just how he liked it. He ran up to surprise his dad as he walked to the front door.

But his dad shoved him away. 'Bloody hell, look at the state of my fucken uniform,' he said, wiping at the smears of jam Craig had left on the pristine blue uniform shirt.

'I'm sorry, Dad,' Craig said.

'You're a pain in the fucking arse,' his dad replied. He left the house in a temper, slamming the door in Craig's face as he went.

Craig threw the drawing in the bin. It had jammy fingerprints on it now as well. He couldn't do anything right.

'Can I help you?' an overweight, flustered middle-aged woman in a damp-looking, hand-knitted jumper called across the counter. Then: 'Excuse me, can I help you?' she asked again, not as friendly the second time around.

Watson jerked back to reality, blinked and shook his head.

'Ah, yes,' he said. His mind was completely blank. He pulled out his notebook and checked his notes.

'I'm here to see the General Manager, Sam Nefarian, about an incident that occurred yesterday,' he managed.

The woman looked like she was about to burst into tears. The colour drained from her face. 'Um, do you have an appointment?' she asked nervously.

Watson looked up to the ceiling, gathering himself then, still sitting, he pulled out his badge and held it in front of him.

He couldn't be bothered standing up or approaching the counter.

'Detective Senior Constable Watson. Just tell him I'm here.' Then he added, as an afterthought, 'Waiting.'

Sam Nefarian was a thirty-something bundle of thin brown energy. He bounded out into the reception area only a minute after 'Debbie from Reception' had called him on an internal telephone. He was stick-thin, in a short-sleeved purple shirt and skinny black trousers with a shiny silver belt buckle. Sam had his hand out apologising when he was still six steps away from Watson.

'G'day, Detective Watson. I'm Sam Nefarian, General Manager. So sorry to keep you waiting. Come in. Come in.' He was bouncing on the balls of his feet.

Watson followed Nefarian through a maze of hushed corridors; most of the office doors were closed. The ones that were open were mostly empty.

'We've given most of the staff the day off,' Nefarian explained. 'The flood situation, you know.'

They ended up in a corner office on the ground floor, the walls covered in colour-coded maps and diagrams of places and things that Watson had no interest in.

'Yeah, we've had a very exciting last couple of days, haven't we?' Nefarian began. 'No doubt a lot worse to come, though, hey? We've got crews out . . .'

Watson was hearing white noise, beginning to shake. He needed an Oxy badly. He held his hand up, palm out, the international signal for *shut the fuck up*.

'Sam,' he managed.

Nefarian's verbal diarrhoea tailed off. He stopped talking and started staring, wide-eyed.

'We received a report of a disturbance here, yesterday afternoon,' Watson began, reading from his notes. 'At three fifteen p.m. The report says you were assaulted.'

'No, no. Look, it was all just a big misunderstanding. Assault? There was no assault. It was nothing, truly; we'd just like to forget about it.'

Watson swallowed hard.

So why the fuck did you call?

'Yeah, that's all well and good,' he said, 'but a complaint has been received so we have to follow up. Why don't you just tell me what happened?'

'Ha ha.' Nefarian impersonated a laugh. 'It was just a couple of guys from outside of town who had some issues with the flood mitigation work. They were blowing off a bit of steam. No harm done.'

'Names,' Watson said, pen poised.

'Ah . . .' Nefarian held his chin in his hand, doing an even worse impersonation of a person trying and failing to remember something. 'I don't think I got their names.'

Watson said nothing, just kept looking at Sam, tapping his pen on his notebook.

'Ah, Jim—that was one of them. Jim Banks,' he said proudly, apparently expecting a pat on the back.

'And?' Watson prompted.

'Oh, the other one. Ah, yeah, I think that was Chris Wordsworth.'

'Banks and Wordsworth.' Watson wrote the names down. 'And what was their issue with the flood mitigation?'

'Oh well, you know, it's not an exact science, is it?'

Watson gave no response.

'Well, we do our best—I've had a big team working on

it—but you're never going to be able to stop a flood once the river gets up, are you?'

Watson had no idea, but it seemed a reasonable assumption.

'So, what was their problem? Mr Banks and Mr Wordsworth?'

'Well, their places have gone under. They thought the mitigation work was going to mean that they were safe, you know? Outside the flood zone.'

'Why would they have thought that?' Watson asked. 'Had someone told them that?'

'Oh, I very much doubt that, Detective Watson. I mean, like I said, it's not an exact science, is it?'

'No, I don't suppose it is,' Watson said. He wanted to wrap it up but there was something about Nefarian that just didn't seem legit. He waited a moment to see if the gears clicked into place . . . Nope, nothing.

Nefarian looked like he was going to start speaking again so Watson cut him off.

'Well, if you're happy to leave it at that, then we've all got more important things to be getting on with.' He snapped his notebook shut and stood. Nefarian rose too, to walk him out.

'Don't get up,' Watson said. 'I can find my own way.'

He couldn't tell whether Nefarian looked relieved or disappointed.

———

Debbie was still standing at the counter when he returned to the reception area, wearing the same deer-caught-in-the-headlights expression on her face. He gave her a brief nod as he passed and her hand sprung up to her mouth.

As he was about to exit the building, he heard someone clearing their throat behind him. He turned and saw that Debbie had followed him to the door. She was holding a rolled-up cylinder of large laminated sheets. She glanced fearfully over her shoulder then thrust the rolled-up papers at him. He reached for them automatically and then, without a word, she hurried back into the silent depths of the building.

He stood for a moment, confused, then made the dash out to his car in the pouring rain.

11

The office was empty and whisper-quiet when he returned. Ellie and Larissa were out. He had passed them on his way to the station, their high-vis vests to the fore, marked cars with the full flashing lightshow happening: the evacuation protocol— whatever that entailed. There was probably an email about it somewhere.

Watson was feeling good, buzzing nicely. He had dropped into the barracks and had two Oxys and then grabbed a McFlat White with three sugars and some salted caramel macarons for lunch.

He made himself comfortable in his cubicle and slid the elastic band off the cylinder Debbie had given him at the council chambers. There was more to it than he'd first thought. The bundle, unrolled, comprised a single A4 sheet, about half-a-dozen poster-sized laminated sheets and about the same number again of unlaminated poster-sized sheets. He had to push aside the clutter of empty coffee cups and junk that had accumulated on his desk to spread them out fully, then weigh down the ends to stop them rolling up again.

The first sheet was a large map. Gloster and the coast were on the bottom left and the Gloster River snaked its way diagonally up and across to the top right of the page. It was black and white, no topographical information, just roads and rivers. There were tables full of numbers, measurements and volumes and arrows pointing to different sections of the river.

The second sheet was similar to the first but it was an aerial photograph of the same area with the same tables and measurements overlaid.

The next six sheets were all detailed schematic diagrams. They set out construction plans for channels to be dug to specific depths for specific distances and to drain into new dams that were to be constructed. There were pipes to be laid, underpasses constructed under existing roads, land cleared, tunnels dug and gradients flattened. It was, he realised, a massive scheme designed to channel and dissipate floodwaters before they could inundate and destroy low-lying farmland.

The final sheet was a clear plastic overlay with a complex pattern of shaded boxes, dates, numbers and hieroglyphic symbols that Watson could make neither heads nor tails of. On a whim, he laid the clear plastic sheet over the black-and-white map of the town and the river. This brought it all together. The shadowed boxes and the dates related to the entire scope of the Gloster Region Flood Mitigation Plan. It showed the size, placement and extent of each of the individual projects to be completed as part of the plan and the date of completion of each part of the project.

The single A4 sheet was a photocopy from a year-old issue of the local newspaper, *The Gloster Gazette*, celebrating the completion of the project. There was a grainy black-and-white photo accompanying the article and there, smiling widely, shaking hands with his boss, Sam Nefarian, was the man responsible for the outstanding achievement—Anthony Sweeney: Manager, Infrastructure Delivery. Father of Laura, Tayla Howard's best friend.

'Something stinks,' the old man—Sweeney's father-in-law—had said.

There's something there, Watson thought. *What am I missing?*

He was losing his buzz.

Raised voices made their way up from downstairs. He did his best to ignore them.

Think!

There was a crash, and a scream, and then his phone started ringing.

Fuck it.

He didn't race downstairs; he got up slowly and waited, just in case.

There was another crash, shouted obscenities.

Damn.

He walked out into the hall and stood at the top of the stairs.

No, it definitely seemed to be picking up steam again.

He walked down one step at a time until he was five or six steps from the bottom, then he bounded down onto the ground floor like a man on a mission to find Philby on the floor in the corridor. His shirt had come untucked and his flabby white gut was spilling out over his belt. He had a small skinny woman in a bear hug, his big salami arms wrapped around her while she struggled and kicked and screamed and tried to bite him.

Watson couldn't help but laugh out loud.

'For fuck's sake, don't just stand there—give me a hand,' Philby commanded, all red-faced and breathless.

Watson unhooked the handcuffs from his belt and approached the writhing couple. But as he caught sight of the woman's face he hesitated. It was Jenny Howard.

He pocketed the handcuffs and knelt down in front of her.

'Jenny, come on,' he pleaded. 'It's going to be okay.'

'Fuck you,' she spat, then subsided, her energy more or less expended. 'Fuck you,' she whimpered. She was limp now.

Philby extricated himself and rolled back into a sitting position.

Jenny Howard lay on the floor, sobbing. 'You said you were going to find her,' she gasped, wrapping her arms around herself, her eyes closed, tears running freely.

Watson glanced at Philby, raised his eyebrows. *What the fuck?*

'We just had to inform Mrs Howard,' Philby wheezed, as he heaved himself first to his knees and then to his feet, 'that the, ah, the search for Tayla is, ah, being put on hold, just for the moment.' He avoided Watson's eyes.

Briony, the daytime civilian receptionist, was standing at the end of the hallway, her hand to her mouth. Philby angrily waved her away back to reception.

Watson rubbed Jenny's arm, doing his best to console her.

'Jenny, it's going to be okay. Like I said, teenagers go missing all the time. Tayla will show up. She's probably just caught up at someone's place now—you know, caught in the flood.'

'It's not like that and you know it. I heard her on the phone. I told you! Someone's taken her.'

Watson had no answer. He looked up at his boss.

Philby just held out his hands, like, *What can I do?*

Weak as piss.

'Jenny, don't worry, I'm going to keep looking for Tayla,

okay?' He stared at Philby as he said it. 'We're going to do our best to find her.'

The sergeant wouldn't meet his gaze.

Jenny dragged herself up off the floor and Watson put his arms around her shoulders and helped her back to the reception area.

'I'm going to do my best,' he assured her again as he opened the door for her.

She put her arm out and patted him on the chest, her head down, then she stepped out into the rain.

Philby was dabbing at a vivid red scratch on his cheek with a tissue when Watson went back and stood in the doorway of his office. Philby glanced at him and shook his head; he seemed close to tears. He pulled on his old gravy-stained windcheater and Watson noticed there were a few new stains down the front of it. They could have been blood.

Watson stood aside as Philby passed him and headed out the front door of the station without another word.

12

The rain had reduced to a light drizzle by mid-afternoon, but the damage was done. According to the weather reports, enough rain had been dumped on the ranges west of town to keep the river rising, despite the conditions easing in Gloster.

Meanwhile, Watson had found Jim Banks, one of the local landowners with whom Nefarian had had a 'misunderstanding', in the state's criminal database. He was mid-fifties, and had a record for assault back in the 1990s over a boundary dispute with a neighbour. He had received a twelve-month good behaviour bond for the assault and had no other record on file.

Banks had an address listed as a property about ten kilometres west of town. Watson checked the SES database and found that the road directly west of the property was now closed due to flooding, but he could potentially access it by heading north up the highway from Gloster and then taking a secondary road— still open, according to the SES—out to the west.

Heading over the bridge out of town, he fought the urge to just keep driving all the way back to Sydney, forget he had ever set eyes on the merry municipality of Gloster. He was still feeling tempted when he pulled over to the narrow, gravelled kerb at the highway intersection.

Larissa stood on the road, in the drizzle, in front of a marked police vehicle with its red and blue lights reflecting off her yellow high-vis vest. She was holding a bright orange traffic control torch and waving away sightseers and anyone else who wasn't a resident or didn't have urgent business in town.

He was still feeling a bit sheepish after his no-show the previous afternoon, but he need not have worried. Larissa smiled up at him from under her sodden hood as he approached across the road.

'Hey,' she said.

'Hey,' he responded. 'Okay?'

'Oh yeah, great,' she said. 'You just here to hang out with me or are you heading somewhere?'

'Yeah, I just decided to pack it in,' he said. 'Heading back to Sydney.'

She looked at him, her expression serious, and then must have seen something in his eyes. 'Dickhead,' she said, lightly donging him on the head with her torch. 'Where are you going?'

'A bloke called Jim Banks. A property called Berimma Station on the Yulong Road. Heard of it?'

'Nope,' she said, 'but be careful if you're heading out Yulong Road—it's pretty bad even when it's dry.'

'I'll bear that in mind,' he said.

'You do that. Hey, you should come around again—that was fun the other night.'

'It was, wasn't it?' he said, feeling . . . something.

They stood there for a moment, smiling awkwardly at each other, then he gave her a little salute and headed back to his car.

———

The Yulong Road was sealed for the first fifty metres off the highway before it turned into a narrow muddy track. Watson was about sixty metres off the highway when he started to think that maybe heading out to the Banks place wasn't such a great idea. The road had some serious dips and climbs in it. In the bottom of most of the dips there was brown running water, the depth of which was impossible to determine.

The morning's fine drizzle gave way to heavier rain the further he headed west and the windscreen wipers, like the tyres of the car, were having trouble dealing with the volume of water being thrown about. When the car lost traction on a steep uphill stretch and started sliding towards a waterlogged ditch on the side of the road, Watson made the decision to turn around. There was no point getting himself stuck out here in the middle of nowhere in the pissing rain.

As he crested the rise, looking for a place to turn around, the Banks property came into view. Even to a born-and-bred city boy, the drama of the landscape was striking. The land stretched away in front of him, deep green and shining wet, as far as the distant foothills of the misty, cloud-covered ranges just visible to the west. On his left, the river had broken its banks to become a raging torrent, swirling whirlpools of debris, covering long flat stretches of land into a rippling inland sea of dark, dirty flood-water. To his right, the land climbed slowly away from the river, the water giving way to small green paddocks and then dense bushland. The paddocks were crowded with seemingly thousands of drenched and immobile sheep and cattle moved up from the lower-lying fields.

The Banks home was only a kilometre further on, up a short gravel driveway. It stood stark and white against a carefully tended patch of dark green lawn. As Watson crunched his way up the driveway, a small four-wheel-drive vehicle detached itself from a huge mob of sheep in a paddock not far from the home-stead and headed in his direction.

Watson half lowered his window as the quad bike pulled up beside him.

'Can I help you?' the figure on the bike shouted over the thrumming of his own engine, the wind and the rain.

'Jim Banks?' Watson asked.

'Yeah.'

'Detective Craig Watson. We need to have a word.'

Banks stared hard at the badge and then glanced down towards the mass of brown water inundating the majority of his property.

'Follow me,' he said.

Banks pulled into a large corrugated-iron shed standing behind the homestead. There was room enough for four or five cars, but the shed was mostly empty, just a collection of tools, something that Watson assumed was a plough, and large drums of oil and diesel. He parked just inside the shed door and approached Banks, who had dismounted from the quad bike and was removing a thick yellow rain jacket and gloves.

The wind was gusting hard outside and the rain was ham-mering against the sides of the shed. It was freezing cold. Watson fought the urge to shiver and fold his arms.

Banks dug his hands deep into his pockets and glared at Watson as he approached. 'This about the other day, is it?' he demanded. He had a large round head, bald, with thick features.

His lips were cracked and bloodless and Watson had the impression they didn't smile much.

'We are following up a complaint received from Gloster Council, Mr Banks,' Watson said evenly. He was in an oddly positive frame of mind.

'Fuck me. Who are they to be making a fucking complaint? Have you seen the state of my fucking stock?' Banks said, taking a step towards Watson, getting right up in his face.

Watson ignored the advance. His original intention had been to keep things informal, just fishing for information. But fuck it. His good mood was evaporating rapidly.

He took his notebook from his pocket. Reading from his notes, he said, 'We received a complaint that you attended the council offices, intimidated council staff, acted aggressively and may have committed an assault, Mr Banks.' He looked up into Banks's narrowed eyes. He could smell sour tea and cigarettes on the man's breath. 'So, we can either do this here, now, or you can accompany me back to the station. It's up to you, but I'd suggest you might want to back off.'

Banks took his time, then wrinkled his nose and shook his head. His hand rustled inside his pocket and he produced a battered packet of cigarettes and a lighter. He took a step back, turned away from the wind howling through the shed door, and lit a cigarette.

'What do you want to know?' he asked, exhaling a thick pall of smoke while gazing outside, over Watson's shoulder.

'Well, let's start with why you were there in the first place, shall we?'

'Because those cun –' He stopped, took a healthy drag of his cigarette, then started again. 'Did you see the state of the property when you drove in, when you came over the rise?'

'Yes, I did,' Watson said.

'Then you can see that I'm fucked, that everything from here down to the river is underwater.'

'Yes, I saw that.'

'Well how much do you know about the flood mitigation plan?'

'A fair bit actually,' Watson said.

Banks raised an eyebrow at that. 'Well, why don't you come inside, and I'll show you something.'

Watson nodded and returned his notebook to his pocket. Then they both made a dash for the back door of the homestead.

———

There was a good fire burning in a combustion heater, and Banks quickly opened the door and tossed another split log inside before flipping the kettle on in his small bare kitchen. The home was clean and neat, but it was clearly the lodgings of a recently single man. Furniture was sparse and utilitarian. There were obvious indentations and unworn squares of carpet where now-missing furniture had once stood. There were piles of books, mostly military history, and an obvious lack of any attempt at decoration.

Banks made his guest a coffee and himself a mug of black tea, while Watson stood as close to the heater as he could bear. Banks placed the cups on an empty kitchen table and left the room. He came back with a bundle of paperwork which he placed neatly in front of him as he sat down.

He looked up at Watson before he started. Watson could tell he would have been a good-looking man once. Rugged, tanned, with a strong square chin and vivid green eyes. But he looked more tired than angry now, maybe even slightly embarrassed when he met Watson's eyes.

'This is all correspondence from the council,' Banks said, indicating the stack of paperwork sitting on the table in front of him. There would have been at least five hundred pages.

'Okay,' Watson said. He could see Banks wanted to talk.

'This all started six years ago'—Banks ran his thumb up the side of the pile of paperwork—'after the last big floods we had out here. Half the farms went under. Not just underwater; I mean financially. Gone. You see, the river narrows around here, it picks up all the water coming out of the hills and flows downstream until it gets about five mile upriver from here and then *bang*. If there's too much, it just spills over and, well, you can see for yourself what happens.'

'Yeah, I can,' Watson said.

'So, six years ago we all got together, all the property owners out here on the river and the council, and said, you know, how do we stop this sort of thing happening in the future? And they did this big study and spent all this money and came up with this plan—the flood mitigation plan.' He looked up at Watson, to check that he was following.

Watson nodded, sipped his coffee.

Banks lit another cigarette.

'Then they bring in all these experts, hydrologists and whatnot, and say they can fix the problem with the flooding but it's going to cost us, you know? Cost us big time, because the council can't afford all this new work. I mean, look at the state of the bloody roads, right? Anyway, we came up with a plan, the council upped the rates, and all the properties with a river boundary had to pay an extra levy.'

'And it all went ahead?'

'Too right it did. Five years they've been working on it. Fleecing us dry, overrun after overrun, cost blowouts. They kept on coming back with their hand out and it's bloody hard enough trying to make a living out here as it is.' He stabbed his cigarette out into the ashtray and glared around his semi-abandoned home.

Watson, seeing that the man's eyes had started to glisten, gave him a moment before he said, 'Obviously it hasn't worked.'

'Hasn't worked?' Banks looked up, a shattered man. 'It would've fucking worked, if it was ever fucking finished.'

Banks took Watson through the main points of the paperwork. He showed him well-thumbed, notated sheets of correspond-ence, pointing out where changes had been made to the project throughout the course of construction. They were subtle but they were constant. Over the course of five years, the original scope of works had been altered almost beyond recognition from what was originally envisioned, costed and agreed upon.

'We had no say,' Banks said. 'These things would just turn up in the mail. They wouldn't discuss any changes. If you didn't look closely yourself, you'd never even know the changes were happening, but bit by bit we got less and less, and by the end of it . . . well, you can see the result of it.'

'Yes,' Watson said, 'you sure can,' and he grimaced as Banks cracked the knuckles on his massive scarred fists.

'So, about the other day then?' Banks asked, as Watson pushed his chair back.

'What about it?' Watson said, gathering his things and heading for the door.

Banks looked relieved.

'Oh, there is one other thing,' Watson said as he reached the front door. 'I didn't see a car in your garage. How do you get around?'

He caught a flash of something in the other man's eyes.

'It's, ah, in for repairs,' Banks said.

'Oh yeah? Have an accident?'

'Yeah, just a small one.' The man's tone had changed.

'What sort of car is it?'

'It's a Camry, Toyota Camry.'

'Colour?'

'Red.'

13

The drive back to the highway was a blur. A couple of times Watson had to use the wipers to wash mud off the windscreen when he hit water in the dips of the road, but his mind was elsewhere.

Anthony Sweeney must have been rorting the council's flood mitigation works; there was no other logical explanation. There was the half-built palace on the hill, the new Jaguar, the accident that could be a murder. The motive? Banks had motive in spades *and* he had a red Toyota. Watson had asked for details of the smash repairer before he left, citing 'routine enquiries', and Banks had looked like he was going to shit himself.

Ellen Sweeney—he had to talk to Ellen Sweeney. *Something stinks!* Someone had kidnapped Tayla, and her best friend was murdered. *Something stinks!*

His phone buzzed with an incoming text and he glanced at it, lying on the passenger seat beside him: *Not long now faggot!*

What the fuck?

Seething, Watson stopped the car and reached for the phone,

started to key in a reply: *I know who you are. I know where you live* . . . Fuck it—he didn't send it.

He was doing one-sixty when he passed the Gloster turn-off. He kept driving towards Sydney.

An hour down the highway, he pulled in at a well-patronised truck stop and cruised around the back to where the big rigs were parked. He needed sustenance; his head was on fire. It was never hard to find it if you knew what you were looking for, and sometimes it was easier than others.

A shiny new SS ute with all the trimmings and the silhouettes of two heads inside was sitting in the back row, trying to look inconspicuous. He parked his car well away from the ute and watched it through his rear-view mirror. Five minutes later, a sagging, crook-backed truck driver approached the passenger side of the ute and had a quick conversation. They went through the time-honoured ritual. The truckie and the passenger shook hands once as the money changed hands, and then they did it again to exchange the drugs. All the while the truckie looked innocently out into the car park. They couldn't have made it more obvious if they tried.

Watson gave it five more minutes and watched one more deal just to be sure, then he got out and approached the ute himself. He could see the two occupants stiffen in their seats as he walked straight up to the front of the vehicle. They clearly didn't get too many customers in suits.

He walked around and tapped on the driver's-side window, pulling his coat back so that his gun and handcuffs were clearly visible on his belt. The window came down slowly, about halfway.

'How can we help you, officer?' The voice came with a cloud of cigarette smoke.

'I think it's fairly fucking obvious how you can help me, fellas,' Watson said, leaning down to look inside the car. As expected, there were masses of tattoos, goatees and tombstone stares.

There was a plastic shopping bag sitting at the passenger's feet that he was doing his best to cover with his legs.

'The bag,' he said. 'Give it here.'

Neither man moved.

Watson pulled his right hand back to rest on the butt of his pistol. 'Are you sure you want it to go this way, boys?' he said.

The passenger leant forward and reached towards the bag.

'Uh-uh,' Watson said. 'You'—looking at the driver—'reach over with your left hand, pick up the bag and pass it to me. You'—motioning to the passenger—'keep your fucking hands where I can see them.'

The driver did as instructed while Watson watched on carefully.

When the bag was in his hands he peered into it greedily. 'Right, what have we got here?'

There were twenty or so little deal bags of speed, probably about the same amount of pot, about ten deal bags of ice and a small automatic pistol. Watson picked up the pistol with two fingers, then he looked at the two men in the ute.

'Fellas, really?' he said.

The driver gave him a *well, what's a guy supposed to do?* look before Watson tossed the pistol into the trash-filled garden behind the ute. Then he took a big handful of everything, had a quick look at his haul, and dumped three deals of pot back into the bag. He then stuffed the remainder into his pocket and dumped the bag back onto the driver's lap.

'Now, fellas, that'll do you for this afternoon. Take off and don't let me catch you around here again.'

The driver gave him a practised death stare and said, 'We'll see you round, pig,' as he reached for the key. The ute rumbled into life and Watson let it get well clear before he made a move back to his own car. His heart was racing.

———

He hit the outskirts of Sydney just on dark. It was drizzling, he was sizzling. He'd chopped up and snorted two of the bindles of speed. It was jaw-clenching, heart-poundingly powerful stuff. He sat fidgeting and mumbling to himself in the peak hour bumper-to-bumper traffic. His GPS blinked away at Jeremy Landers' Bondi address.

It took more than an hour to cross Sydney from north to east. Another fifteen minutes of cruising around the block before he found a parking space with a view of the property his mate from the Drug Squad had texted him. It was half a red-brick semi-detached Federation-style home. The letterbox was hanging lopsided off the collapsing front fence. The small patch of lawn had probably died before the Depression. All of the lights were off. He sat and watched and waited.

It was another two and a half hours before a taxi pulled up in front of the house and Jeremy Landers and a young woman jumped out. They put their arms around each other and went laughing up to the front door and into the house. Watson had been grinding his teeth and sweating for hours. He pulled out the last of the bindles of speed, stuck a rolled-up twenty-dollar note straight into the bag and snorted it. He saw colours. He lost his mind.

He jumped out of the car. Jogged across the road. Banged on the front door.

It wasn't answered quickly enough so he banged again harder, faster.

'Hang on, hang on,' an angry voice yelled from inside. 'Who the fuck is it?'

'It's the police—open the fucking door!' Watson raged.

The door didn't open immediately, so Watson stood back and smashed his fist through the opaque glass feature in the wood. There was a scream from inside. He heard running feet on hardwood floors. He kicked at the door once and it cracked. Twice, and it cracked some more. He heaved himself at the door and it smashed wide open.

He lost his balance and went sprawling down the hallway. A woman was screaming hysterically from a room at the end of the hall. Landers was crouching down in a corner with his hands up, utterly terrified.

Watson's phone had been flung from his pocket when he flew through the door. When he stooped to pick it up, he saw it was buzzing.

There was a message.

You can run but you can't hide.

His heart spasmed. He coughed. His vision was blurred, but he could see that Landers didn't have a phone in his hand. Landers was crying. The girl was screaming. He ran blindly out of the house.

14

He pulled into the same truck stop he had stopped at on the way down. The digital clock on his dashboard read 10.30 p.m.

It can't be!

He checked his phone. Only three missed calls, two voice-mail messages. The time on the most recent text message, the one that had seared his brain in Jeremy Landers' hallway, was 9.25.

The drive from the city to the truck stop normally took two hours. He had done it in just over one. He had no memory of the trip and he was coming down hard.

His jaw ached; he was completely dry. Both eyes had a pulse, a thumping, red pulse. Rain was coming down heavy in the bright lights shining down into the almost-empty car park. He didn't venture out the back.

In the roadhouse they had Visine and fast-acting Panadol. He applied the meds while he ordered a quarter chicken and chips. He couldn't even remember the last time he'd eaten.

He listened to the two messages. Larissa: *Are you okay?*

Where are you? Philby: *Where the fuck are you? Get your arse in here—it's an emergency.* Ellie: hang-up.

He got a quarter of the quarter down with a few chips, then he hit the road.

———

He was stopped by a glowing orange traffic torch waving in the rain at the Gloster turn-off. He pulled up short and opened his window a crack. It was hammering down. The face under the bright yellow hood didn't belong to Larissa or Ellie.

'The road's closed,' the young constable shouted through the rain.

'Detective Senior Constable Watson,' he said. 'What's the situation?'

'Oh right, we're evacuating. It came up much faster than everyone expected. There's an incident van down at the bridge.'

Watson headed slowly down to the mass of flashing blue and red lights.

There were a dozen police vehicles pulled up on each side of the road at the highway end of the bridge. There was a team of three blocking the road into town, and taking names and details from the residents as they crossed the bridge towards the highway.

He added to the pile of cars and ran the thirty metres to a large bus that was the local area incident van. He pulled up short under a tarpaulin that had been erected just outside the door of the bus and shook off the freezing rainwater.

There were four men in the harsh white light in the bus, all of them senior to Watson. Three of them ignored him completely and continued with their rushed conversations on mobile phones and police radio. Philby turned and glared. 'Where the fuck have you been?'

'I got bogged out on the Yulong Road,' he lied. 'There was no reception,' he added before he was asked.

'What were you doing out there?'

'Following up an assault complaint from the council yesterday. A bloke called Jim Banks.'

Philby looked sceptical. 'Well, there're more important things to be going on with,' he said. 'We're evacuating. The river came up faster than it should have.'

'Yeah, so I heard,' Watson said.

'It's only just over eighteen metres, but it's broken its banks the entire length. We've got blackouts, we've had a few small fires, the grid is shorting out all over the place. There are boats lost out at sea. We've only got all these blokes until midnight, then they have to head back to their own areas. Cameron and Brookes are going house to house. We have to get everybody out—the town is about to be cut off.'

'Righto, where do you want me to start?'

'Cameron and Brookes are here, Marsden Street,' Philby said, pointing to a spot on a large situation map of the town pinned to the wall. 'Get over there now and coordinate with them. We have to make sure everyone is out and then we have to get out ourselves before this bridge goes under. You got me?'

'Got ya. I'll get going right now.'

'Good man,' Philby said, and Watson could see the fear in his eyes.

———

The municipal park on the town side of the bridge was under-water and most of the main street was a rapidly expanding puddle. The drains were gone, filled to capacity; there was more water spurting out of them than flowing into them. The main street of Gloster ran parallel to the river, the main residential areas were behind the centre of town and slightly more elevated. The flooding would hit the main street and the shopping precinct first before flowing out into the houses.

He followed the flashing lights to Ellie and Larissa's patrol car two streets back from the centre of town. They were helping an elderly couple, rugged up in blankets, into a police van. As he approached, Watson heard the driver of the van say, 'Okay, that's it for us, we have to make a move.' When it pulled away, he stood facing Ellie and Larissa, deep under the hoods of their soaking rain jackets.

'Where have you been?' Larissa asked. 'We've been worried!'

Ellie looked unconvinced.

'I got bogged,' he said.

The women looked at each other.

'I told you that would happen,' Larissa said.

Ellie still looked unconvinced.

'Well, you know men—we never listen,' Watson said.

Ellie might just have smiled.

'So where are we up to?' he asked.

'We think we've got everyone,' Ellie said, 'but we don't know who left before we started taking names at the bridge, so we're checking all the at-risk people, mostly the elderly. We've got'—she stopped and pulled a soaked piece of paper from her pocket—'five more to do. There's two in the caravan park. Why don't you go and do those, and we'll look after the other three.'

'Okay,' he said. 'What numbers are they, and where will we meet after I'm done?'

'Eleven and thirty-three,' Ellie replied. 'Just catch us on the radio—the phones are patchy because the towers are down.'

He drove through darkened, waterlogged streets to the caravan park, closer to the beach end of town. A police cruiser passed him going back towards the bridge and the occupants gave him a farewell wave and flashed their high beams.

The Panadol had had only minimal effect; his head was fragile, his mind was numb, he was working on autopilot.

He turned in through the main gates of the caravan park and idled in front of the manager's residence. The park was in complete darkness; none of the cabins appeared to have any lights on. He could see wind-rippled puddles of black water across the surface of the rough roadway through his rain-spattered windscreen. He hit the high beams and rolled forward.

His headlights carved a cone out of the blackness and the falling rain. Number eleven was only four cabins further on from the manager's cabin; he stopped outside it and shone a torch up through the rain at the front door and windows. Nothing. He sounded his horn. Nothing. He started to drive on. Then he stopped.

Bloody old people.

He got out and immediately went down, ankle-deep into a puddle of freezing rainwater.

Fuck.

He slammed the car door closed and hunched under his hood as the wind and the slanting rain did its best to rip it off his head. He leapt the four stairs to the front porch in two steps and hammered his torch against the door and then the front window. He shone his torch in through the window. It was dark, no movement; the place was definitely empty.

He jumped back into the car, managing to avoid the puddle outside his door this time, and moved on, headlights blazing into the dark, counting the numbers aloud as he went. Number thirty-three must be at the end of the line, he realised.

The car thumped into a particularly deep pothole hidden under the floodwater and the left side of the car went down; there was a scraping sound under the car.

Fuck this.

He reversed back, attempted to drive around the invisible pothole.

The right wheel went down.

He was still a good ten cabins from number thirty-three. He stared hard down into the cone of light penetrating the darkness. The windscreen wipers were barely keeping pace with the rain. Small shrubs and trees were whipping furiously around on the edge of his vision, just beyond the reach of the light.

But there . . .

A flicker of something near the edge of the light. The car wouldn't move further forward without grinding against the edge of a major deformation in the road under the water.

There! A face?

He shook his head. He must be seeing things.

Right then, he saw a person come running out of the darkness, flash across the roadway between the cabins at the end of the park and disappear into the darkness on the other side.

He threw open the car door, jumped out, and was immediately submerged to mid-calves.

'Hey!' he screamed. 'Police! Stop!'

He shone his torch in the direction the person had run. He saw a flash of eyes in his torch beam, and then the figure bolted away.

'Hey!' he yelled again uselessly into the howling wind.

He tried to follow, but the water deepened steadily the further he went, splashing up under his waterproof jacket and into his face.

It was pointless anyway; whoever it was had gone. He stood at the edge of the limits of his headlights and shone his torch into all of the dark places between the cabins. Nothing. He was soaked. He was freezing.

'Fuck you then,' he yelled into the darkness. 'Stay here!'

Number thirty-three was only two cabins further on. It was empty.

He sploshed his way back to the car, shivering and swearing.

―――――

The barracks was on one of the highest streets in the town. Although the ground was saturated, there was no floodwater running through the property. He pulled into the carport and called Ellie on the radio. Told her he'd gone under and needed to change his clothes. He didn't bother running for the door. It wasn't possible to get any wetter.

As soon as he entered, he could tell something was wrong. The house was dark but there was a clattering noise coming from the kitchen. There was a presence in the house. Not rats this time. He threw on the lights and drew his pistol simultaneously.

'Police, don't move!' he screamed with fear-fuelled adrenaline. Moving to his left, his pistol trained on the kitchen door.

'Police, don't move!' he yelled again as he took two big strides into the kitchen.

It was empty. The back door was wide open. The rain-filled wind was slamming the door into a cupboard and the raggedy curtains were streaming in sopping tatters across the room.

'Oh God,' he moaned as he kicked the door shut. He laid his head on the bench as he looked down at the floor, at the trail of muddy footsteps coming in from the yard.

Fuck.

He spun around, pistol out in front.

'Police, don't fucking move!' he screamed.

The hallway, the bedroom, the bathroom, the lounge, the second bedroom—something flashed. Nothing. He wanted to cry.

He fell down onto the lounge. His pipe was still there, stuffed between the cushions where he had left it. He reached into his pocket to retrieve the few bags of rocks that he had crammed in there at the truck stop. The deal bags were sopping wet, open and empty. He held his head and moaned.

He spent the obligatory five minutes waiting for the hot water and then another five under the steaming flow before it ran out. He towelled off quickly, dancing on the freezing cold tiles. He exited the bathroom just as the front door opened. There was a direct line of sight between the two. He froze. Larissa entered first and then Ellie. They stood and watched, smiling wide, while he stood semi-paralysed, swinging in the breeze.

———

'Must have been the cold,' Ellie said to Larissa when he re-entered the lounge room, dressed. Larissa snorted, smiling his way. It took him a moment, then he smiled himself.

Whatever.

They had made coffee, instant, and were hunched together on the lounge with his little heater on full. He snuck a hand down and carefully manoeuvred his crack pipe further back under the cushions.

'Could be the only street that still has electricity,' Ellie said.

He took the cup of coffee they had made for him and held it between his hands, soaking up the warmth.

'So, what's the story now?' he asked.

'We just wait until five a.m., then we head out as well,' Ellie said. 'They reckon the bridge will be under by eight. If anything comes up between now and five, we'll have to deal with it but other than that we might as well just hang out here.'

Watson told them about seeing the person in the caravan park and then showed them the muddy footprints in the kitchen.

'We've had three reports of burglaries this afternoon and tonight,' Ellie said.

'Arseholes,' Larissa said. 'But they're scraping the bottom of the barrel here, aren't they?'

Then the thought seemed to strike all three of them at the same time.

'We've got a proper coffee maker, too,' Ellie said.

They poured their thin instant coffees into the sink, raced out into the rain and drove to Ellie and Larissa's place.

No sign of forced entry. It was all good.

Ellie got the king-size gas heater happening while Larissa got the percolator perking. Watson dropped himself into the big plush lounge in front of the fire. Ellie dropped a mohair blanket onto his lap.

'Try this on for size,' she said, and he did. It was toasty.

It wasn't long before Larissa entered, carefully holding out three steaming mugs and with a packet of Tim Tams stuffed under her arm, one biscuit already hanging out of her mouth.

'Move over,' she muttered around the biscuit, and she squeezed herself under the blanket to Watson's right. Ellie had already made herself comfortable under the blanket to his left.

They sat in silence, sipping their coffee, eating their biscuits, entranced by the hypnotic glow of the heater.

'Three-thirty,' Ellie said eventually. 'An hour and a half to go. I'm just going to close my eyes for a minute.'

Watson felt Ellie's weight gradually lean into his side and a bony elbow grind into his ribs as she relaxed into a deep sleep. She was snoring lightly within minutes.

'It didn't look that cold to me,' Larissa whispered in his other ear, and he felt her warm breath against his neck. Two minutes later she was asleep as well, snuggled up close with her head on his shoulder.

The New South Wales Police Force Academy was a breeze. It was everything he had hoped for. Most of the instructors there knew the old man. 'Watto's boy' they called him. He'd invited his father to a little family get-together the night before he was due to leave for the Academy, but he didn't show.

There was nothing he didn't excel at. The physical fitness side of things was a bit of a joke. He actually had to slow himself down on a few occasions just so people wouldn't think he was big-noting himself. He applied himself hard to policing theory and legal studies and was running at close to a hundred per cent in every test he took. He was absolutely killing it.

There was a four-day block of leave scheduled at the end of the first month's training. He was glad to be heading home for a few days but he also wouldn't have minded if they just kept on going.

He got in late on a Thursday afternoon. He hadn't teed anything up with his mates and his mother was working a late shift at the hospital. He hung around at home by himself for a little while before meeting a mate, Mark, at the Rex Hotel for a couple of after-work beers. Mark couldn't hang around, though, as he was meeting up with a girl. People were moving on; the town was changing.

He noticed Alison right away. Remembered her from school. She was waitressing at the pub and she delivered his meal to him at his table. She remembered his name, but he had to read her name tag. She told him she had started at university, was studying radiography. He wasn't sure what that was but it sounded impressive. He kind of remembered she was one of the smart girls.

She delivered meals to the tables all around him and smiled at him each time she passed. He liked her smile; it looked happy and sad and serious all at the same time. He asked her if she'd like to sit with him after she had knocked off. She didn't look certain, but said she might.

She was paler than the girls he usually went for and she wasn't a glamour. He didn't mention that he was kinda sorta seeing someone else at the time. After all, it was only a casual thing, they hadn't agreed they were exclusive or anything. He hadn't even told the other girl he was coming home on leave. So he told Alison he was single, that he was focused on getting through the academy, which was more or less the truth.

Alison asked questions about the training course, and he found it hard to get it all out by closing time. She seemed genuinely interested, and she had a way of looking at him, half serious, half smiling. He took her number and thought about her before he went to bed. He sent her a text, just a smiley face, but she didn't respond.

He sent her a text in the morning, saying, I might see you tonight.

That evening, he met up with Mark and the boys for Friday night drinks. Most had serious girlfriends, some were turning into losers, he couldn't work out which were which. He thought about Alison, remembered that she knocked off at nine thirty, so he got there at nine. She came straight over, looked surprised to see him. 'Of course I came,' he said. 'Did you think I wouldn't?'

She looked different when she came and sat with him that night. Her hair was out, long and wavy and light brown, and she had put lipstick on. They resumed their conversation from the previous night—at least he did—and it was as if he hadn't drawn breath. He told her all about himself. She listened intently.

'I'm tired,' she said after last drinks were called.

She must have seen something in his face. 'You can come back to my place.' She said it seriously. It seriously turned him on.

'It's just me and my mother.' Her eyes flashed when she said it.

He felt a stirring beside him.

'Come on, it's four thirty,' he heard, and his eyes snapped open.

Ellie was standing in front of him, dressed, ready for action, two steaming mugs in her hand.

'It's black,' she said. 'No milk.'

Larissa mumbled incoherently and tried to pull the blanket back up over herself. 'I don't want to go to school,' she whined.

Watson watched Ellie's face soften into a smile.

'Come on, get up. The bridge will be under by eight—we've got to get out of here.'

Larissa threw the blanket off. 'If you put it that way,' she said. 'Can you imagine being stuck here?'

Ellie called in on her large police walkie-talkie. Static. She tried a few more times and got the same result.

'It looks like all the towers are off the air,' she said. 'We've got no comms. Phones are down as well.'

Watson pulled his phone out of his pocket to double-check. No bars, no reception.

He stood outside the house's only bathroom while Larissa took an inordinate amount of time to go to the toilet. He was just contemplating the backyard when the toilet flushed and the door opened. She had fixed her hair and make-up. She looked him in the eye and touched a finger to the end of his nose, just lightly.

They made a dash for their cars in the freezing wet darkness and took off for the bridge, the women in front.

Ellie's brake lights flared unexpectedly, scattered red in his windscreen. It took him a moment to realise she wasn't slowing down—she was stopping. He stamped his foot hard on his own brakes and only just missed slamming into the back of the other car.

What the fuck?

They were two hundred metres from the bridge, just short of the town's main drag. Ellie and Larissa climbed out of their car. Watson got out and joined them. The road they were on dipped down into the intersection before climbing again slightly to the bridge. From a couple of metres in front of Ellie's cruiser to as far as the eye could see, the road was awash.

The bridge was gone.

They all turned and looked at each other, then turned back again to face the spot where the bridge used to be.

There were no lights on the other side. There was no one waiting for them.

'Philby,' Watson said. 'What the fuck?'

Ellie shook her head, speechless. Larissa had tears welling.

Ellie jumped back into the patrol car, flashed the high beams, turned on the lights, gave the siren a burst. It turned the area into a flashing red-and-blue psychedelic lightshow, but there was no response from the other side of the river.

'They've left us,' Larissa said. 'They've fucking gone and left us here.'

He could hear Ellie yelling into the two-way radio in the patrol car, but there was no answer.

They were on their own.

15

Insipid dawn light was doing its best to break through the gloom when they pulled up outside Ellie and Larissa's. The power was out. They stood around in the lounge, directionless, breathing out frost until they got the heater cranked up again.

'At least we have gas,' Ellie said, toasting her hands over the heat.

'I'll make us some breakfast,' Larissa said.

Watson and Ellie followed her into the kitchen; it seemed they all felt the need to stick close together.

Larissa pulled eggs and bacon, tomatoes, mushrooms and cheese out of the fridge, took a large frying pan out of the cupboard, and asked, 'So what are we going to do?'

'What *can* we do?' Ellie responded.

'We'll just have to wait it out,' Watson said, stating the obvious. He frowned. 'Philby,' he said, then, staring hard at Ellie, 'what the fuck is going on?'

She shook her head.

'Come on, Ellie, you act like he's carrying Ebola, you can't stand to be in the same room as him, and as far as I can see he's shit scared of you.'

'We don't know what his problem is,' Larissa jumped in. 'We just know he looks at porn—a lot.'

'He's disgusting, makes my skin crawl,' Ellie added. 'And there's something else . . .'

'What?' Watson and Larissa both said it at the same time.

'I'm not exactly sure, but I think there was something going on with Alan Bishop.'

'He's a pig,' Larissa muttered.

'Like what?' Watson asked.

'I don't know,' Ellie said, 'but I heard them fighting in Philby's office with the door closed. I think Philby was scared of Alan, or Alan had something over him. It was just after the big accident.'

'The accident? Out on the highway?' Watson said.

'Yeah, that afternoon, and then he was gone. I haven't seen him since.'

'I've seen him,' Larissa said. 'He was hanging around outside the station in his car.'

'When was that?' Ellie asked.

'Monday, the day that Craig started. He was just sitting there watching.'

'Christ,' he said, and moved back to the heater.

He had to pull over on the side of the highway, driving back to the academy that first time—after Andrea on the lounge.

He couldn't concentrate. He kept getting pictures in his mind. Kept hearing her voice, laughing at him, teasing him. It was like he was naked to the world for the very first time. Everyone would be able to see straight through him. See the bullshit. See his act. They would know that he was terrified. Know that 'Watto's boy' was nothing but a pale, hopeless imitation of his father.

Watto had treated him like a mangy mutt that had followed him home one day. He hardly even visited after he'd left them. He'd left Craig sitting on the wall outside his mother's house for five hours one day, hoping his dad was going to turn up for his scheduled visit and take him somewhere. He'd cried for days afterwards.

Sitting by the side of the road, he did it again: he held on to the wheel tight, and he sobbed.

There was an exam that first week back from leave. He hadn't studied, he hadn't really slept, he didn't even finish it, let alone pass. A few of Watto's old mates pulled him aside, asked him what was going on. They looked concerned. 'Woman trouble,' he told them, and they chuckled. 'Just like the old man, hey?'

Alison was like a lifeline. She was back at uni now and working nights, but they'd speak most evenings and she'd tell him how much she missed him. She made him feel better about himself.

Two weeks back at the academy, and he was called up to see the Superintendent, who wanted to talk about what was going on. 'Why the failing grades?' he asked. 'You were at the top of the tree.'

He gave the Superintendent the same story: he had broken up with a girl, it was nasty, but he'd bounce back, there was no need to worry.

Three weeks in and he had started to get on top of things again; he'd got some pills to help him sleep, and they helped to calm him down. He started to study and got back to the exercise. He was passing again; there were smiles all round.

Then one Wednesday afternoon he had a message from the office. His mother was coming to pay him a surprise visit; she'd be arriving at five thirty to take him out for dinner.

He waited in the reception area and at five thirty on the dot a car pulled in. A brand-new Mercedes. Behind the wheel was Andrea, smiling widely.

'It's only going to go off if we don't eat it all now,' Larissa said, cracking more eggs into the frying pan.

Watson was shovelling it down; he couldn't remember the last time he had an appetite. They sat and they ate until none of them could eat any more.

'Oh my God,' Larissa said, rubbing her stomach. 'What did we do that for?'

'That was great,' Watson said, then, feeling he should contribute, 'I'll make coffee.'

'There's no milk,' Ellie said. 'I can't drink coffee without milk.'

'Well, I think the shops might be shut, El,' Larissa pointed out.

'The station,' Ellie said, not even bothering to acknowledge the interjection. 'There's plenty of milk there. I got a large bottle yesterday. I'll just go and get it.'

Watson knew better then to offer. Knew she wouldn't appreciate any show of chivalry. Equal rights and all that.

Ellie grabbed the keys and went for the door, letting in an arctic blast of cold air and rain before it slammed shut behind her.

Larissa scraped the plates into the bin and rinsed them in cold water before loading them in the dishwasher. Watson was wrestling with the hand-cranked coffee grinder.

'It's not that hard,' she said, standing at the sink watching him, hands on her hips.

He suddenly felt flustered, nervous. It was the way she said it, the way she was standing.

Larissa must have noticed, because she walked over to him. Stood behind him. Put a hand on his shoulder. 'What's the matter?' she cooed. 'Is that big old machine too complicated for you?'

He felt her other hand slide up and start to lightly massage his neck and shoulders. He could feel her heat close behind him.

'Is that good?' she whispered in his ear, closer now.

'Oh yeah,' he managed.

These girls are seriously confusing.

She dug her fingers in a little harder. He turned to face her. Her eyes were smiling, her lips slightly parted, curving at either end. He slid his hands around her waist, then slowly down to her firm round rump, and pulled her to him. He moved his face closer to hers until they shared each other's breath.

'You're a naughty boy, Craig,' she said, stepping backwards, just out of reach.

Watson took half a step forward, then reconsidered, stopped, dropped his hands and his head.

'Yeah, I suppose I am,' he said, trying to smile. There was an awkward silence. 'I'm sorry,' he said.

'Don't be,' she said, meeting his eyes, her expression warm, placating. 'It's just not the time right now. Not the place.' She smiled then walked towards the door, holding her palm in front of her open mouth. 'And I've just got to brush my teeth,' she said.

———

Twenty minutes later they were sitting at the kitchen table, all awkwardness gone, chatting like old pals. It struck them both at about the same time: *Ellie should really be back by now.*

'I'm starting to get a bit worried,' Larissa said.

'Yeah, she's been gone a while,' he said. It was only a two- or three-minute drive to the station.

'Something might have gone wrong—she could be bogged or something,' Larissa said.

'Should we go and have a look?'

Larissa didn't answer; she just stood up, wrapped her utility belt around her waist and grabbed her rain jacket off the back of a chair.

Watson drove. It was slow going. The station was only one street back from the river and the floodwater was coming up fast. Rapidly flowing, debris-filled brown water was swirling through the streets and running freely into shops and businesses that hadn't had time to sandbag or barricade their doors.

Close to the station, the water was up to the bottom of the car doors. The slightly elevated car park at the rear of the block was only ankle-deep. Ellie's patrol car stood silent and empty at the back door.

'Oh good, she's still here,' Larissa said, relieved.

Watson didn't say anything.

'What?' she asked.

'I dunno,' he said. 'I've just got a feeling.'

They pulled up beside the patrol car. When they got out, Watson released the catch on his safety holster, allowing easy access to his pistol.

'Just keep behind me,' he said when he saw the concerned look on Larissa's face.

The back door was closed but unlocked. Not unusual. He pushed the door open a crack, stood silently and listened. Nothing.

He pushed the door fully open and entered the kitchen—his chest thumped. The kitchen was wrecked. There was a large bottle of milk lying in the middle of the floor. There was blood smeared on the fridge door, spattered on the cupboard doors, and there were drops on the floor.

His mouth dry, he pulled his pistol. Beside him, Larissa held her hand over her mouth, hyperventilating.

'Stay here,' he mouthed to her, and motioned for her to pull her pistol out of her holster.

He moved towards the hallway. Two, three steps, Larissa right behind him.

'Stay here,' he whispered again.

She shook her head. Her eyes were wide with fear.

He continued into the hall, Larissa holding on to the back of his jacket, holding in sobs. They carried on in silence to Philby's door. A step short of the entry, Watson stopped. Listened. Still nothing. He stepped forward, pistol leading.

Philby's office had been ransacked. All the furniture was up-ended and smashed. Files were ripped and scattered all over the floor and the remains of the desk. The computer had been totally trashed, smashed to pieces.

They moved on. The interview rooms were empty. Upstairs was clear. The station was deserted. Ellie was gone.

16

'Larissa' he said, 'you're going to have to get your shit together.'

Watson had gone back through the station from top to bottom, front to back. As far as he could make out, Ellie had been surprised by someone who was already in the station when she got there. Someone tearing Philby's office to pieces, by the looks of it. Thieves? Vandals?

Whoever it was would have seen Ellie's patrol car approaching through the window in Philby's office. Watson guessed the intruder must have then hidden and waited for her. It looked like it happened just after she had pulled the milk out of the fridge. He was no blood-spatter analyst, but it appeared that Ellie had put up a hell of a fight. There were three clear, distinctive areas around the kitchen where fighting and bleeding had taken place. Ominously, there were drag marks on the floor leading to the rear door. Any clues as to what occurred outside had been washed away by the incessant rain.

The entire time he had been searching the station, Larissa had been down on her haunches in Ellie's workstation with her arms wrapped around herself, sobbing helplessly.

'Arsehole,' she said now, getting to her feet. She blew her nose loudly into a tissue and dried her eyes.

He put his arms around her and she leant into him, still holding the tissue up to her nose.

'Someone's taken her,' he said. He deliberately did not mention that he suspected Ellie had been badly injured. There was a lot of blood. 'Why would someone do that?'

Larissa didn't respond; she slumped down into Ellie's chair.

Watson paced back and forth across the room. 'I think they were in Philby's office. Destroying it.'

'Probably after his filthy porn,' she said. He wasn't sure if she was joking or not.

His head hurt. His hand automatically went to his pocket for an Oxy. He had none. He was getting anxious. He had no crystal either. *Shit*. He felt a panic attack coming on. He walked out of the office into the hallway. Held on to the wall.

Deep breaths. Deep breaths.

He heard the creak as Larissa got up from Ellie's chair. He straightened himself up. Wiped his eyes.

'Hey, are you okay?' she asked, following him into the hall.

'Yeah, yeah,' he said. 'Just felt a bit . . . you know?'

'Yeah, I know,' she said, leaning the top of her head into his chest. 'Let's get out of here.'

———

'You take Ellie's car,' he said when they stepped out into the car park. 'We'll cover more ground that way.'

'No.'

'No? What do you mean no?'

'No way. This is what happens in the movies. You split up and something bad happens. I'm not doing it; I'm not going anywhere by myself. We can look together—the town isn't that big.' To make her point, Larissa opened the passenger-side door of Watson's car and climbed in. He got in himself and looked across at her, speechless. She stared straight ahead, no eye contact.

'Well, come on, let's go,' she said angrily, tears welling up again.

The town of Gloster had no more than twenty streets and the four or five of them closest to the river were now underwater or impassable. Most of the town's long streets ran parallel to the river, with shorter streets connecting the long streets in a grid pattern. The only exception was a single long road running up onto the headland close to the beach; it was the furthest from town.

'We'll start up on the headland and work our way back down through town,' Watson decided, turning left out of the station driveway.

Larissa sniffed. Her nose was running and she didn't have any more tissues. It wasn't often that he felt like the grown-up.

Watson needed an Oxy so badly he thought he was about to vomit.

He drove fast to the beach end of town. Sand had been washed across the road and sat in piles up against the sides of the Surfside Hotel. There was a huge muddy brown stain out in the ocean where the river emptied into the sea. The beach was covered in tree branches, sticks and leaves and what looked like an entire oyster lease that must have been washed down the river by the flood.

He gunned the motor through a low dip in the road and they went down to the bottom of the doors, sending a massive spray of dirty brown puddle water into the air on either side of the road.

Larissa started, covered her face with her hands and wiped her brow. He thought she was about to cry and was seriously considering putting her out of the car. His hands were sliding on the steering wheel, made slippery with his own sweat. He swallowed back acid-tasting bile.

'Keep an eye out,' he said harshly.

She gave him a sullen look.

The road leading up to the headland provided a spectacular vista out to their left, down the coast and out to sea. Low cloud and rain squalls obscured the horizon. The sea reflected the grey clouds overhead and was flecked with white caps and a chaotic heaving swell. No ships could be seen, there were no helicopters or planes in the sky. The wind was howling up over the cliff tops, buffeting the car and hammering into the impressive-looking two-storey houses on their right.

He slowed the car at the top of the road, where it ended in a wide circular dead end. A little park with a couple of picnic tables backed onto thick coastal scrubland that covered the cliffs. Turning the car around, they had a panoramic view back over the town itself.

They both saw it at the same time. The river, wide in flood, streaming through the main shopping precinct and extending as far back into the misty fog and gloom as they could see. The leafy residential streets running parallel to the river before petering out into flooded farmland further to the west and, from one house, just in fits and starts, smoke.

'There!' Larissa yelled, pointing. 'Smoke!'

Watson hammered it.

They hit the puddle in the road doing one-twenty. The noise was horrendous. Larissa stifled a scream. Held on to her seat. Watson was grinding his teeth. Sweating up a storm.

'Which street, which street?' he yelled over the racing motor and the gushing spray.

'Turn here,' she yelled. 'Second on the left.'

He threw the car into the turns.

'Look for the smoke,' he told her.

'There,' she said, craning her neck.

'Where?'

'We just went past it.'

He threw the car into reverse. Backed up two houses along the abandoned residential street.

They flung open their doors and charged in. It was a typical three-bedroom weatherboard. A short driveway running up the side to a separate garage at the rear.

Watson drew his pistol.

'I'll head out the back,' Larissa said, sprinting for the driveway.

Watson leapt the waist-high front fence and went for the door.

'Stop! Police!' Larissa's voice, urgent, panicked.

Watson smashed his foot into the door. It didn't budge. Solid. *Fuck.*

Bolted for the driveway. Larissa vaulted the back fence. He went after her.

He leapt at the fence, scrabbled over, regained his balance. Kept going.

Larissa's yellow rain jacket disappearing around the side of the house to the rear. A blur of movement.

By the time he reached the front yard of the next house, Larissa was going hard, up the side of a house on the other side of the road.

'Stop! Police!' she yelled again.

He felt a rush of hot liquid steaming up the back of his throat. He spasmed in the middle of the road and projectile-vomited. Eggs, bacon and tomato. He kept moving. Up the side passage of the house across the road. The backyard was empty.

He ran for the back fence. Larissa was already in the next yard. She turned and walked back towards him.

'I lost them,' she said.

He bent over and unleashed hell onto the lawn.

———

They jogged back to the car using the same route through the houses and over back fences. His head was a blinding mass of pain. They did half-a-dozen laps of the surrounding streets, got out and checked a couple of garages and overgrown gardens, but found nothing. They kept cruising up and down, around and around.

'Kids,' Larissa said. 'Two kids. A boy and a girl.'

'Anything else? Specific?'

'Um, teenagers. Youngish teenagers. The girl was leading the boy—that's a bit unusual.'

'What were they wearing?'

'They both had on hoodies, that's why I didn't get a good look at them. Hers was pink, his was blue. And they could really run,' she added.

'And jump,' he said.

A flash of pain jolted his head forward.

'Oh my God, are you all right?' Larissa asked, touching her hand lightly to his shoulder.

'I'm – no, I'm not,' he said. 'This migraine is killing me.'

'We have some Panadol back at our place,' she offered.

'No, I've got Panadol,' he said. 'It's not enough. Not nearly enough.'

She looked concerned. He was having trouble seeing.

'Oh God,' she said, jamming her hands down between her legs.

'Chemist,' he said. 'I need to go to a chemist.'

'Down here.' She pointed. 'Turn right at the end.'

There were two chemists in Gloster. The one on the main drag was waist-deep in water, but the other one was a street further back from the river, slightly more elevated. It was only knee-deep.

He pulled up a further street back from the pharmacy.

'Wait here,' he said.

She didn't respond, just got out of the car and followed.

They sloshed along the footpath up to their knees, careful to avoid potholes and the masses of floating debris. The flood-water was like a swirling mobile rubbish tip. Larissa stumbled over a piece of submerged rubble and he turned and caught her. They made the last twenty metres to the chemist with their arms intertwined.

The chemist had a large display front window and a firmly barred and bolted front door.

'Out the back,' he said, and led the way down a narrow driveway between the buildings.

The back door was also heavily barred. There was no window.

'Shit,' Larissa said. 'What do you want to do?'

He led her back to the street and walked just a little further down to a cement rubbish bin container. He pulled the metal bin out of the cement container and emptied the rainwater and sopping garbage into the swirling flood at his knees.

'Stand back,' he said.

'I don't know if this –'

The bin made a horrendous smashing clashing sound as it went through the front window. Watson smashed off the jagged bits of glass with his baton and climbed in.

It was dry inside; the owners had done a good job sand-bagging the doors, and the base of the window was above the flood level. He made his way straight to the rear, behind the prescriptions counter, where he found a large padlocked cabinet. He grabbed a fire extinguisher from the wall and battered the padlock into submission.

His heart skipped a beat when he opened the cabinet. Xanax, Vicodin, OxyContin, Buprenorphine—it was an Aladdin's cave of goodies for the prescription-addicted. His mouth was watering as his hand hovered over the array of glorious opportunity before he selected two boxes of twenty Oxys and another two of twenty Xanax. He pocketed the boxes, turned, then turned back and grabbed another box of Oxy—just to be on the safe side.

He made his way back to the front of the store. Larissa was standing in the middle of the shop with a plastic shopping bag stuffed to the brim with deodorants, make-up, perfumes and what looked like a new hairdryer, still in its box.

'Get what you need?' she asked.

He didn't know whether to laugh or cry. He laughed.

'Yep. Let's get going.'

———

He swallowed an Oxy and washed it down with some bottled water. By the time they arrived back at the house they had just chased the children from, he was starting to feel calm, his head was clearing, he no longer felt nauseous.

The back door of the house remained open; it was obvious where the frame of a pet door had been removed to gain entry.

'Would have to have been a skinny kid,' Watson said.

'The girl,' Larissa said. 'Built like a whippet.'

They entered straight into a kitchen. There were the remains of a couple of meals. Bacon-and-egg sandwiches and a bowl of cereal by the look of it. A frying pan on the gas cooktop still retained some heat. The rest of the house looked relatively untouched: just some blankets in front of the dying embers of a fire in a small combustion heater.

'You know, I get the feeling they weren't here that long,' Watson said.

'Me too,' Larissa said, returning from a quick scout of the house. 'None of the beds have been slept in.'

'The cooktop is still warm, and this fire doesn't look like it's been going too long. Any idea whose house it is?'

Larissa found a pile of recently opened mail on the kitchen bench.

'Karen and Michael De Jong,' she said, and shook her head. 'Never heard of them.'

Watson inspected an array of family portraits arranged along a wall in the hallway. They were all fairly recent, and showed a young married couple, a dog, no children.

'They've come in through the pet door, had a feed and tried to warm up with this fire. They've heard us pull up outside and bolted.'

'Jesus,' Larissa said. 'We're supposed to be the good guys. What would they be running from?'

'I don't know, but the same thing happened to me at the caravan park last night. It's like they're scared of us.'

'The caravan park?' Larissa said.

'It's worth another look.'

———

The flooding hadn't got much worse in the park since the night before. It was up to Larissa's knees and only just below his. The floodwater somehow seemed dirtier in the caravan park, murkier, and Larissa crinkled up her nose as she waded along.

They went from cabin to cabin, having a quick look through each front window before trying the door. Watson had the safety catch released on his holster. They were four from the end, and Watson was wading towards the next cabin, when a movement caught his attention. He froze, held his hand out to his side. Larissa stopped moving behind him.

'What?' she asked softly.

'The last cabin,' he said, 'on the other side of the road. Something moved.'

He saw it again: a flash of blue material.

'Curtains?' Larissa said.

'The door's open,' he whispered.

He pulled his pistol out and waded slowly to the other side of the road, where they could not be seen from the front of the supposedly empty cabin.

'Someone could have Ellie in there,' he said, looking Larissa in the eye and then shifting his gaze down to her still-holstered pistol.

Her eyes widened with fear. She reached down and wrenched her pistol from its holster on her hip, her hand shaking.

'We'll make our way up to that cabin slowly and quietly, okay?'

She nodded.

'When I say go, we steam in yelling, *Don't move*. Got it?'

She nodded, and he saw beads of sweat on her forehead despite the cold.

He moved off slowly, careful not to make too much noise or splash too much water around as he went. They stopped hard up against the cabin next door. He turned his head quickly.

'Ready?'

A quick nod.

'Police, don't move!' he screamed and bounded up the four steps to the cabin's porch.

Larissa had lost the power of speech but followed him to the door.

'Police, don't move!' he screamed again, and went in through the door pushing the flying blue curtain aside. The main room was empty.

'Cover that door,' he yelled at Larissa, pointing to the bathroom door at the back left of the cabin, then he charged into the bedroom.

Nothing.

He went straight to the bathroom door, swung his pistol in.

Nothing.

Fuck.

Larissa dropped to a knee, holding her chest. Watson leant against the kitchen counter, catching his breath, waiting for his heart to stop pounding. There was a flash of purple on the kitchen counter, just next to where his hand was resting.

An amethyst.

17

He had been looking forward to his mother's visit. He came straight from class, thinking she might like to see him in his uniform. He had lost a little bit of weight since starting at the academy but had put on some lean muscle. The hard work and outdoor activity had bronzed his already olive skin.

Andrea smiled at him as he approached her car. Had she told them she was his mother? Or had they just assumed? He knew with every fibre of his being that he should turn around and run a million miles from this situation. Instead, he got in the car.

She turned and faced him, regarding him critically from behind large, expensive, gold-rimmed sunglasses.

'Put your belt on, Craig,' was all she said before she put the car in gear and took off. Fast.

A few minutes later she pulled into the forecourt of a newish-looking motel not far from the academy. It was where the parents and friends stayed when there was a graduation parade.

'Get us a room,' she said. 'The best they've got.'

He was on autopilot, numb.

'A double suite with a hot tub,' the man behind the counter responded to his query. 'Comes with a complimentary breakfast.'

'I'll take it,' Craig said, passing over his card. His hand was trembling.

'Take my bag, Craig,' Andrea said. She was standing at the back of her car, smoking a cigarette. She dusted some non-existent lint from the shoulder of her white suit jacket. As he bent down to pick up her overnight bag, she dropped the cigarette and carefully ground it out with the toe of her high-heeled shoe.

He dropped the overnight bag just inside the door and stood next to it. She shut the door and walked past him into one of the double bedrooms that opened onto the main lounge and dining area.

'Come here,' she said, and he walked further into the room and stood where he could see her, sitting on the end of the bed with her legs crossed.

'Do you know why you are here, Craig?'

He shook his head. 'No,' he muttered, uncertain. 'I don't.'

She looked disappointed. 'I'm here to teach you. You know that, right?'

Unsure what to say, he just nodded his head slowly.

'Because you've been getting away with a lot of crap, haven't you, Craig?' She was raising her voice now.

He stared at her. She leant back, her left arm resting on her crossed legs, her right arm stretched out on the bed behind her. As he watched, she uncrossed her legs. He glanced down. She slowly widened her legs, stretching the brilliant white material across her tanned thighs.

'I said you've been getting away with shit for years now, haven't you, Craig?'

He didn't know what to do, what to say; his mind was buzzing, his palms sweating badly.

'What do you think about when you're fucking my daughter,

Craig?' she spat. 'Who do you think about? Who do you think about when you're shoving—it—into—my—daughter?' Every word was punctuated with venom.

'I don't. I don't,' he said. His mind was ablaze. This was so fucking wrong, he knew that, but still . . . He clenched his hands into fists. She shouldn't be talking like that, saying those things, but somewhere, buried very deep, he felt that maybe he deserved it, and that it all made sense.

She stood up quickly, walked the two paces to him and slapped his face hard.

He reeled back.

'You fucking –' He never finished the sentence as another stinging slap whipped across his cheek.

'Don't you ever raise your voice to me, Craig.' She said his name like it was poison.

He felt powerless, hopeless.

'Get undressed,' she ordered, her hands on her hips, her vivid green eyes burning holes in his skull.

He hesitated, but only for a moment. He needed this, he realised.

He unbuttoned his uniform shirt and pulled it loose from the top of his pants while she watched on, expressionless. He was breathing hard, his chest expanding, his abdominal muscles clearly visible with the rise and fall of his chest. He bent down and untied his boots, kicked them off and pulled off his socks.

When he straightened up, he caught the slightest trace of a smile at the corners of her mouth. It calmed him. It started to feel right.

He undid his belt and unbuttoned his pants, opened the zipper and let the pants fall to his ankles. He stepped out of them and glanced quickly at her face to see if he was pleasing her. He could see her breathing was growing heavier now.

He hooked his fingers into the waistband of his neat white boxers and slid them down over his thighs then stood before her, semi-erect, thick and rapidly filling with heat and blood.

'Now me,' she said, still expressionless.

He looked at her quizzically, unsure what she wanted.

'Undress me, Craig.'

He slid her white linen suit jacket from her shoulders and she let it slide off her arms.

'Hang that up,' she said. She watched closely as he walked across the room to put her jacket on a hanger then returned to her.

Next he unbuttoned her silk blouse and peeled it from her shoulders.

'Put that over there.' She gestured to the back of a chair.

'My shoes now,' she said, and he dropped down to his knees. She lifted her left foot and then her right so he could slide her shoes from her feet. He set them aside.

'Go around the back,' she commanded as he reached for her bra.

He stepped around behind her and unhooked the pale purple scrap of lace. Her head jerked back involuntarily, just slightly, when his hardness brushed against her lower back.

Her breasts were heavy but firm, with large, dark areolas and thick, hard nipples. He reached out to cup them but she slapped his hands away.

She undid the button and the small zipper on the side of her short skirt, then he slid the skirt off and placed it with her blouse over the back of the chair.

She placed her hand on his shoulder and with light pressure guided him down to his knees.

He hooked his fingertips in the waistband and slowly pulled down her purple lace panties, revealing a soft brown bush of hair.

As the panties dropped to her ankles, he wrapped his arms around her and leant his cheek into her warmth. She pressed her hands onto the back of his head, holding him there. He turned his face into her. She shuddered.

'Fetch my bag, Craig,' she said quietly.

He moved quickly to where he had left the bag by the door and brought it over to her.

She turned and went into the bedroom and lay down on the bed on her back, her left arm behind her head on the pillow.

'Open it,' she said.

There was a change of clothing in the bag, but on top of the clothes was a shiny, silver metallic vibrator, a tube of lubricant and a pair of handcuffs.

'Just bring the vibrator over here,' she said.

He obeyed, then stood beside the bed looking down at her. He was throbbing.

She took the vibrator and turned on the switch at its base. 'Get on the bed,' she said.

He climbed onto the bed on his knees beside her. She handed him the vibrator and said, 'You know what I want.'

He started with her breasts, running the lightly buzzing instrument around the sides of her pale fleshy mounds before touching the tip to her nipples and then lowering his mouth to her again. She moaned deeply.

He used the vibrator on her softly, patiently, then with more urgency as her breathing and her moaning increased in tempo and intensity. He alternated between the vibrator and his tongue, bringing her higher and higher, her thighs spasming, her hips bucking wildly, grabbing at his hair, forcing him deeper and harder against her until she heaved and moaned then let out a cry of relief and flung him aside.

She lay on her back breathing heavily for two or three minutes. He knelt beside her, watching her, holding himself, iron-hard, in his grip.

'Get the handcuffs and the lubricant,' she said when she had regained her breath.

He went to the bag and grabbed the cheap metal handcuffs and the tube of KY.

She sat up when he handed her the cuffs and said, 'Now turn around and get on your knees.'

18

He stood as close to the heater as he could without setting fire to himself while Larissa took a quick shower. They were both soaked through with freezing, smelly floodwater. He took the opportunity to check his phone. No bars. No texts.

That's one silver lining.

He heard the bathroom door open down the hall and footsteps clump their way to a bedroom further along. He hadn't checked out the sleeping arrangements in the house; he wasn't even sure if Larissa and Ellie had separate beds. He had half a mind to walk down there and find out.

Maybe that's what she wants me to do?

He hadn't heard a door close, he realised.

It was just another imponderable. Another confusing, energy-sapping mystery that he had no answer for.

What the fuck was this morning all about? And last night? And Ellie the other night?

He felt for the pills in his pockets. Just knowing they were there brought him relief.

'I don't have any socks,' she said, rushing past him through the kitchen to the small laundry.

His own socks and the bottoms of his trousers had begun to steam in the heat emanating from the fire. They stank of stale pond water.

Something stinks, the old man had said. Anthony Sweeney's father-in-law, Laura's grandfather, the owner of the cabin.

He felt the sharp edges of the amethyst in his pocket.

The river came up faster than it should have, Philby had said. Eighteen metres was four metres below the point at which they were supposed to start evacuating, but the town was already in flood.

'So, what are you thinking?' Larissa asked. She had come up behind him, giving him a start.

'It's all connected,' he said.

She stood beside him facing the fire.

'Connected how?'

'Fuck knows. I'm not sure.' He put his hands up to his face and rubbed at his eyes, trying to clear his mind. 'The amethyst, Tayla, the cabin, the Sweeneys, the car crash. Fuck, what have I walked into here?'

She put her hand on his shoulder.

'What did Ellie walk into?' she said.

'Christ, Philby's office. It's not like they were looking for something, it's like they were destroying it. And he just fucking left us here.'

'Maybe the river came up too quick,' she said. 'The bridge went under and they couldn't get in contact with us—the radios were out, remember.'

'Maybe,' he said doubtfully. 'And there's another thing:

you said the river had to be at twenty-two metres before we start evacuating. The place was underwater at eighteen. Who did those sums?'

'The council,' she said. 'There was a big meeting about it with the SES and all those guys. They had a big study done, put all these plans in place.'

'Jesus, and those kids,' he said. 'What the fuck are they doing?'

'They might have got left behind.'

'So why run away from us? What's the story with that?'

'I don't know.'

'I mean, one thing's for sure: they don't have Ellie—which means someone else here does. Someone trapped on this side of the river with us has Ellie. Have you thought about that?' He turned and went into the main room then slumped down on the lounge.

She sat down beside him, her hands jammed firmly between her knees.

'So, what do you want to do then? We can't just sit here.'

He could see fear in her eyes. He reached over and touched her arm.

'The council,' he said.

'What about the council?'

'It all starts there somewhere, I'm sure of it.'

She looked at him, questioning.

'So, let's go visit the council then,' she said.

————

Being slightly elevated, the council chambers hadn't flooded. Watson put his metal baton through the thick glass on the sliding front doors to the reception area and then kicked in more glass to allow them entry to the building. He was certain that had there been any electricity he would have triggered an alarm.

'Hope no one calls the cops,' he said, stepping inside.

Larissa smiled nervously and followed him in.

It was hushed, with the peculiar atmosphere of a place usually busy and filled with life now empty and quiet.

'Where do we start?' Larissa whispered, keeping as close to his back as possible.

'There's no need to whisper,' he replied, but as soon as the words left his mouth, he felt the same strange reluctance to speak in a normal tone.

'This way.' He nodded, choosing to say less rather than lower his voice.

He walked along the dim, carpeted corridors, trying to remember the route to Sam Nefarian's office. All of the doors leading off the hallways were closed and most appeared to be locked.

'Here,' Larissa said, stopping in the centre of a long stretch of hallway and gesturing to a sign attached to the wall beside a stairwell entrance. It was a directory of departments and office numbers. Being a senior manager, Sam Nefarian's name was listed with his office number, 132, but Watson's eye was caught by an entry near the bottom of the list—Infrastructure Delivery Team, office number 214.

'That's where Anthony Sweeney worked,' he said, pointing to the name on the list.

'All these numbers start with a one,' Larissa said, looking down the hallway. 'Two-fourteen must be upstairs.'

Watson pulled open the heavy fire door to the pitch-dark

internal stairs. Larissa was halfway in when she turned in a state of semi-panic and put her shoulder against the automatic-closing door about to click shut behind them.

'Shit. You go up,' she said. 'Imagine if we got locked in here. I'd die.' She pulled a small torch out of her belt and shone it up the stairs for him while she stood shoulder up against the door.

'It's all good,' he called out from the top after opening the door into the first-floor hallway. She sprinted up the stairs, through the door and out into the hall while he held the door open.

'I can't be in those kinds of places,' she said breathlessly.

'It's all good,' he said again, placing a hand on her shoulder.

Number 214 was another nondescript locked door in a quiet corridor not far from the staircase. After jiggling the handle and giving it a few good, firm shoves, Watson said, 'Look out.' He took a step back and rammed the heel of his boot into the door, just below the handle.

It opened with a resounding snap and part of the lock went pinging off across the floor inside the office.

It was a large room, with windows at the far end looking out over the flooded town centre and down to the river. There were four desks, one in each corner of the room, and each with a desktop computer and a selection of filing cabinets. The walls were lined with charts, plans and maps similar to the documents Watson had been given by Debbie the receptionist on his way out of the building on his last visit.

One of the desks stood out quite clearly from the other three. It was in the furthest corner from the door, under the windows. Aside from the computer, the desk and the walls behind it were completely clear.

'So, what exactly are we looking for?' Larissa asked.

'I don't know,' he said, stopping at the closest desk and shuffling some papers. 'A note saying, *I'm a dodgy prick*, and a map leading to Tayla and Ellie?'

Larissa shook her head. Didn't answer.

'This desk belongs to John Derrick and he's an engineer,' Watson said reading from a printed email.

Larissa rifled through the contents of the next desk. Not speaking.

Watson went to the clean desk. A piece of tape stuck to the bottom of the computer screen had *Sweeney* printed on it, with a combination of letters and numbers written underneath in thick black texta.

'This is his desk,' he said. 'Anthony Sweeney's.'

Larissa ignored him.

Fuck.

'Okay, look, I'm sorry,' he said.

She waited a few seconds, then spun around. 'What did you say?'

'This is Sweeney's desk,' he said, gesturing.

'No, after that,' she said, putting her hand on her hip.

He went blank momentarily then realised. 'Sorry,' he mumbled.

'That's okay,' she said, moving closer to him. 'But don't treat me like an idiot.'

'Sorry,' he said again. He needed another Oxy badly now.

'So, what have we got?' she asked.

'It looks like it's been cleaned out.'

The desk drawers were unlocked, as was the set of filing cabinets against the wall behind the desk. Other than dust, pencil shavings, the odd paperclip and a random five-cent piece, they were all empty.

'Like he never even worked here,' Larissa observed.

'That's what I was thinking,' Watson said. 'Let's go and see what his boss has to offer.'

They went through the same process as before with the stairs: Larissa holding the door to the first floor open until Watson had opened the door to the ground floor hallway. They followed the numbers to 132, and Watson let Larissa do the honours with a boot through the locking mechanism.

'We want things with dates and things with dollars, preferably both together,' Watson told her. 'This has got to be about money.'

Watson went through the desk while Larissa broke open the cheap filing cabinets with a few well-placed cracks with her metal baton and some levering. Other than some invoices and a personal bank statement with a disappointingly low balance, Watson came up empty-handed.

'What about a set of keys?' Larissa said, waving a small brown envelope. 'These were stuffed right at the back of the files in there.' She dropped the keys into his hand. There were two keys on a single key ring.

'I've seen plenty of these,' he said, holding up the larger of the two keys. 'It's for a gun cabinet. And the other one looks like it might be for a strongbox or something like that.'

Larissa nodded, returning her attention to the files. She pulled out a manila folder containing dozens of personal bank statements similar to the one Watson had found in the desk.

'Well, I doubt it's here in the council building, but it looks like we have his home address,' she said, holding up one of the statements.

'And you don't seem averse to a bit of break and enter,' he noted.

'Maybe Ellie . . .'

'It's as good a place as any right now,' he said.

She led the way out the door.

———

Sam Nefarian's place was a couple of streets back from the river on the western edge of town, just where residential blocks became hobby farms, before they became real farms further west. The house was elevated and dry, but access from the street at the front of the house was blocked by floodwater. They parked and made their way over a couple of back fences to gain entry to the house through the rear.

The back door and ground-floor windows were all covered by metal security grilles, not that uncommon in the properties close to the edge of town. Watson gave Larissa a leg-up to a first-floor balcony, and she shimmied over a railing and smashed her way in through a set of glass doors.

Watson went in first, hard and fast, clearing every room with his pistol drawn. No Ellie.

'It'll be in a bedroom wardrobe or in the garage—they always are,' he said, once they had completed their initial walk-through.

They had a quick look around the single downstairs bedroom before finding the internal door to the double garage next to the kitchen.

'Jackpot,' he said. A large metal gun cabinet stood directly beside the door. And under a protective sheet, on the other side of the garage, was a new-model Toyota RAV4. Red.

19

Watson tried the larger key in the gun safe; it slotted straight home and turned. The cabinet was as big and wide as a standard metal locker and it held two pump-action shotguns and a bandolier of ammunition. He took out the shotguns and handed them to Larissa, who placed them on the floor.

'Aha,' he said, once he had lifted the weapons out. 'What have we got here?'

'Gimme, gimme,' Larissa said, grabbing the keys from his hand. She lifted out a grey metal strongbox that the guns had been sitting on and carried it to a wooden workbench running along the back of the garage. She inserted the key and popped it open.

'Look!' she said, removing a thick sheaf of documents.

Watson moved over to stand behind her, looking over her shoulder.

'*Incorporation of a Company*,' she read off the first sheet of an official-looking form. '*Gloster Hydrology Proprietary Limited.*'

'And check out the directors,' Watson said, pointing at the bottom of the page.

'Anthony Sweeney and Sam Nefarian. Shit, you were right—dodgy as. And look at all these,' she said, flicking individual pages from the stack down onto the bench. 'Invoices, heaps of them.'

Watson picked up one for the supply of twelve hundred metres of a special type of plastic piping. The invoice was for $30,000, and it was by no means the largest amount contained in the thick ream of paper.

'Christ almighty, look at this one,' Larissa said, holding up a large, monogrammed invoice for him to look at. 'Who would have thought hiring machinery was so expensive?' It was an invoice for more than $600,000.

Next in the pile of paperwork were Business Activity Statements and other tax-related forms, and at the bottom of the pile were bank statements. The most recent balance for Gloster Hydrology Pty Ltd was just shy of $3 million.

Larissa held the statement, her hand slightly trembling.

'It could be enough to get you killed,' she said.

Watson had already turned and was walking to the other side of the garage. He pulled the cover off the RAV4. It was missing almost its entire front end. The bumper bar, the grille and the plastic surrounds were all gone.

He took one of the shotguns with them when they left.

———

The rain was falling steadily and although both of them were wearing their thick police-issue rain jackets, they were both wet from the waist down by the time they had leapt two back fences and ran back across three waterlogged yards to their car.

Larissa had the documents stuffed down the front of her

jacket to keep them dry and she pulled them out before she climbed into the passenger seat.

'Shit, let's just drive around for a while,' she said. 'See what we can see. Ellie's got to be here, somewhere. I'll go mad sitting at home.'

They cruised Gloster's unflooded residential streets for close to an hour. Avoiding the same potholes on the long parallel streets and choosing different connecting streets to add some variety. The windscreen wipers added a monotonous slapping beat. They talked about Sam Nefarian and Anthony Sweeney, they dissected the details of the crash that took Anthony and Laura Sweeney's lives. They talked about John and Eunice McCann, and Jim Banks and the documents they now had in their possession that screamed Motive. But it got them no closer to Ellie, and Tayla seemed a million miles away.

'Fuck, I need a drink,' Watson said.

'Yeah, we could do with some ice too,' Larissa said.

He nosed in close to the roller door securing the entrance to the drive-through bottle shop at the Surfside and got out. There was a large padlock connecting the base of the door to a steel ring set in concrete in the driveway.

'I don't think we're going to be able to open that,' he said, returning to the car. 'It's too bloody thick.'

They sat for a moment, pondering.

'Well, this looks like an emergency,' Larissa said. She reached into the back seat and grabbed the shotgun he had placed on the floor there. 'And desperate times call for desperate measures, right?'

'Yeah, you're dead right,' he said, looking at her in astonishment.

'Well, here you are. Don't think I'm going to shoot it,' she said.

'Oh, right. Yeah. Okay,' he said, taking the shotgun and opening the door again.

He lined up the padlock from two metres back, pumped a shell into the chamber and pulled the trigger. The blast was deafening and the effect was catastrophic to every part of the concrete surrounding the padlock, but the lock itself seemed hardly scratched.

'Jesus, it's a tough one,' he said.

He took a step forward and let fly again.

'Shit, what's this thing made of?'

He racked another shell into the gun and moved closer again.

His third round was the charm. It disintegrated the padlock. Unfortunately, it also took out the passenger-side headlight and flattened the left front tyre of the car. Larissa screamed and took shelter in the footwell under the dash.

He stood for a moment, assessing the damage.

Larissa popped her head above the dash again and, satisfied that he wasn't planning to fire again, got out of the car.

'You shot the car,' she said, gesturing towards the rapidly deflating tyre.

'Yeah, I didn't mean that,' he said.

She gave him a wide berth as she walked up to the roller door and heaved it up chest-high.

He helped her shove it the rest of the way up.

'Probably best if you leave that in the car,' she said, nodding towards the shotgun.

'Oh, yeah, good idea,' he said with an embarrassed laugh.

Larissa shook her head and walked into the bottle shop.

'So, what do you think?' she asked, standing at the counter taking in the wide assortment of beverages on display.

'Well, since we've been left to our own devices it's only fair that we go top shelf,' he said, strolling behind the counter to lift a bottle of Jack Daniels from a display rack.

'Oh, very nice,' she said. 'We'd better get some ice too, or all the food we have at home in the freezer is going to spoil.'

They found an ice-making machine still half full of unmelted ice at the back of the public bar and filled half-a-dozen plastic bags with ice cubes.

The public bar faced out onto the beach with the headland road off to their left and the river running brown and muddy into the sea about a kilometre down the beach to their right. The water was grey-brown and wind-blown; a new front had arrived in the time it took to open the roller door, and the rain was slamming down hard in impenetrable sheets across the debris-strewn beach.

'Jesus, have a go at it,' Watson said, stopping to take in the view. 'It's like the end of the bloody world.' He had to talk loudly as the wind and the rain hammered into the front windows of the pub and a searing white bolt of lightning arced across the darkening sky outside. The resulting crack of thunder rattled the bottles and glasses behind the bar.

Larissa stared wide-eyed. 'How the fuck are we going to find Ellie in this?' she said, panic rising.

Watson suddenly felt the need to hold on to one of the raised tabletops. Another bolt of lightning hit close overhead; the air fizzed. They both instinctively ducked.

'We can't,' he yelled as the booming echo of thunder receded. 'We'll just have to wait until this passes. There's nothing we can do now.'

'Yes there is,' Larissa yelled, her eyes glowing in the deepening darkness. She walked quickly to the bar and grabbed two glasses from a rack. Returning to the table at the window she slammed the glasses down and said, 'You pour.'

———

They were on their third. They had dropped the first couple like shots. The heavy squall had set in and showed no signs of easing, although thankfully the lightning had moved further out to sea.

They had talked the Nefarian–Sweeney case to a standstill. It was clear to both of them what must have happened: the two men had set up a company and used it to rort the council's flood mitigation works. They had made millions but then there had been some sort of falling-out, ending up with Nefarian, deliberately or not, running Anthony Sweeney and his daughter off the road to their deaths in the river.

'It seems fairly straightforward now,' Watson concluded, absent-mindedly pulling his box of Oxy from his jacket pocket.

'Hey, what are they?' Larissa asked, reaching over and grabbing the box out of his hand. She seemed to have hit her three-drink sweet spot and was getting hyperactive. 'OxyContin,' she said, reading the label. 'What are they for?'

'They're pain relievers,' he mumbled, taking the box back and self-consciously popping a capsule out. Downing it with a mouthful of bourbon and warm Coke.

'And you're supposed to take them with bourbon, are you?' she said, snatching the box back.

'No' he said, 'it's probably not the ideal way, but—hey! I don't think that's a great idea . . .'

'Well, I've got a hangover coming on,' she said. She popped a capsule into her mouth and swallowed it.

There was no immediate effect, but over the next twenty minutes her speech slowed noticeably from the hyper-verbal three-bourbon level, and she wore a blissful smile.

'How are you feeling?' he asked, taking in her dreamy expression.

'Craig, you are a naughty, naughty boy, aren't you?'

'Well, I try,' he said.

'No, you don't.' She beamed at him. 'You're very naughty, and I like that you know?'

'Do you?' he asked.

'Yeah,' she said, hiding her smile behind her glass as she tipped in another good slurp of bourbon.

He was momentarily struck dumb. Ill at ease with emotion. Suddenly feeling naked.

'And Ellie, she likes you too, you know?'

He didn't answer. Nodded. Avoided her eyes.

'What?' she slurred. 'What's wrong?'

'Huh? Nothing.' He faked a laugh, avoided her eyes. 'What is it with you two, anyway?'

'Me and Ellie? Oh, we're great big lezzos—didn't you know that?'

He said nothing.

She laughed and had another good mouthful of her bourbon. 'No, we had a little fling, that's all. I was curious, you know, and she was too. She was so good to me when I first got posted here, really looked after me.'

He couldn't help but laugh.

'Not like that, you dickhead! We only tried it once, but it wasn't very good. We just couldn't get into it. But sometimes we sleep in the same bed. It's just nice to have someone, you know?'

'Yeah, I know,' he said, softening.

'And Ellie doesn't care if everyone thinks she's a big lez; she reckons it keeps the dickheads away ... Hey, is someone out there?'

The sky had begun to brighten a little, the front passing out to sea again. Larissa was squinting through the rain-spattered window.

'Where?' he said, with a sudden jolt of adrenaline.

'Out there on the beach, heading up into the bush.'

'Fuck. Quick!' he yelled, jumping up from his stool and rushing to the window for a better look.

They were hard to see. Two or three hundred metres away. Two figures just disappearing into the bush at the headland end of the beach.

Watson started to move. Larissa spun her legs around from under the table and just kept spinning all the way to the floor.

'I'm okay,' she said as he reached down to help her up. She held on to his shoulders and tried to take a step, but if he hadn't been holding her, she would have slid straight back onto the floor.

'Shit, how good are those pills?' she slurred.

He could see over her shoulder that the figures were gone.

'Fuck,' he spat.

Larissa was a deadweight and was mumbling incoherently in his ear. He carried her out to the car and laid her on the back seat, then went to work changing the flat tyre in the pissing rain.

20

He thought it must have been written all over his face when he got home for his next weekend leave. He thought Alison would see straight through him and the thought of that scared him more than just about anything had ever scared him in his life.

He had decided to break it off. It was all too much. He rehearsed his speech in the car on the way home that Friday night. His mother was working, so he was expecting the house to be empty when he arrived, but when he pulled up he saw Alison sitting on his front porch waiting for him.

He got out of the car full of determination: he was going to do it, just tell her. He wouldn't tell her the real reason why, of course, couldn't mention Andrea. She probably wouldn't believe him if he did; he'd just end up looking like a weak, pathetic fool.

But there she was. Sitting on a garden chair under the porch light. As he walked towards her she smiled at him. When he reached the top of the steps, she threw her arms around him. Kissed him and held him close.

He could feel her heat right down the front of him. She smelt of shampoo and goodness.

'I missed you so much,' she said, and he gripped her shoulders and stepped back slightly, looked into her eyes and said, 'Me too.' And that was that.

Alison couldn't let go of him while he opened the front door, couldn't stop touching him, and he couldn't keep his hands off her. He dropped his bag and led her straight to his bedroom. She stood in the doorway, looking at him, then she turned and shut the door.

He moved to her.

'No' she said. 'I want to . . .' And she backed him up against the wall and let her tongue melt into his mouth while she slid her hands up under his shirt, peeled it off over his head. She kissed his neck while running her hands over his chest, his stomach and up his back. She licked him and bit him hard and he jerked and she giggled. Got down on her knees.

She looked up at him, smiling. He placed his hands on her face and she shook them off.

'Just let me,' she whispered.

She kissed his stomach and rolled her tongue on his skin as she slowly unbuttoned his jeans and pulled them to his ankles. His white briefs stood out starkly against his deeply tanned flesh and the sparse smattering of black hair running down from his belly.

She took him hungrily in her mouth, working her tongue and her lips to maximise the sensation; maximise his pleasure.

He groaned and his knees buckled. 'Oh God,' he moaned. 'Oh God, Alison.'

She let him slip from her mouth and she ran her tongue expertly up and down the length of him. He banged the back of his head against the wall as she slowly took him in again.

'You'll make me come if you keep doing that,' he gasped.

'I want you to' she said, momentarily releasing him, looking up into his eyes. 'I want all of you.' And she took him back into her mouth and he groaned and she cupped him in her hand and his hips bucked involuntarily once, then twice, and on the third time he exploded, violently, spectacularly, jerking and spasming until he was completely drained.

They spent the rest of the night and most of the next morning in bed. Exploring, experimenting and giving themselves to each other completely. They got up to have lunch with Craig's mother before she headed off to work again on Saturday afternoon, then he dropped Alison home to shower and change, making an excuse not to go in. When he picked her up again two hours later, she was home alone; Andrea had gone out and Alison looked upset.

'She's just such a fucking bitch,' was all she would say. He didn't push for details.

They went out for dinner, avoiding the pub and the usual haunts of their old schoolmates.

'Why don't we hang out with your friends?' she asked.

'I think I've outgrown them,' he said. 'Plus, I just want to be with you.'

They drove up to the lookout after they had eaten. It was busy on a Saturday night: cars squeaking on their suspension, sweaty hand-prints on the windows.

'Let's go for a walk,' he suggested. 'There's a place I used to know.' And he led her out of the car park out along the cliff tops on a narrow track through the bush. The place he was thinking of was an old gun emplacement, built during one of the wars but reclaimed by the weather and the vegetation. There was a little shelter built right up against the cliff edge; you could only find it if you knew it was there.

'Where are you taking me?' she laughed as he took her hand and stepped off the overgrown track.

'It's just through here,' he said. 'It's a secret spot that nobody knows about anymore.' And when they broke through the bush there was just the cliff ledge, the little open-ended shelter and the twinkling harbour lights spread out before them.

'Oh my God,' she said. 'It's beautiful.'

'And so are you,' he said, and he kissed her deeply, passionately, then he laid her down on the edge of the cliff and slowly made love to her there under the stars.

When they returned to the car someone had let down both of their front tyres. He could see broken twigs jammed into the valves—it was clearly no accident, and he could only think that it must have been her, Andrea.

They caught a cab back to his house.

'I can sort it out tomorrow,' he said, and they showered together and went to bed.

She had tears in her eyes when he dropped her at home on Sunday. He could still smell her perfume all the way back to the academy.

21

'I'm okay,' Larissa said when he opened the door of the car for her.

They had just arrived back at her place.

'I just felt dizzy and a bit out of it,' she added.

He took her hand and helped her to her feet, just in case, then they walked quickly to the front door and let themselves in. She made it to the big lounge in front of the fire before she had to sit down again, then, with some slovenly rearrangement of cushions, lie down.

'Hey, where are you going?' she yelled when he left the room.

'To get the ice out of the car,' he called, exasperated.

'Oh. Okay.' She subsided into the cushions.

Once he had the contents of the fridge and freezer packed in ice, he returned to the lounge. Larissa appeared to be dozing. He stood over her, staring down. Her dark hair had mostly fallen out of its complicated knotted arrangement, and loose strands had fallen across her face. Her mouth was slightly open.

She's beautiful, he thought. A sharp pain stabbed him in the chest.

His eyes were watering when he reached down and gently tugged a length of hair out of her mouth. She opened her eyes slightly and mumbled, 'Don't go anywhere, all right?'

He grabbed the mohair blanket and draped it over her, then he gulped down one of the Xanax and relaxed into the armchair.

It was mid-afternoon on a Thursday. There was a call from the administration office; he was required urgently, there was some sort of problem. He was filled with a sense of dread as he hurried over. He checked the car park on his way up to the main admin block. Sure enough, Andrea's car was parked in a handicapped space.

He was shown into a conference room where Andrea was seated with his course adviser, Robert Mueller. Neither of them smiled when he entered. Mueller waved him to a seat.

'Mrs Fuller has brought a very serious matter to our attention here, Craig,' Mueller began. 'She says you are harassing her daughter, making unwanted advances, texting and calling incessantly.'

Andrea's hair was tucked back behind her left ear to reveal a gold teardrop earring. Her eyes were peeling him open.

He gaped at the pair of them. 'What? No way!'

'I'm afraid we take allegations like this very seriously, Craig,' Mueller continued. 'Indeed, if Mrs Fuller were to make a formal complaint, then you would be immediately suspended pending a full investigation. I have recommended to Mrs Fuller that she do so, but she wants to give you the benefit of the doubt. She says she is reluctant to ruin your career.'

'But this is all bullshit!' Craig exclaimed. 'It's her. She ...' His face was burning, his head was throbbing.

Mueller held up his hand. 'She has shown us the texts, Craig, and the log of calls. If Mrs Fuller decides to proceed with a formal complaint, you will have every opportunity to defend yourself. To tell your side of the story.'

'No. I don't want that.' He couldn't swallow; he could hardly breathe.

Andrea spoke up for the first time. 'I would like to have a word with Craig alone before I leave,' she said.

Mueller frowned. 'I wouldn't advise that,' he said officiously. But he melted under her imperious gaze and left the room.

She said nothing for a good sixty seconds. Craig kept his eyes fixed on the table.

'Look at me,' she ordered.

He raised his head, tried to glare, defiant.

She just laughed.

'I want you to know that I can and will destroy you, Craig, if you should ever displease me. Do you understand that?'

He nodded.

'If it ever crosses your mind to tell my daughter what you have been up to, Craig, I want you to remember this moment.'

He nodded.

'If anyone, ever, hears of this, you are finished.'

He nodded.

'Be at the motel, in the same room as before, at five o'clock,' she said. Then she stood, picked up her handbag and left the room.

He was there at five sharp, too frightened to disobey. The key was in the door and there was a note waiting for him when he entered.

Get in the bath. I will be there at 6.

He filled the bath with steaming-hot water, got undressed and climbed in. He wanted to cry, he wanted to scream, he wanted to slide under the water and suck in big lungsful and never come up for air.

He flinched when he heard the door open.

Andrea strode into the bathroom.

'Empty the bath,' she said.

With a trembling hand, he pulled the plug and started to clamber out of the tub.

'No, stay where you are,' she commanded. He could smell wine on her breath.

When the tub was drained, she stepped up over the side and stood astride him. She lifted her skirt; she was wearing no underwear.

'Don't move,' she ordered.

He was stunned speechless, mortified. He went to a place where there was no light, no sound, no emotion. A cold, dead place where no one could see him, no one could touch him. No one could harm him. He hugged his arms around his knees, all but unconscious of his surroundings; oblivious to the perversion taking place.

When Andrea was finished, she stepped out of the bath, unrolled some sheets of toilet paper and wiped herself. She flushed the toilet and without speaking or looking back, walked out of the room.

When Larissa woke him, it was going on dark.

'Hey, Craig, are you still with us?' She was looking deeply concerned.

He came back to consciousness with a start. He had been in a deep, deep sleep.

'Yeah,' he said groggily. 'Yeah, I'm awake. What's happening?'

'We've got to get moving,' Larissa said, 'Ellie's out there somewhere. She needs us.'

'Yeah, right,' he said, sensing her urgency, climbing quickly to his feet. As he came upright, his vision dulled and he momentarily lost his balance. 'Whoa,' he said, grasping the edge of the couch.

'What's wrong?' Larissa asked, moving quickly to support him.

The dizzy spell was over as quickly as it had come on. Slightly embarrassed, he said, 'I don't know, I just . . . Christ! When was the last time we ate?'

They both took a moment.

'Early this morning,' Larissa said. 'We'll just have something quickly before we head out. Are you hungry?'

He wasn't really. A good Oxy and Xanax mixture will kill any appetite.

'Yeah, I am,' he said.

She stood close beside him, not speaking, waiting for him to start moving towards the kitchen. It took him a minute to work out why.

She's afraid of the dark!

His tongue felt like it had been sandpapered. His head felt like it had been stuffed with cotton wool. He half remembered, guiltily, that he had helped himself to another bottle of Jack Daniels before leaving the Surfside.

He followed her powerful torchlight into the kitchen and stood near the sink, uncertain what to do next.

'Just sit down,' she said. 'You'll only get in the way.'

She fired up all four of the gas rings, filling the kitchen with a soft, flickering bluish light. He sat himself down at the table and cracked open the fresh bottle of Jack Daniels while Larissa busied herself inspecting various items he had packed in ice in the fridge.

She shook her head and raised her eyebrows when she saw him pouring the bourbon.

'Christ, Craig. We need to focus on Ellie!'

'Yeah, I know. I'll just have one,' he said sheepishly. 'I feel like shit.'

'Yeah, well, that's not going to help.'

'You'd be surprised,' he said.

She stood watching him, trying and failing to hide her disappointment, as he downed a neat shot in one gulp.

'You're going to have to lift your game,' she said.

'I am. I will,' he said.

'I mean, if we're ever going to . . .'

The sound of the hissing gas rings suddenly filled the blue-lit space, the kitchen seemed smaller, closer.

'Do you feel like anything in particular?' she asked, breaking the spell.

'No. Whatever you want is good for me.'

She selected a packet of sausages and turned back towards the cooktop.

'Hey,' she said, peering at the lino near the back door. 'Have you been out the back?'

'No,' he said, draining the bourbon and exhaling vapour. 'Why?'

'Because there's footprints.'

His heart skipped as he jumped to his feet. 'Where?'

'Here.'

He was no expert, but in the half-light they looked to him exactly like the prints he had noticed at the barracks door.

He reached for his pistol only to find he wasn't wearing it. He grabbed Larissa's arm and dragged her into the lounge.

'Grab your pistol,' he said, pulling his own out of the holster he had discarded on the lounge room floor.

'Fuck, fuck, fuck,' she chanted as she shakily pulled out her own gun.

'Sit here. Don't fucking move,' he ordered. Then, when Larissa started to protest: 'Don't argue—just fucking stay there and look out.'

'We're armed,' he bellowed down the hallway. 'We are armed police officers. Lie down on the floor and do not move.'

He made his way slowly and methodically down the hall, clearing each room as best he could with his pistol and torch. The door at the end of the hallway was closed. He stopped hard up against the wall beside it.

'Larissa, is this last door usually closed?'

'No, I don't think so,' she called from the lounge room.

Fuck!

'This is the police—we are armed. If you fucking move in there, I am going to fucking shoot you.'

There was no sound from within. He went to open the door, pulled his hand back.

'Are you fucking sure it's normally closed?' he called.

'Yes. No. It is sometimes.'

For Christ's sake.

He put his hand on the doorhandle.

That's a start.

He felt like he was going to vomit.

'Hurry up!' Larissa wailed.

'Fucking shut up!' he yelled.

He threw open the door. Shoved his hand in with his torch. Quickly poked his head in.

Nothing.

He vomited onto the carpet.

22

'I'm sorry. I'm so sorry,' Larissa said, standing up straight and wiping tears from her eyes. He couldn't help but think that in the not-too-distant past a parent would have been admonishing her to 'be a big girl'.

'I wanted to be a paramedic you know?' she said eventually, sniffling and wiping her eyes with a tissue. 'I just wanted to help people, so I applied for the ambulance service and the police. The police got back to me first. And now I'm the worst police officer in the world,' she said, trying to smile.

'No, no,' he said. 'There's probably a worse one somewhere.'

She slapped his shoulder. 'Shut up, you don't have to agree with me.'

They stood facing each other. He reached out and lifted her chin gently until she looked at him and smiled, then they fell into each other's arms, holding each other tight. She sniffed loudly in his ear.

'God, your breath stinks,' she said, but she didn't loosen her grip.

He reached an arm up and breathed into his hand.

'Jesus, you're right.' He moved his head slightly towards her and deliberately breathed into her face.

'Oh God, get off me,' she said, wriggling out of his grasp. 'Go and brush your teeth or something.'

He rinsed his mouth two or three times with icy water from a bathroom tap and rubbed at his teeth with toothpaste on his finger. Larissa stood quietly just outside the bathroom door.

'Let's have a look at these prints,' he said, leading the way to the kitchen.

They were clearly made by boots, muddy and covered in grass.

'You know what that looks like?' Larissa said. She quickly left the kitchen, returning a few seconds later with one of her own boots which had been drying in front of the fire. 'It looks like one of ours.'

Watson inspected it closely. It was similar, but it wasn't exactly the same.

'Yeah, it could be,' he said. 'It definitely could be. But one thing's for sure: it's not those kids.'

'Do you –' She stopped and grabbed hold of his shirtsleeve, swallowed hard. 'Do you think he came in when we were both asleep?'

Watson looked down at the muddy boot prints. He was standing almost on top of them; his own boot, parallel to one of the prints, was a good five centimetres longer.

'Who says it's a he?'

———

They half ran, half walked down to the back fence and climbed over into the rear neighbour's yard. 'I know where they keep a spare key,' Larissa said approaching the back door of the house. She absolutely refused to sleep in her own home now, and as much as Watson felt like a coward, he was exhausted and the prospect of a few more hours of peaceful sleep overcame his reluctance to leave.

'The old lady who lives here told me where it was just in case of an emergency,' Larissa whispered, reaching her hand inside a disused bird cage.

Watson held two doonas and pillows while Larissa opened the door. Larissa had thought it would be inappropriate to use the old lady's bed linen as well as her bed.

They did a quick scout around the little home before settling on the master bedroom, which had a window facing out onto the street. Larissa stood peeking through a gap in the curtains while Watson peeled off his damp boots, trousers and shirt and climbed in under the two doonas in his underwear and t-shirt.

The room fell into complete darkness when Larissa pulled the curtains back into place and approached the bed. He listened to her pulling off various layers of clothing and stifled a laugh when she stumbled while getting her boots off.

'Shut up,' she whispered, climbing in under the doona. He was lying on his side facing her, she rolled herself into the same position with her back to him, and he put his arm over and around her. She wiggled her bum against his crotch and he felt a semi-hardness start to arise.

'I'm sorry,' she said, grabbing his forearm where it rested lightly across her chest. 'I just feel so guilty and bad about Ellie.'

'I understand,' he said. 'We'll just get a few hours' sleep and then go and check out where those kids went.'

It was like a dream. He was half awake in the pre-dawn light, lying on his back in his own bed. Alison was kneeling on top of him her face only inches from his own, staring intently into his eyes. Her hand was gently kneading him into hardness down through her own legs. He could feel her heartbeat through her breasts, lightly rising and falling against his own.

'I love you,' she said, and she lightly touched her lips against his before he could say anything back. 'I love you,' she said again, and she moved her hips down and guided him inside her and slowly, very slowly, sank down on top of him, engulfing him.

He came awake dreamily. It was still dark. He guiltily placed his hand down over his crotch. Larissa had rolled forward a little bit onto her stomach so thankfully she couldn't feel the pounding erection that filled the front of his briefs. He rolled over and sat up on the edge of the bed. She stirred.

'Are you okay?' she murmured.

'Yeah, good,' he said. There was a soft sliver of light creeping into the room through a gap in the curtains. He glanced into the large dresser mirror sitting against the wall at the end of the bed and he could just make out Larissa lying there staring at his back. It was hard to tell in the half-light, but she looked like she was smiling.

———

They had breakfast back in Larissa and Ellie's kitchen. Larissa cooked up the sausages she had left out the night before and some eggs. He toasted some bread over a hotplate, holding the slices with a pair of tongs, and then boiled water in a saucepan for coffee.

Watson needed to get back to the barracks for a change of clothes and a shave, but they checked out the back door before they left. It had been expertly jemmied; Watson had to look closely to see where a thin sheet of steel—like a spatula—had been jammed into the locking mechanism.

'Well, I'm pretty sure they didn't get in while we were asleep yesterday afternoon,' he said.

'How can you tell?'

'This way of opening the door, with a steel jemmy, it's loud. You have to jam it in hard and then shove the door to make a gap. It's not easy and it's noisy.'

When they arrived back at the barracks the first thing they did was check the back door there. Same deal.

'It must be the same person. These boot prints look identical.'

'God, this place gives me the fucking creeps,' Larissa said. 'I hated it here. Was anything taken?'

'Not that I could tell,' he said. 'Things had been tossed around, like at your place. It was like they were looking for something.'

'Like a search?' she asked.

'Yeah, just like a search. Except there's nothing here to find.'

He grabbed a pair of jeans and an old flannelette shirt, the last pieces of dry clothing he had available. Most of his clothes were either still wet or at the laundromat. Larissa stood in the bedroom doorway smiling at him while he shed his dirty damp clothes and re-dressed in a goosebump-covered frenzy.

He was considering skipping the shave but his whiskers had just reached the awkward length where they were itching and sticking into his neck.

She followed him into the bathroom, where he ran some icy water into the sink, his breath frosting against the mirror.

'I see you've been dealing with the rats,' she said, leaning up against the doorway, her arms folded.

'What do you mean?' he said, daintily splashing his face with the frigid water using only his fingertips.

'The manhole,' she said, glancing up.

'Oh yeah,' he said, and followed her gaze in the mirror. The manhole was half open. He felt a jolt and stopped. He turned. Looked. There were muddy tracks on the side of the bath. There was something just on the edge of his consciousness. He looked up again at the half-open manhole cover.

'What?' Larissa asked, sounding concerned.

'That,' he said, looking up and pointing. 'I closed it.'

He stepped over closer to the bathtub, reached down and picked up a scrap of grass from a faint muddy print on the edge of the tub.

Fuck.

'What?' she said again.

'Out the back,' he said, charging past Larissa towards the back door. He flung the door open and rushed out into the soaking wet knee-high grass and weeds. It was raining steadily onto his dry clothes.

'Look,' he said. 'I tossed an old sack out here. The rats had eaten it.' He paced furiously up and down in the long grass searching.

'Is that it?' Larissa asked, pointing into the weeds further down the yard.

He quickly walked over. It was hardly recognisable, a pile of lighter brown scraps down in the mud.

'Yep, that's it,' he said, and he bent down and scooped the soggy mess into his hands.

———

He carried the rotten heap back into the kitchen. It was mostly paper scraps, rat shit and chewed pieces of sack, but there was a clump of paper still stuck together, probably by a combination of damp and rat piss.

'Oh my God.' Larissa heaved and held her hand over her mouth. 'That is so fucking rank.'

Watson pulled at the wad of papers with the very tips of his fingers and separated it from the rest of the disgusting mess, his face a tight grimace of revulsion.

'Go and get my shaving kit from the bathroom, will you?' he said, trying not to breathe.

When she returned, he took a pair of tweezers from his toiletries bag and attempted to gently prise off the top piece of the chunk of twenty or so layers of paper. It continually ripped and came off in little pieces as he grabbed at it.

'Shit, this isn't going to work,' he said. 'It's too soggy.'

'Try to grab a few pieces at once,' Larissa said, holding her nose. 'It might be drier towards the middle.'

He did as Larissa suggested and carefully dug the bottom prong of the tweezers between bits of paper in the middle of the stack.

'Yep, that's it,' he said as he began to prise the stack apart. The edges of the paper revealed nothing, but as he peeled more away, he could see colour.

'What are they?' Larissa asked.

'They're photos,' he said as he peeled the stack completely in half. It was only a portion of a colour photograph and it was badly bleached by time and decay, but what you could see was not good.

'That's someone's leg,' Larissa said.

Watson knew he had seen something very similar to that leg not too long ago. He carefully peeled the photo off the pile, exposing the next one.

'Oh, hello,' Larissa said.

It was obviously the same scene, the same person, but this section of photograph showed the upper legs and naked, shaved vagina of what appeared to be a teenage girl. Watson looked up at Larissa; her eyes were wide with revulsion. He shook his head and peeled off the next photograph. It was a headshot, from the neck up, a different girl, and her hands were tied to bedposts behind her head.

Larissa let out an involuntary groan and held both hands over her eyes.

'Hey.' He stood up, putting his arms around her.

She uncovered her eyes, left her hands resting on her cheeks, and took a deep breath.

'That's Laura Sweeney,' she said, breathing out. 'And, oh fuck.' She leant in closer. 'Oh no.' She turned and walked out of the kitchen, motioning for Watson to follow.

She led him down the hall to the second bedroom. 'Here,' she said. She threw open the door and pointed a shaking finger at the narrow single bed and the pieces of coloured cloth holding the ratty, thin curtains open.

23

Watson walked back into the kitchen, ran some water into a glass, drank half, and then popped an Oxy. Larissa stood behind him, seemingly in a trance. He picked up the bunch of photographs and walked back into the bedroom. There was no doubt it was the same place.

'I bought those curtain ties,' Larissa said. 'I left them here when I moved out.'

He turned to face her. 'How long ago did you move out?'

'A year—just over a year ago.'

'And who has been in here since?'

'No one. Just you.'

'Philby. He has the keys to this place and I saw something like this on his computer the night you saw me coming out of his office.'

'Oh God. Really?'

'Well, who else could it be?'

'God no, he's . . . old.'

'What about the other bloke—Bishop? You and Ellie said they were close.'

'He was a sleazy arsehole, but this?' She indicated the room, the pictures.

'Fuck knows,' he said. 'Let's go through the rest of these and see what we can find.'

Most of the photos they could salvage were body shots of Laura Sweeney on her own. Except one.

In one photo there were two sets of legs intertwined, both obviously female. It was taken on a different day, at a different time, judging by the light. One pair of legs belonged to Laura, but the other woman was clearly a lot older, her legs more toned, fit-looking.

'Anything?' he asked, staring hard at Larissa.

Larissa shook her head. Her eyes were terrified.

'Do you know where Philby lives?'

'Yeah, we had to drop him off a few times after he passed out at the pub.'

'What about this Bishop character?'

'I know he lives up on the headland road. I'm not sure where exactly, but it's a nice house going by the way he kept banging on about it.'

'And those kids—I remember Tayla's mother, or maybe it was her brother, saying something about a place up there on the headland where kids go to hang out. Maybe that's where they were headed when we saw them yesterday, on the beach?'

'Yeah,' she said quickly. 'So where do you want to go first?'

'Philby. He had access to the house. He left us here. He had these photos on his computer. He's involved.'

Larissa looked like she was going to be sick. She shook her head. Walking over to the sink she ran a glass of water and had a sip, staring out the window into the grey and the rain and the soggy unkempt grass.

He felt for the Xanax in his pocket, thought about offering her one, to numb the pain. He left them there.

'Are you okay?' he asked instead.

She turned and nodded, smiling weakly.

'I'll be all right,' she said, and he felt the floor move under him, just slightly. He held out an arm and she walked into him and they wrapped their arms around each other. Clinging on for dear life.

———

It was miserable, low clouds dripping, drizzling and freezing cold when they made their way out to the car. Larissa tried the police two-way radio: nothing. The walkie-talkie: static. She checked her mobile.

'Fucking hell!' she yelled jamming the useless phone back into her pocket. He had already checked his. Same result.

'Which way?' he asked.

She sniffed. Gathered herself.

'Just go straight,' she said. 'It's not far.'

Philby's home, it turned out, wasn't far from Nefarian's; only a two-minute drive. Again, they needed to jump a back fence to gain access as the road at the front of the property was underwater.

'Jesus, they don't mind locking up around here, do they?' Watson observed, surveying the security grilles covering the doors and windows at the back of the smallish single-storey weatherboard.

'It's okay,' Larissa told him. 'Like I said, we've had to drop him home heaps of times. He's usually passed out.' She led him around a side passage, slightly overgrown, and reached up on top of an external hot-water tank. When she pulled her hand back she jangled a small set of keys.

When Larissa inserted the key into the rear security door it was immediately apparent that it was already unlocked.

'Hello,' she said pulling the grille open and trying the door-handle. She looked back at Watson with raised eyebrows as it slid open as well.

'Just be careful,' he said as he followed her into the house.

It was a small kitchen, with old-fashioned appliances and well-worn cabinetry. The sink was stacked with empty beer bottles, a dozen or more.

Larissa gagged, holding her hand up to her mouth. There was a thick, sickly aroma. They had both smelt it before.

Watson took the lead, walking out of the kitchen and down a short hallway to a bedroom at the front of the house. The smell was eye-wateringly powerful as he pushed open the bedroom door.

It was as he'd expected. Philby was there. Hanging by his belt from the clothes rack in his wardrobe.

———

'You should probably just take half,' Watson cautioned as Larissa popped the Xanax tablet into her mouth.

Ignoring him, she swallowed the whole thing with a mouth-ful of water.

'They're pretty strong,' he said resignedly, and then swal-lowed one himself.

'I don't care,' she said, slumping down at the kitchen table.

Larissa had walked out of the house immediately after they'd discovered Philby in the bedroom. Watson stood at the back door and watched as she walked two or three laps of the well-tended back lawn, alternately mumbling to herself and clutching her chest, trying not to throw up.

After swallowing the pill, he went around the house opening all of the doors and windows.

'I'll do a quick search,' he said. 'Do you want to wait in the car?'

'No, I'll help,' she said. 'Just not that room.'

Like a lot of divorced blokes, Philby didn't have a lot. The bedroom gave up a dog-eared collection of old porno magazines—*Hustler*, *Penthouse* and the like—but nothing that got them any closer to Ellie or Tayla.

There was no suicide note. No signs of a struggle. He was dressed in his full uniform, less his jumper and rain jacket, which they found lying on the bathroom floor. Watson reached out gingerly and felt the bottoms of Philby's trousers; they were still slightly damp.

His face was horribly swollen and had taken on a dark bruised purple colouring. His eyes had almost detached themselves from their sockets; most of the intraocular veins had burst, giving them a demonic red glaze. Blood had seeped out of his eye sockets and his nose and had run dark red tear tracks down to the collar of his light blue police shirt. His tongue had swollen to twice its normal size and it was poking pornographically out through his blood-coated lips.

Watson stood back, rubbing his eyes, trying to take only shallow breaths. Clearly Philby had cleared his bowels into his pants sometime during the horrifically painful few minutes it would have taken for him to literally choke himself to death.

He had hanged himself from less than head height, simply fastening the belt around his neck, attaching it to the clothes rail, and then basically sitting down as far as he could, using his own body weight to tighten the belt around his throat. His backside was suspended thirty centimetres off the floor, his legs protruded stiffly out of the wardrobe, his feet resting on their heels on the carpet.

Watson took a step forward and placed his boot up against one of Philby's. There was not a lot of difference; not nearly enough for Philby's boots to have made the tracks in the barracks and Ellie and Larissa's place.

Larissa was standing at the door watching him silently. He looked up at her, moved his foot back and shook his head.

'Check the light switches,' he said.

She immediately looked at the switch just inside the doorway she was standing in.

'It's on,' she said, then went to investigate the rest of the house.

Most of the other lights were switched off, except for the kitchen.

'The heater,' she called from the lounge room. 'It's still in the on position.'

He came to stand with her next to Philby's little bar heater and surveyed the room. There was a TV, an old record player, some scattered newspapers and an empty beer bottle and glass on a small side table next to a tattered recliner lounge. There was a small puddle of water, most likely condensation that had run off the empty bottle.

'What time did the power go off the other night, do you remember?'

'Um, it was on when we got up and went to the bridge—I remember turning the light on to go to the toilet before we left,' Larissa said.

'And it was off by the time we got back. What would that have been about five thirty?'

'That's right.' She nodded. 'I wanted to cook everything out of the fridge for breakfast because the power was out.'

'Shit,' Watson said, rubbing at his face again. 'So, he's packed up everything at the bridge, probably told the other crew that he was coming over to get us.' He looked down at the beer bottle and the glass. 'He's come straight back here, had a beer in front of his little heater and then decided to go and top himself.'

'He was probably already dead when we were standing at the bridge wondering where everyone had gone,' she said softly.

'Yeah, maybe we should have checked here earlier,' he said.

There was no response from Larissa.

He turned. She was standing in the middle of the lounge room, contemplating the carpet. The Xanax had kicked in.

24

He graduated in the bottom third of his class. A major disappoint-ment. Mueller had recommended he see the police headshrinker, guaranteed it would not go on his personnel file, nor would it effect promotion or postings in the future. Bullshit. He didn't go. His mother had a six-month supply of Valium left over from a bitter break-up with a boyfriend a couple of years back. He went through the lot in six weeks.

He was posted to the City Central Command and worked out of Central Station in the middle of the CBD. It suited him just fine; it was the biggest and busiest station in the state and he could get lost in the crowd. He had found a regular source of Valium, Oxy and Xanax among the deadbeats and low-lifes he dealt with on a daily basis as an inner-city cop. And of course, there was Jeremy Landers for coke. He was barely able to function most days: his memory was shot, he was anxious and depressed.

Andrea, meanwhile, had made the leap from local council to state politics and been swiftly bumped up the pecking order. She was being touted as the next big thing, and her party was backing her to run for a blue ribbon seat in the upcoming elections. To his relief, Craig hadn't seen or heard from her since he left the academy.

He had his first holiday three months after starting in the city. He doubted his colleagues would miss him; his first probationary performance report had rated him as barely adequate. He took Alison to Fiji. It was a special deal at the travel agency near the station; there was no way he could have organised it himself. The first couple of days were a nightmare. Coming down off his regular opioid cocktail, he didn't sleep, but by day three and then four and for the rest of the fortnight it was the best time of his life.

They sometimes lay in bed until the early afternoon, then it was cocktails and bar snacks by the pool, being waited on hand and foot. They went on a rainforest trek and on a day trip out to the remote islands, where they snorkelled among the coral reefs. They went canoeing and on one particularly memorable day he got his bum badly sunburnt while they made love on a deserted beach, miles from anywhere.

He started counting the days until they were due back, but hid it from Alison. She had changed. When she laughed now she just seemed happy: not happy-sad, not even happy-serious, just happy.

When they took their seats on the plane for the flight home it felt like the first time he had breathed out for a fortnight. He held his face against her freshly tanned cheek and then he turned his head further and whispered into her hair, 'I love you.' She squeezed his hand and wiped away the tears making salty tracks down to her chin.

25

'So, Bishop lives up on the headland?' he asked.

They were sitting at Larissa's kitchen table. It had taken her a good two hours to resume normal transmission after falling down the Xanax hole in Philby's lounge room.

'Yes, one of the big houses with views down the coast, he was always making a big thing about it, wanting us to come around, but Ellie couldn't stand him.'

'Oh yeah, what about you?'

'I didn't give a shit about him. He's ugly, and short, and bald. He tried it on when I first started here, but he gave up pretty quickly when I moved in with Ellie. Thought we were both lesbians, probably.'

'Do you reckon the kids we saw could have been heading up to his place?' he asked, just throwing it out there.

'No,' she said dismissively. 'They wouldn't have anything to do with him.'

'Yeah, why not?'

'Oh, I don't know—just too up himself, you know? Too'—she paused, looking for the right word—'self-centred.'

Watson took a moment, letting a thousand different scenarios play out in his mind. He sighed, rested his elbows on the table, took his head in his hands and scratched at his scalp. His hair hadn't seen shampoo for a week. Something clicked. His head snapped up.

'What?' Larissa said.

'I don't know. Something just . . .'

'What were you thinking about?'

'I dunno. Shampoo . . .'

Fuck.

'The photos,' he said rising quickly and heading for the lounge room where they had left the stack of photographs drying in front of the gas heater.

'Here,' he said, shuffling through the stack of prints. 'And here, again,' he said, holding two of the snapshots up for Larissa to inspect.

'What?' she asked, exasperated.

'The shadows,' he said. 'The photographer's shadow falling across the bed, across the girls. Look closely.'

Larissa leant in. Stared intently at the dark silhouette, standing out in stark contrast against the girl's pale flesh. Her hand went to her mouth.

'Oh my God.'

'That's right,' Watson said. 'The prick is bald.'

26

Andrea sent him a text the week after he returned from Fiji. It contained the name of a hotel, a room number and a time. He wasn't going to go, he decided. He'd had enough; he had finally started to feel good about himself after Fiji. If someone like Alison could love him, then surely he must be worth something?

Andrea called him three times that day, as if she could read his mind.

He ignored the first two, but answered the third call.

'Don't even think of not showing up,' she said.

He folded. She had a hold on him that was too deep to fathom. He took two Oxys before he left work.

Fuck her, *he thought,* I won't even be able to function.

He knocked on the hotel room door. It was a very expensive affair, a suite overlooking the harbour. It was opened by a woman he had never met before.

He stepped back, about to apologise, presuming he had the wrong room.

'Come in, Craig,' the woman said.

She was maybe in her mid-fifties. Slender, but the skin on the tops of her arms was loose. She was wearing a long, close-fitting shiny dress, her hair was long and too dark to be natural, she wore too much perfume, too much make-up and her eyes were glazed.

Andrea was seated in an elaborate straight-backed armchair in the large main room of the suite. She held a flute of champagne, and there was a bottle seated in a bucket of ice on a table beside her. There was another bottle upturned in a bucket next to it.

'So, Craig, this is my friend Cynthia,' Andrea said too loudly.

He looked at Cynthia, who was coyly taking a sip from a wine-glass. There were two wine bottles sitting on a cabinet near to where she was standing, surveying him.

'Say hello to Cynthia, Craig, don't be rude.'

'Hello, Cynthia,' he said, rocking forward on his toes.

'What the fuck's the matter with you, Craig?' Andrea snapped. 'Come over here so I can look at you.'

He stepped over into the light, closer to Andrea. She stood up, swaying slightly on her feet, and looked into his eyes.

'Oh no, no, no, this won't do,' she said. 'This won't do at all.'

He was having trouble staying upright.

She slapped him hard across the cheek. Cynthia let out a little shriek.

Craig just smiled; he was numb.

'Don't move,' Andrea said. She went into the bedroom and came out with her handbag.

'You really are a shocking disappointment, Craig,' she said, producing a small pill bottle from her bag. 'Here.' She shook out a pink pill and handed it to him. 'Take that.'

He tossed the pill into his mouth but had trouble swallowing it.

'Oh, for fuck's sake,' Andrea said, handing him her champagne.

He swallowed the pill and polished off the rest of the glass for good measure.

'Cynthia?' Andrea said, offering her friend the vial.

'I don't mind if I do,' Cynthia said, downing one of the pills herself.

She had moved around in front of Craig now and was looking down at his crotch.

'It looks like he has taken something before he arrived, doesn't it?' Cynthia drawled. She had a posh accent, Craig noted.

'He has,' Andrea said. 'He's got a pill problem. Haven't you, Craig?'

He was guessing it was ecstasy he had just taken; whatever it was, it was fast-acting, because it was undoing his Oxy buzz and sending pins and needles up his spine.

'Yes, I do,' he said, smiling.

'We can fix that for you, sweetheart.' Cynthia went to the sideboard and retrieved a shiny black handbag. She rummaged around inside and pulled out a box clearly marked Extra V.

'They're double strength,' she said, smiling at Andrea, 'for twice the fun.' She pulled one of the diamond-shaped blue pills from the packet and slipped it halfway between her lips. Leaning forward, Craig took the pill in his own lips, followed by Cynthia's tongue.

He was starting to see colours and his balls were tingling.

'Get undressed, Craig,' Andrea said as both she and Cynthia refreshed their glasses then moved over to a large hard-backed leather couch set against the wall of the main room.

The two ladies clinked their glasses, smiling at each other.

'I didn't expect him to be so pretty, Andrea,' Cynthia said.

'Don't say that. He'll get a big head. Won't you, Craig?'

He didn't answer, he just continued to unbutton his shirt. Surges of intense euphoria were flowing through him. He was rock-hard.

He kicked his shoes off then reached down and removed his socks. When he stood up, he saw colours bouncing off every surface of the room. He dropped his pants and kicked them away.

Cynthia gasped. Andrea sneered. He had to grab hold of himself, he was pumping, thick and ready to burst.

'My God, you've been keeping this all to yourself. You lucky bitch.' Cynthia's voice had dropped an octave, becoming husky.

'Come over here, Craig,' Andrea commanded.

He walked over and stood before them. He was floating on air. Cynthia reached out and wrapped her cold little hand around his hardness. Her hand took up half his length and she could barely wrap her fingers all the way around. Try as she may she could not make an impression on the rigid length, no matter how hard she squeezed.

Cynthia's eyes were glazing over. Andrea's lips turned up in a snarl.

'Eat her,' Andrea commanded.

He knelt down in front of Cynthia, who quickly lifted her hips and hiked her dress up to her thighs. He shoved the skirt higher and lowered his head to her. She was soaking wet and ready. He went to work furiously.

Cynthia was bucking and moaning, screaming with ecstasy. He was involuntarily grinding himself into the base of the lounge. His head was spinning, flashing with bright colours. He pulled his head back, eyes ablaze, and used his fingers, up and down, in and out, one, then two, then three. Cynthia's head was back, her hips straining off the lounge, squealing.

Suddenly Andrea stepped between them. She was naked. Grabbing him by the hair, she wrenched his head around and shoved his face into her. She held him there, grinding herself against him

186

so hard he found it difficult to breathe. He was beyond rational thought, starting to lose consciousness. Andrea must have felt him go limp, because she stepped away from him again.

'Fuck her,' she ordered, slapping the side of his head.

He grabbed Cynthia's calves and pulled her down further onto the edge of the lounge. He placed her ankles up on his shoulders, grabbed at himself and rammed inside her. She screamed and bucked. Holding on to her legs, he withdrew and plunged in again, withdrew and then plunged, harder and faster, a madness overcoming him. Cynthia's mouth was wide open, her eyes were squeezed shut, and every time he rammed home the breath would heave out of her throat.

Then Andrea was behind him, reaching around to force another pill into his mouth. He was aware of her rubbing something cold and wet onto his behind. He looked up into the large picture mirror above the lounge and saw her adjusting some sort of strap-on apparatus. She shoved him forward and held his hips with her hands, slowing his rhythm, and then he felt something penetrate him, going deep, and his teeth were grinding and he bucked and fucked and fucked and fucked while Andrea fucked him.

Completely.

27

They stopped outside the Surfside. Sat there in the car with the motor running, checking out the road ahead. There was a stiff wind blowing in off the ocean, and the beach was a mess. White-caps and muddy waves pounded the beach, while the wind buffeted the side of the car and pelted the rain into their windows.

From the pub car park, they could see the headland jutting out into the sea. Thirty or so big houses lined the right-hand side of the road snaking up it, backing onto the thick coastal vege-tation running steeply down the cliffs to the beach. The other side of the slick, black road was just a narrow grass verge with some tough vegetation hanging on for dear life at the edge of a sheer cliff face.

'What are you waiting for?' Larissa asked.

'He'll see us coming if we just go driving straight up there now,' he said.

'But Ellie might be there,' Larissa pleaded.

'Yeah, I know,' he said, nodding, turning to face her. Trying to think. 'Those kids—they went up a back way from the beach.'

He cleared a small hole in the condensation fogging up the windscreen and looked out to where the bush tumbled down to rocky ledges where the sand met the cliff.

'He won't see us if we go up that way,' Larissa said.

He nodded.

'Come on,' she said.

They threw their doors open to the gale and hurried across the road to the beach. The wind was howling in their ears, pulling at their hair and their clothes as the icy rain stung their faces. Watson led at a slow jog across the damp sand to the rock shelves a hundred metres or so along the shore.

The wind abated slightly when they reached the shelter of the cliff face.

'We'll just take it pretty slow, okay?' Watson said, raising his voice to be heard over the wind and the crashing surf. 'It'll probably be pretty slippery.'

They found a well-worn path in and around the boulders and the rock shelf at the bottom of the slope. They dodged large puddles and rock pools formed in the cracks and fissures on the surface leading up into the thick bush covering the slope.

It was steep, muddy, slippery going once they entered the dark vegetation clinging to the side of the incline. Many times they would take two or three steps only to lose their footing and come sliding back in to each other, or fall forward, banging a knee. They grabbed on to the thin straggly tree trunks and prickly branches, usually bringing torrents of freezing water down onto their heads and the backs of their necks.

After ten minutes of winding their way up the slope, Watson called out to Larissa, who was a couple of metres ahead. 'I've just gotta rest a moment,' he gasped, his head pounding.

Larissa slid back down the slope to him and rested at his side on her haunches.

'I'm so unfit,' he said, pinching the skin between his eyes.

'It's okay,' she said, 'I think I can see some back fences just up there a bit further.'

Watson sat until he felt the spongy wetness soaking through to his underpants and his bum started to go numb with cold. He clambered to his feet and sucked in a deep breath, then frowned. 'What's that?'

'What?' Larissa asked, alarmed.

'That smell.'

Larissa stood silently, breathing in deeply through her nose, looking quizzically at Watson. 'Is it smoke?' she whispered, squatting down on her haunches again.

'Yeah, I think so,' he said. 'It's coming from up ahead. Go slowly.'

He reached down and released the safety on his holster and glared at Larissa until she did the same. He took the lead; the ground was beginning to flatten out a little bit. The undergrowth and the canopy of trees above them became thicker as they moved forward.

After another ten metres, Watson saw flashes of a wooden structure in the bush in front of them. He stopped and Larissa hunched down close beside him, their arms touching.

'There's something there,' he whispered.

'I know. Is it a fence?'

'It's not a fence. It's a shack or something.' He felt her start to tremble.

'I'm going to have a look,' he said. And before she could object, he added, 'Just keep right behind me. And don't shoot me in the arse.'

He turned to face her. Their noses were only centimetres apart.

'Okay?' he said.

She nodded.

He stood up and they moved forward.

The wind, the rain and the thrashing trees above their heads made it possible to move without being heard. As they edged along the path, a small shack came into view among the thick undergrowth.

They stopped, and squatted in the bushes to scope out the small structure. Even calling it a shack was generous. It was made up of random fence palings, a few wooden crates, timber scraps and tree limbs trimmed to order. It was the size of an average suburban bathroom, but a fully grown adult would have difficulty standing upright in it. The roof was piled high with what looked like recently cut green foliage, and faint wisps of wood smoke were seeping out, only to be torn away immediately by the howling wind.

Watson tugged his pistol out of the holster on his hip. Larissa pretended she didn't notice and left hers where it was.

'Just stay here,' he whispered directly into her ear. 'I'm going to crawl up there and see what I can see.'

Larissa stared at him wide-eyed and nodded furiously.

He began to crawl forward, doing his best to keep his pistol out of the mud.

He could hear nothing except the wind rushing through the trees above and streams of water cascading down the hillside. The ground around the shack was well trodden and muddy, and there were reasonably fresh woodchips scattered around. There were no windows on the side of the shack, so he climbed to his feet to avoid crawling through the slurry of mud and sand.

He made it to the very side of the shack and looked back to check on Larissa. She hadn't moved.

He found a gap in the haphazard woodwork and was leaning forward to get a sneaky peek inside when he heard someone scream: 'Run!'

There were two of them. He recognised them straight away: the pair of kids from the backyard marathon, the same two they'd seen from the bar at the Surfside. And they were off!

'Don't move,' he yelled as the two hooded individuals turned and seemingly hit a full sprint in a single movement.

Larissa was off and moving at the same time. She passed Watson before he had gone five metres, moving fast and athletically through the undergrowth.

They were running up towards the end of the headland, flashes of pink and blue hoodies through the bush. They were drawing away from Watson, but Larissa was gaining ground.

'Just stop,' she yelled.

Watson caught a whipping, wet, spiky branch across his face and seriously considered letting off a few rounds in their general direction.

'Just stop,' Larissa yelled again into the wind. 'We only want to help you.'

She had stopped running. Watson eventually caught up with her.

'They just disappeared,' she said. He leant against a tree, put his head down and tried to suck in some deep breaths. They were in particularly rugged country, steep, with large exposed rock faces. A small waterfall was cascading off a rock shelf to their left, forming a fast-running channel in the muddy ground at their feet.

'They can't have gone far,' he wheezed.

Larissa looked at him disdainfully but said nothing.

They both sensed it before they actually saw anything. Movement at the top of the closest rock face, close to where a waterfall was tumbling off the cliff top. A shriek. A flash of pink against the grey and the green, bouncing, and then a body plummeted down the cliff face to lie lifeless in the tangle of bushes.

Larissa screamed. Watson froze.

A boy stood at the top shouting: '*Tayla!*'

28

'Leave her! Leave her alone,' the boy yelled as Watson and Larissa tramped through the sopping undergrowth to the thicker rock-strewn clumps of bush at the base of the drop.

'Just fucking calm down, Shaun,' Watson called back up towards the cliff top. 'We're only here to help.'

Shaun Howard's voice confirmed what Watson had first suspected the previous day.

'Leave her alone,' Shaun wailed. 'Please. Don't hurt her.'

They ignored him, hastening through the bush to where Tayla lay moaning, bleeding from innumerable cuts, among a huge tangle of lantana.

Shaun was sobbing incoherently.

For fuck's sake.

'It might help if you came down and gave us a hand, Shaun,' Watson shouted.

Ya fucken drop kick.

Larissa gave him a scathing look. Together they held up, twisted aside and snapped off enough sharp, stinging lantana limbs to get to Tayla, who was suspended in the mess of vines a metre or so off the ground.

'Tayla . . . Tayla, honey, we're coming to get you out,' Larissa said soothingly as she reached the girl.

Tayla turned her head to look at Larissa. She appeared stunned, her jaw slack, her eyes unfocused.

'Help me here,' Larissa said, putting both of her arms under Larissa's body, supporting her weight.

Watson did his best to free Tayla from as much of the lantana as possible. It was wet and spiky and it sliced into his fingers and his hands, drawing blood.

Tayla was coming back to reality. She started whimpering.

'Tayla, honey, everything will be okay, we've got you now,' Larissa reassured her.

Tayla put her arms around Larissa's neck and cried into her shoulder while Watson freed her from the last of the vines. Over Larissa's shoulder, he could see Shaun now standing just outside the mess of lantana, frozen, staring intently at them as they carefully released his sister.

Larissa started to back out slowly while Watson did his best to clear a path for her. When the way was free enough, he supported Tayla's legs until they could lie her on the sopping earth.

Shaun backed off, just out of reach.

'It's okay, Shaun. No one's going to hurt you,' Larissa said, concentrating on Tayla.

Watson just held his hands out to his sides where Shaun could see them. 'You all right?' he asked the boy.

It was difficult to tell with the wind blowing a fine misty rain into his face, but Shaun appeared close to tears.

He looked pleadingly towards his sister, lying helpless on the wet ground. 'Is she badly hurt?' he asked, his voice choked.

'I'm okay, Shaun,' Tayla said huskily. 'The lantana broke my fall.'

Watson moved out of the way to give Shaun a direct path to his sister.

The boy rushed over and knelt at her side. 'Oh shit,' he said. 'I thought you were . . .'

Tayla struggled to sit up. Larissa helped with her hand on Tayla's back.

'No, I think I'm okay; I just hit my legs and my back,' she said, peeling open a large rip in the front of her skin-tight jeans. Her bright pink hoodie was a write-off, torn and muddy, and the jeans weren't much better. Damp strands of her dark auburn hair were pasted to the sides of her face and down her neck. There were vivid red scratches visible on her pale cheeks.

Watson noticed Tayla stiffen suddenly in Larissa's arms as she took in her rescuers. Shaun glared at them.

'Guys, it's okay,' Larissa said forcefully. 'We're here to help you, I promise.'

They both looked hard at Larissa, their expressions softening, then all three of them glanced over at Watson as he casually popped an Oxy out of its cellophane packaging and shoved it into his mouth.

———

It took them a good three-quarters of an hour to negotiate their way back down the slope and along the beach to the car. Tayla was dizzy and unstable on her feet. Larissa found an egg-shaped swelling on the back of the girl's head.

At the last moment Shaun appeared reticent to get into the car; he stood by the front passenger door as if weighing up his options. But the sight of Tayla in the back seat, resting against Larissa's shoulder with her eyes closed, appeared to make up his mind for him. Watson started the engine and Shaun climbed in.

Back at Larissa's place, they gathered all the large saucepans they could find, and Watson and Larissa heated up enough hot water on the gas stove for Tayla and then Shaun to have a warm bath. Larissa selected an assortment of Ellie's clothes for Tayla to try on. She ended up in a pair of black gym tights covered with dark blue tracksuit pants, two t-shirts and a thick woollen jumper. Shaun wasn't so lucky; they just did their best to dry his clothes in front of the heater while he soaked in the bathtub.

Larissa cooked up a storm of fried eggs, sausages, bacon, mushrooms and tomatoes which the two youngsters demolished while sitting under a blanket in front of the fire. When they were finished, Watson boiled water for coffee, made four mugs, and pulled two armchairs up in front of the lounge.

He looked at Larissa questioningly. She nodded and blew on her coffee. He took a moment, making sure he had everyone's full attention.

'So, Tayla, Shaun,' he began, 'what's the story?'

It was Tayla who answered, gripping her mug in both hands, staring down into the swirling steam.

'It's Alan,' she said. 'Alan Bishop.' She glanced up at them.

'Go on,' Larissa urged.

'He picked us up one night last year. We were having a smoke down the oval with a few guys and that, and he pulled up in his car. We were all, like, drinking as well. He took everybody's names, said he was going to call all of our parents, but he didn't. Anyway, he told all of the guys to piss off and he said he would take me and Laura home, and he did, it was all cool, he just dropped us off at my place.

'A few days later, Laura told me she got a text from him, like nothing, just checking that she was okay and everything. She thought that was pretty good, you know, someone asking if she was okay. Her parents are just fucked up.'

She glanced up again and Larissa nodded, smiling.

'Well, yeah, Laura started texting him back, and one day he cruised past when we were wagging at lunchtime. I'm not sure, I think they might have, like, set it up or something. He made us get in the car and he drove us back to school, but Laura didn't get out of the car. She said she wanted to hang with him for a while. I didn't. I thought he was creepy.'

The room was silent, just the wind in the trees outside in the street and rain spattering on the windows.

'She started, like, texting him all the time and that, and he was texting her. I told her it was messed up, but she just told me to fuck off. She said I didn't understand, he was really good to her, he was helping her, and she told me they met up at her oldies' cabin and had a smoke together and it was really cool.'

Tayla paused, had a sip of her coffee and stared into the fire.

'I went there once, to the cabin, and we had a smoke. It was really, really strong and I got a bit freaked out, but Laura was just, like, into it, you know. They just had this really deep and meaningful about her parents and stuff, it was weird. Anyway, it started getting late and I had to go, but Laura said she was going to stay. I left, but I couldn't go home straight away because I was too wasted and my mum would be able to tell, so I just hung out in the caravan park for a bit. After a while, I thought I might as well go back to Laura's olds' cabin, but when I got up close to it I could see that they were getting together, you know, like full on.'

Watson sipped his coffee. Shaun stared out the window.

'I just couldn't handle it, you know. I didn't want to see her or speak to her for a while, so I had some days off school. But she told me she was really happy. She reckoned she loved him and that one day they were going to go away together, and anyway, she was my best friend. They started hanging out in that crappy police house, and I went around there a few times and'—she stopped, uncertain—'and anyway, they were like doing stuff there, in bed and stuff, and taking photos and making videos and that . . .'

'Tayla, it's okay. You've done nothing wrong. Do you want to have a break?' Larissa asked.

But the girl shook her head and continued. 'It just all got . . . I don't know.' Tears were streaming down her face now. 'We'd always be drinking and smoking and stuff, and he'd always have this fucking camera.'

She sniffed and wiped her eyes on the sleeve of the jumper.

'Anyway, one day Laura tells me they've had this massive fight. She showed me these bruises on her neck. She said that she had told him that she didn't want to do it anymore unless he got serious, you know? She knew they couldn't be together around here, but she wanted them to go away, live somewhere else, you know? Her mum and dad were just crazy and she needed to get away and she told him he was just, like, using her, and he went off.'

She was silent for a minute.

'So, what happened then?' Larissa prompted gently.

'It started to get really full on. He started hanging outside the school. He changed his phone number about five times and he started sending her texts saying how he was going to hurt her if she didn't shut up and stuff, and then they'd be back together for a week, and then it would all start again. Then Laura said she thought he was seeing someone else, doing the same thing, and then something happened with this other girl. Anyway, Laura decided she was going to tell her dad. She told Bishop that's what she was going to do, and that was the day . . .' She could hardly speak for crying. 'I never saw her again.' And Tayla broke down.

Several minutes passed in which the girl was racked with sobs. Shaun sat stiff and awkward while his sister leant into him and cried with her hands over her face. It was Watson who finally broke the silence.

'Do you think Alan Bishop was responsible for Laura's death, Tayla?'

Larissa shook her head, left the room quickly and returned with a full box of tissues. She pulled a few from the box, handed them to Tayla and left the box on her lap. Tayla dried her eyes and blew her nose.

'Yes. I mean, I don't know. I'm not sure.'

'He said the same thing would happen to Tayla if she told anyone about them,' Shaun interjected for the first time. 'He's a complete fucking arsehole. He said you guys weren't going to do anything about it because you all already knew and you didn't give a shit.'

'Whoa there,' Watson said. 'He what?'

'Alan Bishop said you were all part of it,' Tayla confirmed.

'And that old fat fuck—Philby or whatever his name is— he was definitely part of it, wasn't he, Tayla?' Shaun said.

His sister started crying again.

'It's okay,' Larissa said, getting up and squeezing onto the lounge beside Tayla and taking the girl's hands.

'He stopped me one day after school,' Tayla explained.

'Who?'

'The old guy. Bishop's boss. Just after Laura died. He told me to just forget about everything or there'd be big trouble, and they were the police and everything, you know?'

Watson was pinching at the bridge of his nose.

'So, when I came and saw you at the school?' he prompted Shaun.

'I thought you were just trying to find Tayla so you could tell Bishop.'

Christ.

'I was hiding at the caravan park for a little while,' Laura said, 'but I knew I couldn't stay there, I knew he would look there, so I hid out at the shack.'

'He was following me around too,' Shaun added, 'looking for her, so I couldn't help.'

'I tried to leave. I stole someone's bike from the caravan park, but he was waiting out near the bridge,' Tayla said. 'He ran me off the road and he put his handcuffs on me and took me back to his place. He'—she paused, sucked in a big breath—'kept me handcuffed on his bed.'

Larissa was rubbing the girl's back, making soothing noises.

'I was there for ages; I couldn't even tell how long. He said he was going to throw me in the river and drown me. He was videoing and taking photos and things, and he kept giving me these pills, making me take them, and he was taking them and he was going crazy, and I didn't know what was going on.'

'I was watching his house,' Shaun said. 'I knew Tayla must be there, because I went to the caravan park and she was gone. I saw everyone packing up to leave. I heard you guys on the loudspeakers telling everyone to get out but I could tell that he wasn't getting ready to leave. I hid in the shed down the back of his yard, and when I saw his car leave one morning I broke in and . . . and I found Tayla.' He choked on the last words.

'And then you hid in that house where we found you?' Watson asked.

'Yeah. We freaked when we saw you,' Shaun said. 'We thought you guys were with him, so we bolted.'

'And you've been hiding out in that shack, up in the bush?'

'Yeah, and watching his house,' Shaun said angrily.

'Why's that?' Watson asked.

'Because Shaun wants to kill him,' Tayla said.

'And we think he might have someone else there,' Shaun added.

29

Alison's degree required a six-month residential tenure at a teaching hospital. She was offered a position at a prestigious establishment in Brisbane that was too good to refuse. Left to his own devices, and Andrea's, Craig's downward spiral was swift and severe.

He was working shifts and he was getting more than his fair share of nights and early mornings, so it wasn't hard for him to dodge phone calls and delay responding to Alison's texts. She knew something wasn't right; he had become quieter, much more introverted than the jock she remembered from school, but she put it down to the pressures of the job and even thought he might finally be growing up.

It wasn't so easy for him to hide from his work colleagues and his superiors. He was issued with an official warning, his boss citing his sloppy work and lack of attention to detail, and put on prisoner escort duty, the lowest, most boring job available to a uniformed police officer.

While he was spiralling, Andrea's relentless campaigning and the leg-up she received from a powerful party room faction was ultimately successful in delivering her the leafy north shore seat of

Mosman. Her profile grew; her readiness with a snappy quote or a six-second sound bite on everything from hospital waiting times to naming a new panda at the zoo made her a media darling. She was a sparkling performer and it wasn't long before she was tipped to take up a senior cabinet position—maybe even the top job itself.

Watson woke up with a start when his watch alarm went off at 3 a.m. He and Larissa had taken it in turns to try to stay awake in front of the fire while Tayla and Shaun slept the sleep of the dead, together in Ellie's double bed. Neither Watson nor Larissa had been able to keep their eyes open for more than half an hour. Larissa was slumped beside him, eyes shut, breathing deeply with her head resting on his shoulder. He moved away as gently as he could and laid her down with her head on a cushion. Before moving away, he stopped and stared into her face. He reached out and touched her cheek lightly with his fingers.

He sat in the cold dark at the kitchen table, fidgeting with his boxes of OxyContin and Xanax. He sat there for an hour and then two, as the headaches and the shakes and the gnawing anxiety built up inside of him. As the first weak rays of sunlight brightened the dark corners of the room, he shakily placed an Oxy in his mouth and swallowed it with cold coffee. It was 6.15 a.m.

Three hours he told himself. It's a start.

———

'Just pull in here,' Shaun said, leaning through to the front seat.

Watson turned into a side street a hundred metres short of the Surfside Hotel and parked in a suburban driveway.

They had stopped off at Shaun and Tayla's home so that they could put on some of their own clean, dry clothes. Then they had all sat around the kitchen table and talked about the way forward and how to approach Alan Bishop's house.

'He watches the road,' Shaun had said. 'He has a view down to the pub and up the coast. You have to come up from behind.'

Watson was more nervous than usual; he hadn't wanted them all to come with him, but Shaun and Tayla had refused to stay behind, and he needed them to show him the way.

'Just keep behind me and do what you're told,' he told them as they went through a back gate out into the sand dunes behind the beach. A cold wind whipped the hardy strands of yellow grass that somehow managed to eke out an existence among the dunes. They wrapped their arms around their bodies and ducked their heads into their collars once they were exposed to the full force of the wind out on the exposed shore.

Huge storm seas had battered the beach almost beyond recognition. They had to jump down a two-metre ledge where the waves had cut a swathe through the sand and carried it out to sea. The incoming tide was making the surface close to the water sloppy and boggy and they struggled to make their way up to the bushland at the end of the beach.

They were all breathing hard and straining to be heard above the crashing surf, the howling wind and the rain that was fizzing and stinging against their ears.

'Lead off,' Watson called to Shaun, 'but don't get too far ahead. And watch out—it's slippery.'

Shaun gave Watson a squint-eyed look that said, *I think I know what I'm doing, dickhead.*

As expected, the going was very hard. Watson was grateful that Tayla's choice of footwear was hopelessly inadequate for the task. Her decorated Converse high tops had minimal traction in the slick mud, and every time she slipped back into Larissa's waiting arms he had a chance to pause and heave in a desperately needed breath. Shaun was climbing like a racing ferret and Watson gave up trying to compete with him within the first ten metres.

Shaun stopped and waited for them to catch up not far from where the ground flattened out near the old shack. They gathered in a tight huddle, down on their haunches beneath the dripping trees.

'How far?' Watson asked, using as few words as possible, trying to disguise just how out of breath he was. He had the beginnings of a painful pulse centred on the bridge of his nose.

'It's about ten houses that way,' Shaun said, indicating further up towards the top of the headland. 'All the fences are pretty rotten, so it's easier to go through one of the neighbour's yards. We can stay in the bush until we get all the way there.'

Watson looked from Shaun to Larissa to Tayla. 'Everyone okay?' he asked.

Larissa and Tayla nodded; Shaun just took off up the hill.

They followed him through a skeletal paling fence at the rear of a large two-storey house, and made their way up into a covered entertaining area by the back door. The pebblecrete surface was wet but not running with water, and the chairs of the outdoor table setting had all been tipped forward onto the table to allow the water to run off. They huddled together as close up against the house as they could, well out of the wind and the freezing rain.

Shaun and Tayla looked on wide-eyed when Watson tugged his pistol out of his holster and pulled back the slide a couple of centimetres to make sure there was a round ready to go in the chamber.

'I'm coming in too,' Shaun insisted.

'Nooo,' Tayla whined before anyone else could speak. She stepped towards him and grabbed hold of his windcheater. He didn't try to remove her hands.

'Shaun, someone has to stay here to look after Tayla,' Larissa reasoned.

Watson looked away, knowing his input would probably only inflame the boy's bravado.

'I'm not staying here by myself, Shaun,' Tayla pleaded, and his shoulders slumped.

Larissa put her hand on his back and gave it a quick rub. 'We won't be long,' she promised. 'We just need to know if Bishop's there, and whether he has our friend.'

Shaun nodded, looking down at the sopping floor.

'Okay, let's go,' Watson said, cutting off any further chance of drama.

They slipped through a gap where a sheet of fencing had been torn off by the wind. It was a tall, two-storey, blond-brick affair, built close to the boundary of the property. They were on a narrow concrete path running along the side of the house. There were no windows through which to gain entry.

They edged their way up towards the rear yard. Watson stuck his head around to view the back of the house. There was a small drop down to a covered outdoor eating area, similar to the house next door. It was dark and quiet. He slipped down and moved slowly, quietly, to peer in through the sliding glass door. There were no lights on inside. No sign of movement. He held his ear close to the glass. No sound. He tried the door, but it was locked.

Larissa had slipped in behind him, and together they made their way across the back of the house. All the windows were closed and locked. He felt Larissa tug on his shoulder, and he turned to see her making her way back to the door. She crouched down in front of it and pulled out her plastic warrant card.

'Ellie showed me how to do this,' she whispered. 'It only works on these cheap sliding doors.' She took the credit card–sized piece of plastic and jammed it into the small gap where the door met the frame. She wiggled it around until she was happy with its placement and then thumped the end of it with the heel of her palm.

They both cringed. The door rattled loudly, but the card had slipped in below the locking mechanism. With straining fingers, Larissa manipulated the card upwards inside the doorjamb. There was a faint click. She held on to the card with one hand while with the other she slid the door open just an inch. Then she turned and smiled up at Watson.

She slid the door open wide enough to squeeze through. Stood aside as Watson took a step inside. It was deathly quiet, and dark. He moved through the kitchen with his pistol leading, turned and motioned for Larissa to close the door behind them. They stood completely still, unblinking, straining to hear anything. The house was completely silent. It *felt* empty.

'I don't think there's anyone here,' he whispered, and then he moved off deeper into the house. The downstairs was mostly taken up by a big open-plan lounge/dining area, with only a small bedroom and a locked door that appeared to lead out to the garage beside the kitchen. There was a set of stairs leading up to the first floor. They both hugged the wall. Stood staring up the stairs for a good minute before Watson cautiously took a step up.

There were thirteen steps in all. He wasn't timing it, but he guessed it took him about thirteen minutes to reach the top. Watson was sweating profusely under his layers of clothing. His heart was racing. His head, as usual, pounding.

All of the doors on the top level were open. There was no telltale creaking of bedsprings or loose floorboards.

'Stay here,' he whispered to Larissa when she reached the landing behind him. 'Shoot anything that fucking moves.'

She nodded, eyes wide.

He crept stealthily from room to room. They were all empty.

He was moving back towards Larissa at the top of the stairs when they heard it. A muffled cry. Downstairs. His heart popped.

They stared at each other. Larissa turned and started down the stairs. He was on her heels. They stopped outside the locked door leading to the garage. Motionless. Quiet.

A gasp, a grunt. Something heavy dropping to the floor.

Larissa couldn't stand it any longer. She reached out and slapped on the door as hard as she could with her free hand.

'This is the police! Don't move!' she screamed.

Watson moved to the other side of the doorway, covering it with his pistol.

There was a silence, then, 'Larissa, is that you?'

Ellie!

'Let's smash this fucking thing down,' Watson yelled, and both he and Larissa went at the door with their feet, kicking the living shit out of it.

'Ellie!' Larissa screamed as she slammed her boot into the door.

'Wait! Wait!' came Ellie's desperate voice from inside.

They stopped.

'What is it, El?' Larissa called.

'I've just got to move . . .' There was a thunderous crashing sound, and then the door swung open.

There were three steps down into the garage. The two women met on the middle one, Larissa nearly pile-driving Ellie into the floor. They were both crying hysterically.

Watson drew breath, turned his back on the two women, pulled a Xanax and an Oxy out of their packets and swallowed them both.

30

It only came to Ellie much later; she had plenty of time to think about it, barricaded there in the garage. She had seen Bishop's red Lexus parked out the front of the station when she drove in to get the milk.

She pulled up as close to the back door as possible. She had a premonition before she opened it: there was something wrong, something bad was going to happen, she could almost taste it. She stood in the kitchen, just inside the door, for a moment, sussing the place out. It felt weird, but maybe that was just because it was empty.

Bishop's right fist caught Ellie in the eye as she turned from the fridge. She didn't see it coming. It threw her back into the tables and chairs in the middle of the room. She somehow had the presence of mind to roll right underneath.

'Ya fucking cunt,' Bishop screamed, throwing the chairs out of the way, smashing one against the wall and up-ending the table.

Ellie lashed out with a boot as he came for her, catching him on the side of the knee, slowing him momentarily. Her head

211

was fuzzy, reactions slowed; she was completely blind in her right eye.

Bishop grabbed at her leg as Ellie attempted another kick. He managed to grasp hold of her as she seized hold of a broken chair leg and swung it once, completely missing him, but the second time connecting hard with his forearm.

Bishop grunted and released her.

'You fucking bitch. You're fucking dead!' he screamed, coming at her hard, and though Ellie tried to bring her knees up to protect herself, his kick caught her in the mid-section, lifted her off the ground and drove every piece of wind out of her.

Ellie rolled away as quick as she could, almost blacking out with pain. Vomit filled her mouth and she spat as she hit the wall at the side of the room. She lay there, doubled over in agony, as Bishop lifted her by the collar a couple of feet off the ground, his right fist cocked for another savage, jaw-breaking blow.

There was a needle-sharp shard of wood from a broken chair leg lying beneath her body. She snatched it up as he drew his arm back. She swung hard and jammed the shard into the forearm holding her by the collar until it punched through the skin on the other side of his arm.

Bishop squealed like a stuck pig, dropped Ellie and went bounding around the room.

He picked up the chair leg that she had hit him with and, avoiding Ellie's flailing arms, whacked her a glancing blow across the back of the head.

'You're gonna fucken pay for this, ya dyke cunt,' he spat.

Bishop grabbed Ellie by the collar with his one good arm, and dragged her out the back door, down the side of the station and threw her, semi-conscious, into the back seat of the Lexus.

Bishop was whimpering as he drove the short distance up the headland road to his house, the shard of wood still protruding from his arm.

'You're gonna fucking pay for this, bitch,' Bishop promised, as he dragged her out onto the driveway and up into his house.

Ellie was feigning unconsciousness as he dragged her into the downstairs bedroom, where there was a pair of handcuffs lying ready, one manacle already connected to the bedpost at the head of the bed.

If he gets that handcuff on me, I'm dead, was her only conscious thought.

Ellie waited, lying limp, until Bishop dropped her beside the bed and opened the free manacle of the handcuff. She moved quickly, grabbing his injured arm, smashing the shard of wood deeper into his flesh.

Bishop's ear-piercing scream could have woken the dead.

She sprang from the bed. The front door was deadlocked; she couldn't get out. She turned: he was coming out of the bedroom after her, his eyes insane with rage and pain.

She dodged him, flung open the garage door, jumped down the steps and slammed the door behind her. She was completely unarmed. Hadn't thought to take her pistol to go and get milk. Looking around desperately for a weapon, she spied a dirty shovel leaning up against the wall.

When Bishop threw open the door, the shovel hit him square in the face. Ellie slammed the door shut again as he reeled back, screaming. There was a large metal chest full of power tools sitting on the floor near the foot of the steps. It must have weighed well over two hundred kilograms. She heaved it up like it was a sack of feathers and shoved it against the door.

Bishop came back five times trying to break through the door. No dice. The power was off to the electric roller door so there was no way he was getting in that way either.

Ellie heard muffled voices outside sometime late in the night before there was another frenzied attack on the door. But since then there had been nothing. She had huddled in a corner, wrapped up in an old tarpaulin, shovel at the ready, until she heard Larissa yelling outside the door two days later.

———

Larissa helped Ellie clean herself up as best she could while Watson went and retrieved Shaun and Tayla from the next-door neighbour's yard. They regrouped in Bishop's kitchen. There were a few warm beers in the fridge and half a bottle of Johnnie Walker. Watson helped himself to a mouthful of the Johnnie Walker and cracked one of the beers before pouring four good measures of whisky into coffee cups on the kitchen table.

Larissa and Ellie looked up at him, dismayed.

'Chin-chin,' he said, taking another swig from the bottle.

Ellie couldn't repress a sideways smile. She shook her head and said, 'Chin-chin,' before knocking back her cupful, closely followed by Larissa and the two teenagers, the four of them pissing themselves laughing for the first time in a long, long while.

'It must have been pretty uncomfortable in that shack,' Watson said, more to make conversation than out of any real sense of empathy.

'Yeah, nah,' Shaun said lightly, slightly tipsy from the quadruple shot of whisky he had tipped down his throat in a single fiery gulp. 'There's another, better place right up on the cliffs. It's smaller but it's dry, and it's got sleeping bags and things as well.'

'Oh right,' Watson said, his hand involuntarily going to his chest as his heart surged and a white flash went off behind his eyes.

'Yeah, people go up there to watch whales and stuff. Sometimes kids sleep up there, you know?'

'Yeah, I used to know a place like that,' Watson said softly.

Ellie, Larissa and Tayla waited at Bishop's place—with Larissa's pistol close at hand—while Watson and Shaun went to retrieve the car. Shaun chatted away happily as the two of them half ran, half walked, straight down the headland road together, past the pub and into the side street where they had parked the car a couple of hours earlier.

'Ya know, someone's got to put that dog down,' Shaun said in all seriousness as he climbed into the front seat of the car.

Watson stared into the youngster's rosy-cheeked face and, try as he might, he could not come up with a valid reason as to why that should not be the case.

———

A length of vertical blind streamed out of a shattered front window as they pulled up in the driveway back at Ellie and Larissa's place. The front door stood ajar. Fresh, water-filled tyre tracks made a smooth arc across the front lawn, tracking towards a partially demolished section of their quaint, white-picket front fence.

'Shit.'

They sat there in silence for a moment. Shaun had commandeered the front passenger seat. The three women were crammed into the back.

'Do you think he was watching us?' Larissa asked.

'There's a good chance,' Watson replied, opening his door and drawing his pistol. 'Just wait here,' he said, looking directly at Shaun.

Larissa joined him as he made his way to the front door.

They stood and waited on either side of the doorway, listening intently, but other than the rattling of the blinds against the smashed windowpane there was no noise within the house. Watson glanced at Larissa, who took her place covering the doorway while he stepped in and cleared the house.

'Yeah, he's gone,' he said, returning to the front door.

Larissa breathed out, then motioned for Ellie and the kids to join them.

They left Tayla and Shaun out on the front porch while they hastily tidied the lounge area. A metal garden chair had been smashed through the front window, covering the floor and most of the furniture in shards of glass. There were muddy footprints on the lounge chair, where someone had climbed in through the window.

Larissa stood staring down at the kitchen table, her index finger resting on her lips.

'The photos,' she said. 'They were here.' There were still scraps of paper scattered on the tabletop.

'No, only some of them were,' Watson said. 'Just the leftovers we couldn't separate. I've still got most of them back at the barracks.'

'What photos?' Ellie asked, glancing quickly at Larissa.

'Some photos we found at the barracks of young girls,' Watson said before Larissa could answer. Then he was struck by a sudden thought. 'Oh shit,' he said, hurrying out of the kitchen and up the hall with Ellie and Larissa close behind.

He entered the empty bedroom at the furthest end of the hall. The door was open, just as it had been when he did the initial search, but he knew it had been closed when they left that morning. He stood staring at the empty space behind the open door.

'What?' Larissa and Ellie said simultaneously.

'The fucking shotgun,' he said. 'It's gone.'

———

They did their best to clean up all the shards of broken glass and put the house back together. Things had been thrown and smashed rather than just moved and searched. There were holes in the walls, and drawers had been up-ended and then pulverised with a muddy boot.

They boiled plenty of water for Ellie to have a long hot soak in the bath, and then they polished off the last of the eggs, some sausages, steaks and pork chops that were the final bounty from the now completely defrosted fridge freezer.

Larissa tended to the weeping, jagged tear across Ellie's eyebrow, and gently cleaned the dried blood from her puffy, blackened eye.

They patched up the broken window with tape and cardboard boxes from their garage, then got the heater going and sat in front of it, warming themselves with coffee. But the mood had shifted.

'I don't feel safe here now,' Larissa said.

Shaun and Tayla moved closer together on the couch.

'And we've got no idea who his friends were, where he could be hanging out?' Watson asked.

'There was Philby,' Larissa said, and the room went quiet. They had filled Ellie in on the dramatic demise of Sergeant Philby, and their findings at the council offices and Nefarian's home.

'There was definitely someone there with him,' Ellie said. 'I could hear him whispering outside the door, before he went crazy again.'

'He could have been talking to himself,' Larissa said. 'It sounds like he's lost the plot.'

'Looks like it too,' Tayla said, quietly indicating a fist-shaped hole punched into the wall next to the heater.

There was a muffled thump and then a rattling on the roof above them. They all froze.

'Possums,' Ellie said.

Five sets of shoulders relaxed.

Shaun jumped to his feet. 'Fuck this. Let's go and find the prick.'

No one argued.

———

Ellie drove, of course, and a sulking Shaun was relegated to the back seat with his sister and Larissa while Watson rode shotgun. The police station was their first port of call.

Shaun and Tayla locked themselves in the car while Watson, Ellie and Larissa went single file up to the back door. They entered slow and methodical, guns up.

Nothing.

Once inside, they turned the place upside down, looking for clues, anything that might lead them to a fucking maniac.

Watson jammed a screwdriver into the lock on Bishop's desk drawers and busted them open. There was just run-of-the-mill paperwork, stationery and files.

'He wouldn't be stupid enough to keep anything here,' Ellie said, going through the neat piles of paper sitting in trays on his desk.

'What about his locker?' Larissa said.

Nothing.

'He's cleaned it out.'

'We'd be better off doing a proper search of his home.'

———

'Right, let's tear this place apart,' Watson said as the splintered remains of Bishop's front door flew back on its hinges.

'Anything with an address, photos, names—' Ellie began, but she was interrupted by an explosive crash as Tayla put an ornamental pot plant through an expensive wall-mounted flat screen.

Larissa and Ellie both turned to look at Watson, who just shrugged as Shaun went to town on a top-of-the-line coffee maker before putting it through the kitchen window.

'I'm going to look upstairs,' he said, as Ellie stepped in to try to minimise the carnage.

There were three bedrooms upstairs. He started with the master bedroom, the only one that appeared to be in full-time use. There was an unmade king-size bed with a small bedside table on each side, a walk-in robe and an ensuite bathroom. The blinds were open, letting in enough insipid grey light to work by.

People are reasonably predictable. From a young age, kids always hide things in their bedroom and they either hide things in their drawers among their clothes or in their bed. He started with the walk-in robe.

There were four shelves built into the unit immediately to the left of the door, with neatly folded clothes on each of them. He pulled out every individual garment, shook it, then threw it into a pile in the middle of the room. Nothing.

He moved on to the hanging space. He pulled every coat, shirt and pair of pants off their individual hangers, searched the pockets and then added them to the pile. Still nothing.

Finally, he turned his attention to the long shelf running around the back of the wardrobe and along one side. A variety of boxes were stacked on it.

He knew as soon as he picked up the box that he was on to something good. It just smelt right. A shoebox sitting behind a stack of larger, dusty old boxes containing old trophies, text-books and study guides. There was no dust on the shoebox. He placed it on the bed and opened it up. *Bingo!* More photographs.

He shuffled through the photos quickly, keeping an eye on the door. He could hear footsteps coming up the stairs. There were no photos of Tayla or Laura. At the bottom of the box there were two memory sticks. He slipped them into his pocket just as Ellie stuck her head in the door.

'Anything?' she asked.

'Photos,' he said.

She knelt down beside him next to the bed and grabbed a handful off the pile. They were mostly of girls, mostly bound, some posing, some looking like they were into it, others looking like they'd just realised they'd made a terrible mistake. None of the photos appeared to have been taken in the barracks.

'For fuck's sake,' Ellie said, tossing one back down into the box. It was a picture of Bishop, posing in front of a mirror, a very serious squint-eyed glare, his arms bent at the elbows in the classic muscle-man pose, but totally naked.

Watson added a few similar shots to the pile in the box, and then a few more, probably taken in the same session.

'Fucking filthy fucking prick,' Ellie said, tossing another photo of a bound, helpless girl back into the box with each word. Then she stopped, gasped.

'Hello,' she said and held a photo out for Watson to view.

It was Bishop, wearing a black leather harness which crossed over his shoulders and connected to a leather G-string.

Watson couldn't help but wrinkle his nose with revulsion and he noticed Ellie was holding just the corner of the photo with her fingertips.

There was a woman in the picture, the only mature woman in the entire set. She had largish, heavy breasts with thick, dark brown nipples, and she was wide and fleshy across the hips. She was wearing a leather bikini and fishnet stockings, and though her feet weren't visible her posture screamed sky-high heels. Her face was covered by a black leather mask with cat's eye slits.

Watson looked up, his heart thumping, his mouth sticky and dry.

'These weren't taken here,' he managed. The paint on the walls in the background was a different colour from anywhere in the house or at the barracks.

'Yeah,' Ellie said, and then something appeared to catch her eye. She held one of the photos of the couple up to her face. 'These are fairly recent, though,' she said.

He leaned in closer to look.

'See that tattoo?' She indicated a basic tribal pattern running over Bishop's left shoulder. 'He only got that a few months ago, not long before the accident.'

'Fuck.' Watson shook his head, rubbed at his eyes. 'It must be somewhere local, could be where he is now. Do you recognise anything?'

Ellie shook her head. 'No,' she said, without looking back down at the photo.

Hearing more footsteps coming up the stairs, they piled the remainder of the photos back into the box and replaced the lid.

Larissa, Tayla and Shaun gathered in the doorway. Shaun in particular looked flushed and more than a little pleased with himself.

'How'd you go?' Ellie asked with a tight grin.

'Yeah, we fucked it up real good,' Shaun said, laughing.

'We didn't find anything useful,' Larissa added, looking slightly embarrassed.

'I'm going to look in here,' Watson said, standing up and walking into the ensuite.

'Shaun, just settle,' Ellie ordered, as the boy picked up a pillow and then a bedside clock-radio and threw them across the room.

'Hang on,' Larissa said, and they all stopped, turning to face the bed. 'Put that pillow back.'

When Tayla had retrieved the pillow and placed it back on the side of the bed where it originally lay, it was perfectly obvious what had caught Larissa's attention.

'Two people have been sleeping here,' she said, pointing to the indents on the pillows on either side of the bed.

Ellie picked up the pillow on the far side and inspected its surface.

'Make-up,' she said, glancing at Larissa and then Watson. 'And'—she lifted it closer to her face and sniffed—'some sort of fragrance. Maybe just shampoo.'

'Well, that rules out Bishop,' Larissa observed. 'He's completely bald.'

Watson turned and walked into the ensuite. He felt an overwhelming need to wash his hands after handling the sickening photos of Bishop and his victims. He ran his eyes over the range of male cosmetics, shaving gear and deodorants neatly arranged on open shelves above the sink as he soaped and rinsed. It was only as he was flicking the freezing water off his hands down into the sink that he saw it: a miscoloured hoop across the small metal grid in the drain. He pinched his thumb and forefinger together and attempted to grip the metallic band, but he couldn't get his fingers around it.

'What have you got?' Ellie asked from the doorway.

'I don't know. There's something caught in the plughole here, but I can't get it.'

She moved in and had a closer look, Larissa right behind her.

'Here,' Ellie said, moving in. 'Smaller fingers.' Larissa smiled at Watson in the mirror.

He stepped back and let Ellie go to work. She scrabbled around for a minute or so before finally getting hold of the object and pulling it loose.

'It's an earring,' she announced.

And Watson felt the ground tilt beneath him as she presented the dangling gold teardrop.

31

'Hey. Are you okay?'

He heard it like someone calling to him through a thick blanket of fog.

Jesus!

The world came rapidly back into focus. Watson was sitting on the toilet seat, flopped back against the cistern. Ellie had hold of his shoulders; Larissa was kneeling in front of him with her hands resting on his thighs; Tayla was standing in the doorway, eyes wide, her hand covering her mouth. Shaun just looked disappointed.

'Yeah,' he gasped, regaining his breath. 'I just . . .' He shook his head. 'I don't know,' he lied.

'Just rest for a minute,' Larissa said, reaching up and taking both his hands in hers as he tried to get up.

'No, look, those earrings,' he said. 'They're whatsername's— Caroline. You know: the school principal.'

'What?' Ellie exclaimed. 'How do you know that?'

Tayla took a step into the bathroom, nodding vigorously as she held her arm out, pointing at the golden teardrop that

Ellie was now holding up. 'I fucking knew it,' she exclaimed. 'I fucking knew it.'

Larissa turned to look at the girl. 'What are you talking about, Tayla?'

'I saw them,' Tayla said, 'in her car. The day that Laura'—she paused, drew a breath—'died.'

Larissa went to the girl and put an arm around her shoulders. 'Are you sure about this?' she asked.

'I saw them before as well, coming out of her office. Maybe he'd just come to talk about police stuff, but the way they were looking at each other . . . I just had a feeling. I just knew something was going on between them.'

'Those earrings,' Watson said, getting to his feet. 'She was wearing them the day we interviewed Shaun at the school. I noticed them because someone else I know used to have a pair just like them.'

'Well, I guess we know where the prick is then,' Ellie said.

———

'Whoa. What the . . .' Watson stopped in his tracks as they trooped out the front door of Bishop's house. Off to the west, down the road and past the town to the distant hills on the horizon, a patch of sunlight had broken through the clouds and was shining like the Second Coming on a smoky green patch of bushland.

'Hallelujah,' Ellie said, but as quickly as they had parted the clouds closed in again.

They all stood facing the west, the light of expectation on their faces dimming with the fast-fading cone of light.

'Bummer,' Shaun said, and then, 'What's that?'

Watson held a hand up for silence and then they all heard it: static, voices.

'The radio,' Larissa yelped, shouldering Watson out of the way and sprinting to the car. She threw the front door open and dived into the front seat.

'Gloster two-one-eleven, this is State Emergency Command, do you read? Over.'

'Yes! Oh God. State Emergency Command, this is Gloster two-one-eleven, we read you loud and clear. Over,' Larissa yelled into the two-way handset.

There was a break, some static fizz.

'Welcome back on the air, two-one-eleven. We've been trying to get you for the last couple of days. Thought we'd lost you. What's your status? Over.'

'We got left behind. We've been trying to contact you but our radios have been dead. We have an emergency situation here.' She got it all out in a single breath.

'What is the nature of your emergency? Over.'

'There's a bloody maniac on the loose. We have children with us, too. You have to come get us. Over.'

There was a delay, dead air and static, before the deadpan voice cut through the airwaves once again. 'Do you have an immediate medical emergency? Over.'

'Shit,' Larissa said, turning to face Watson and Ellie, who had both thrown their arms up in exasperation. 'Not yet,' she yelled into the handpiece, 'but there's a maniac running around here with a bloody shotgun and we've got two young kids . . .' Ellie tried to wrest the handset from Larissa's hand. As the two women struggled for control of the narrative, the emotionless electronic voice cut through once again.

'Sorry, Gloster two-one-eleven, we are prioritising medical emergencies only at this time. Unless you are in need of critical medical attention you will have to wait. Over.'

'Are you fucking deaf . . .' Larissa managed to scream into the handset before Ellie wrenched it out of her grasp.

'Look'—Ellie spoke urgently into the radio, holding Larissa at bay with an outstretched arm—'we don't have a medical emergency right at this moment, but there is a very real chance we'll have one soon if we don't get some help in here. We have an armed and dangerous offender at large in the town. Shots have been fired. Over.'

All eyes were focused on the radio. There was another extended delay, then: 'We will communicate your situation to area command, two-one-eleven, but right at the moment we have a long list of critically ill patients awaiting transport to hospital. You'll just have to hold on till we can get to you.'

'When? How long?' Ellie demanded.

There was another delay, then a barely audible voice returned.

'Twenty-four hours. It's the best we can do . . .' And then the voice was gone.

Fuck.

———

'So, we can either wait here for Bishop to come and get us—and he's got a shotgun, remember—or we can go and find him and take him on our terms,' Watson said.

'Get shot on our own terms more likely,' Larissa responded.

The argument had been going back and forth since they'd left Bishop's house. They were now grouped around the heater in Larissa and Ellie's lounge. Ellie had retrieved her pistol from the gun safe built into the wall of her bedroom. Shaun looked on enviously as she expertly slapped a magazine up into the handle of the weapon and racked back the slide.

'Ellie?' Larissa said, looking to her friend for support, trying for a two against one.

Ellie shook her head.

'Why on earth was there an unsecured shotgun in our home?' she said, eyeballing Larissa, then Watson.

'Well, we took it from Nefarian's house,' Watson answered, embarrassed.

'Oh right. Help yourselves to anything else while you were there?' she asked sarcastically.

'No, but there was another gun,' Larissa said.

'What type?'

'Another shotgun, just like the one we took,' Larissa said.

Ellie stood pondering for a moment.

'So, what if we had our own shotgun?' Ellie said, looking from Larissa to Watson.

'It'd certainly give us an advantage,' Watson said.

'I don't care,' Larissa said. 'I say we just stay here and wait. He can't get in with all three of us here.'

'He will come for us, you know,' Ellie said, more to Larissa than anyone else in the room. 'He knows we have the photos and he needs to get rid of us. And if he was listening to his police radio he knows he's only got twenty-four hours to do it.'

'I'm going to get that other gun,' Watson said.

'Yeah, I think you'd better,' Ellie said.

———

He went on foot, over the back fence and through the neighbours' yards. He didn't want to take the chance that Bishop was watching and waiting for them to separate. He took a Xanax before he left, just to calm the nerves. It wasn't a great idea; Xanax made him a bit sluggish and sometimes lowered his mood.

It was probably only five hundred metres to Nefarian's house but he was blowing pretty hard by the time he got there. When he made it over the last fence into Nefarian's backyard he had to stop and suck in some deep breaths. He was feeling particularly light-headed, hopeless, a little bit teary.

They had left Nefarian's back door unlocked when they left the house two days before, so he slipped inside and stood silently in the kitchen, waiting, listening, just in case.

There was nothing, just the wind in the trees out in the yard.

He made his way quickly through the house to the garage and the gun safe standing in the gloom against the back wall. The shotgun was where they had left it, leaning against the workbench. As he gripped its cold wood he was gripped by an overwhelming sense of exhaustion and desperate loneliness. In a searing flash it struck him that in twenty-four hours it would all start again—Andrea, the drugs, the waste, the futility, the crushing, overwhelming guilt.

His head was jolted by flashing lightning images of the cliff; of Alison's beautiful tear-streaked face; of Andrea's bared teeth.

His legs crumpled beneath him and he went down on his haunches on the hard cement, then to his knees. His tears spattered off the cold cement surface. His head was down, resting on his heaving chest, a low, tortured moan escaping him.

He gripped the shotgun hard in his clenched fists, raised his head back and drew in a deep breath.

'Fuck this,' he yelled into the emptiness, and he racked the slide of the pump action, placed the butt of the gun on the floor between his knees and the barrel snugly under his chin. He closed his eyes as his hand slid down the icy metal reaching for the trigger.

With his thumb hooked inside the trigger guard, resting up against the trigger, he felt a warm flood of relief flow through him, as if a million tonnes of grief had been lifted from his shoulders.

It just felt so *right*.

He put the first bit of pressure on the trigger, took up the tiniest bit of slack, squeezed his eyes tight shut—and then moved his head off to the side, away from the barrel of the gun.

'Oh fuck,' he moaned, and then he leant forward to rest the top of his head against the barrel of the gun and he laughed and laughed. He was close to hysterical there in the dark, the tears streaming down his face.

———

There was a substantial bar and drinks cabinet situated in a large downstairs room with a pool table and framed posters of exotic European holiday destinations. He went top shelf, selecting some type of single malt scotch whisky with a faded label and a cork top. He sat on a stool and poured a large measure into a cut-glass tumbler, the shotgun resting up against the bar at his knees.

He observed himself in the mirror behind the bar as he lifted the glass to his mouth. His jet-black hair had gone slightly curly in the constant rain and damp and had fallen loosely over his forehead down to his brows. His eyes were bloodshot, red-rimmed and bruised; his dark tan had faded into a sallow jaundiced colour.

He held the glass up and saluted himself in the mirror, raised eyebrows, the tiniest nod, then he downed the lot and poured another.

He polished off the bottle and was more than sloppy by the time he was ready to leave half an hour later. He banged the shotgun off the wall as he exited the back door and fell heavily on his back into the neighbour's yard as he negotiated the fence at the rear of the property.

It was coming on dusk; the wind had picked up and a light misty rain was floating in the crisp evening air. He was sauntering down the middle of the road, the shotgun dangling from his right hand, his chin hunched down into his collar.

He noticed it because it stopped moving. It just pricked something in the sozzled sensory receptors in his brain. He wasn't alarmed; he was too hammered for that. He kept going until he noticed the dark shadow had what could possibly be—a gun.

Jesus!

He went to move sideways, quickly. Stumbled and fell onto the road. His clumsiness was probably what saved him. There was a bright flash and a dull thud. A sizzling swish as the shotgun pellets flew over his head; if he had still been standing, it would have been a direct hit.

He rolled quickly, dropping the shotgun on the road and coming to an abrupt halt up against the gutter in twenty centimetres of filthy backed-up stormwater.

There was another sharp crack and a flash of light down the road. Pellets splattered into the trunk of a large white ghost gum two metres from where he lay. He dragged himself to his feet and half ran, half stumbled over the front fence of a house as another load of buckshot peppered the ground at his feet.

He careered down the side of the house. Put his shoulder into a large wooden gate that crashed open under his weight. He was in a blind panic, just going as fast as he possibly could. The firing had stopped. He jumped fence after fence after fence, he ran past backyard pools, doghouses, garden furniture and garden beds. His knees and shins were a torn bloody mess, but he kept going until he was sure that no one could have possibly followed his haphazard trail of destruction through the neighbourhood.

He crouched up against a fence in a dark corner of a yard, sucking in air as quick as he could, his heart pounding. He waited. There was no sound, no one leaping fences in any of the nearby yards. He rose to his feet and carefully crept up the side of the house. Peered up and down the street at the front. He was on a parallel street to Ellie and Larissa's, he realised. He got down in a crouch and exploded out of the blocks across the road, through two yards and to the fence at the back of their house.

'Ellie! Larissa! Don't shoot—it's me!' he yelled into the back yard. He could see a dark figure hovering near the back door. He took a chance, scrambled over the fence, sprinted across the yard and threw himself through the quickly opened back door.

———

'Oh my God, oh my God, oh my God,' Larissa was chanting, her left hand over her mouth, her right holding her pistol down by her side. 'Let's go to another house right now.'

'Too late,' Watson gasped. 'He's out there.'

'Get back to the front room and stay there, Larissa,' Ellie commanded.

Watson was on his back on the kitchen floor. Heaving. Ellie hovered over him on her knees. Larissa gave him a desperate look and then headed out of the room.

'Are you hurt?' Ellie asked, laying her palms flat on his heaving chest, searching for God knows what.

'No. No, I'm okay, I think,' he said, still breathless. 'It was Bishop.' He sat up. 'We bloody almost walked right into each other.'

'Shit. He must have been on his way here,' Larissa said, coming back into the room and kneeling beside Watson with a first-aid kit.

Ellie shook her head, stood up and peered out the kitchen window into the darkening backyard.

'Yeah, probably,' Watson said. His head was spinning; he felt like he was about to throw up.

Larissa's expression changed. She leaned in closer to him, smelling his breath.

'What the fuck?' she said angrily. 'Have you been drinking?'

He hung his head; he couldn't look at her. He could tell that Ellie was glaring down at him now too.

'Well?' Larissa demanded.

'Yeah, maybe I had a few drinks at Nefarian's house . . .'

'Fuck,' Larissa spat.

She stood, picked up his unopened boxes of OxyContin and Xanax from the kitchen table and threw them at him. 'I suppose you had a few of these too, did you?'

He couldn't speak, his ears were burning.

'We were here worried out of our minds over you, and you—you just fucking go and . . .' She walked quickly out of the room.

Ellie stood there in the dark, staring at him.

He couldn't breathe. He sat there on the floor in the dark, knowing that if he was to see the expression in the women's eyes, the shame and the guilt and the regret would nearly kill him.

After all, it was only the briefest flash of Larissa's smiling face, and the thought that there could be *something*, that had stopped him from pulling the trigger in Nefarian's garage.

32

He knew it was Alison just by the way she knocked. He hid inside his apartment with the lights off, with the phone on silent, his knees drawn up to his chest, a blackened, spent pipe at his side.

She would give up after a while, but she always came back.

He didn't move. Not for days.

She slipped a note under his door that he didn't read. He held it to his face. Felt her tears.

One night she simply sat there on the other side of his door, said she wouldn't leave until he let her in. He lasted half an hour, shaking there in the dark, then finally he opened the door.

He didn't turn the lights on. They stood there holding each other for what seemed like hours, until the heat returned to their bodies.

'I don't know everything,' Alison said, 'but I know what she's like and I can't help but feel that I have done this to you.'

He couldn't tell her everything; he was too ashamed. But he told her how Andrea watched them and about the motel outside the academy.

'I feel so helpless, so weak, it's like she stripped me, and I can't see a way out other than . . . I can't even say it.'

'She's evil beyond belief,' Alison said. 'But she can't stop me from loving you, and she can't stop us being together.'

She stayed with him that night, and he slept deeply for the first time in a long while.

They were awoken by a steady pounding on his apartment door early in the morning. He recognised the knock, hard and insistent; he knew they were uniforms even before he had put his pants on.

There were four of them, only two in uniform. The man doing the knocking was the second-highest-ranking police officer in the state, and the man standing beside him was the head of the 'Door Knockers', the heavy squad that hunted the most violent criminals in the state.

'You're going to need to come with us, Constable Watson,' the second man said, forgoing any introductions. 'These officers here will see that the young lady makes it home safely.'

Alison stood in the bedroom doorway, wide-eyed and terrified.

Craig glanced from Alison back to the heavy dude. 'Just do what they say, Alison. They'll take you home. I'm just going to have a chat with these guys.'

It was a less-than-subtle warning. They kept him waiting in an interview room for over four hours before the State Assistant Commissioner came in and sat across the table from him.

'This isn't a negotiation,' he said. 'You and the girl, you're finished.' And then he slipped an envelope across the table to Craig. 'This is your promotion to detective.'

As Craig reached out to pick it up, the Assistant Commissioner placed his hand on top of Craig's. 'I don't want to hear any more about this. You got me?'

He froze tight for a second, then nodded and drew the envelope towards him, and something deep inside him died.

33

They had spent the hour Watson had been gone fortifying and barricading their home. All of the bedroom doors were nailed shut and the hallway crammed with furniture. Only the bathroom, kitchen and lounge room were accessible from either inside or outside the house. They had turned the heater down to reduce the light. The rooms were now cold and cloaked in semi-darkness.

Tayla was under a blanket tent on the lounge chair. Shaun had armed himself with a large carving knife and had taken up a position close to the front door where Larissa could keep an eye on him. Ellie remained posted in the kitchen, staring out into the dark. Watson sat at the kitchen table, but if a deep dark hole had opened up for him, he would have gladly crawled in.

They were silent. The kids had heard the argument and were keeping their distance. Larissa had her head down, occasionally sniffing back tears. Ellie was acting all cool and disconnected, like she couldn't even see him sitting there just a couple of metres away.

It started low. Just audible over the distant echo of massive waves crashing on the beach and the water rushing down the overflowing gutters. A car engine. Far off but getting closer. Backs stiffened.

'Don't move,' Larissa said as Tayla popped her head out from beneath her blankets. The roar of the motor increased. They all craned their heads. Straining to see out to the west, through the walls, to where the sound was coming from. And then it stopped. Idled.

'Just stay where you are,' Watson said. Adrenaline had sobered him up. He took a position crouched on the floor in the archway between the kitchen and the lounge, halfway between the front and the back of the house. The lounge was lit by a dull, red glow from the heater. He could just see Larissa's back hunched low behind the front windowsill as she peered intently through a gap in the blinds.

Shaun crept away from the door as the sound of the motor increased again. Suddenly the front of the house was lit by blazing light as the car came screaming down the street, flat out on brilliant high beams.

'Shit, I can't see,' Larissa said, dropping the blind closed as the car screamed past and the front of the house was pitched into darkness again.

There was loud revving somewhere further down the street. Then increasing volume as the car came tearing back down the road towards them again.

'Don't look,' Watson called out to Larissa as the blinding light rippled through the vertical blinds, painting bright shafts across the walls, as the vehicle roared past and then came to an abrupt halt just a few houses up the street. There was more revving and shimmering light through the blinds as the car pulled up, motor running. He could see its headlights through a brilliant rain-flecked halo.

'Don't move, everyone just stay still,' Watson ordered.

'Are you all right, Larissa?' Ellie called.

'Yes,' Larissa answered. He could tell she was doing her best to keep the fear from her voice for the sake of Tayla and Shaun, who were now sitting bug-eyed together on the lounge, staring at Watson.

'We've just got to hold it together,' Watson said as calmly as he could. 'Keep watching the front and back. He can't get in.'

He was sure that the display out the front was just that: a display. Designed to distract them from an attempt to gain entry from the back. As he was about to impart this gem of tactical brilliance a rock came crashing through the front window, throwing the blinds open and illuminating the room. The rock hammered into the floor and bounced, just missing Watson before smashing into the wall in the kitchen.

Larissa screamed as shards of glass rained down onto her hair and down the back of her shirt.

'Just keep low, Larissa,' he yelled and then, 'Don't move,' as Ellie went to leave her post at the back kitchen window. As Ellie stopped in her tracks there was a loud hammering and then the sound of more smashing glass from behind the locked door at the end of the hallway at the other end of the house. Ellie turned in the darkness. Watson could see her pale features as her face darted between him and the other end of the house.

'Just stay here, El—he can't get in that way.'

'I know that!' she snapped at him, her eyes large with fear. Close to panic.

He tasted acid bile at the back of his throat and forced back a mouthful of vomit. It stung his eyes and blurred his vision.

The hammering continued. There was a resounding thump as something heavy hit the floor in the locked bedroom.

He glanced at Ellie. Her eyes were like saucers, reflecting the light beaming through the still-shifting blinds. She turned and, moving almost robotically, headed for the hallway.

'What the fuck are you doing, Ellie?' he shouted.

'Ellie,' Larissa screamed.

A powerful smell suddenly engulfed the house.

Fuck. Fuel!

Ellie stopped at the end of the hallway. Took a perfect combat crouch. Both arms extended. Knees slightly bent. Levelled her pistol down the hallway and opened fire.

The forty-calibre explosions and the heavy slugs tearing through the walls and the door at the end of the hallway were ear-splittingly loud. Ellie kept firing until all thirteen bullets were expended. She hit the magazine release, dropped out the empty and smacked in another full one. She let go again. Adjusting her aim. Side to side. Up and down. Floor to ceiling. She fucking destroyed the joint.

Watson was cringing. Larissa was sobbing with her hands covering her ears. Shaun and Tayla were nowhere to be seen. Ellie turned around, sat down on the floor—and fainted.

There was a slopping, glugging sound coming from the now semi-demolished end of the house. The gasoline smell was becoming close to unbearable. Other than that, the only sound was the car. Accelerating at pace, heading west.

34

He was a pariah, completely friendless and ignored in the detectives' bureau. Rumours abounded that he was engaged to the Commissioner's daughter, that he had blackmail collateral on someone high up in government, that he was the Commissioner's secret illegitimate son.

His immediate superior, Detective Sergeant Roper, went out of his way to make Craig's life difficult. He would gleefully present him with all the jobs no one else wanted to do and the shifts everyone wanted to avoid. Called him Maggot, Faggot and Arse-wipe. He would text Craig, call him, email him at all hours of the day and night. Demand to know where he was at all times.

Other than that, the intimidation was subtle. He would recognise a car from the undercover pool waiting for him to leave home in the morning or sitting out the front when he got home after a shift. Sometimes they would follow him for a couple of kilometres, not caring if they were seen or not. Sometimes they would just pull up beside him in traffic or at the lights, and sit and stare at him through their dark sunglasses.

He arrived home one evening, bleary-eyed and with a cracking headache after reviewing six hours of surveillance camera footage of cars coming and going from a service station, looking for a particular car, with a particular occupant. He almost missed the note that had been slipped under the door. He stood and looked at it for a long time before he picked it up.

Meet me at our place. Tonight at 9.

'Our place.' They had been back to the hidden shelter up on the cliff tops many times since they first met. Alison said that she felt safe there, and that the first time they had gone there together was the best night of her life.

He had been numbing the pain of loss and shame and betrayal with Oxy and Xanax and ice and anything else he could get his hands on, but in the morning it would always be there, sometimes a little bit worse.

He had plenty of time before he had to leave, so he sat on the lounge and picked up his pipe. He held it to his mouth and sparked up his lighter but he didn't touch the flame to the bowl. Instead he concentrated on the pain, his eyes squeezed shut, soaking it up.

At least I'm feeling something real.

He went out the back way and got a cab from a neighbouring street to ensure he wasn't followed. He couldn't find Alison's car in the car park at the lookout when he got there, so he went on alone.

She was standing by the edge of the cliff when he broke through the surrounding bushes, staring out at the twinkling lights in the darkness of the distant harbour. A light breeze ruffled her dress and blew her hair gently back off her shoulders. He felt the pain, he soaked it up.

She turned to face him, but she didn't speak.

After a silence that seemed to last an hour, he said, 'I've missed you.'

He thought he saw her smile briefly. Her lips looked dark against her pale skin in the moonlight.

She nodded slowly; he could see her throat working. She held her hand out. He could see something resting on her palm.

'She gave me this,' Alison said.

He reached forward and took a small memory stick from her hand.

'It's got videos on it. I've watched them. They're of you and my mother's'—she paused, looking for the word—'friends.' It came out like a full stop.

He had no words. He couldn't look at Alison.

'She destroyed us.' He could hear tears in her voice but her face was dry. 'She poisons everything and everyone she touches, and you . . .' She paused. 'She destroyed you, Craig. I'm so sorry.' A sob escaped her then, and she hurried off into the bushes, leaving him there. Eating his pain.

35

He went out the front door alone, his ears ringing.

'Look after her,' he yelled at Larissa, 'and look after them.'

He shut the door behind him.

The car was gone, leaving just a faint waft of burnt rubber and exhaust. He made his way carefully around the side of the house, his pistol leading. There was no one there. He went over the scene with his torch. As he'd expected, the bedroom window had been smashed in and one of the next-door neighbour's lawn chairs had been pulled up against the pockmarked side of the house. A quick inspection revealed numerous holes out through the side fence and matching punctures into the neighbour's home.

He climbed up on the chair and looked inside. A watering can full of what smelt like two-stroke mower fuel had been dropped and had leaked out into the carpet. He had a close look for any blood but found none. When he stepped down onto the soggy ground, he clapped his hands together, rubbing off pulverised woodchips and sawdust. Ellie was standing at the corner of the house.

'How you didn't hit him is beyond me,' he said without thinking.

Her shoulders slumped. 'I thought there'd be a body,' she said softly.

'No. He got away.'

'Fuck him—he's got to go,' she said matter-of-factly.

———

'Take the kids and all of the blankets you can carry and park in the car park at the Surfside. No one will be able to sneak up on you there,' Ellie said. She wasn't asking.

Larissa was shaking with anger. 'No,' she said. 'No way.'

'Bloody grow up,' Ellie snapped. 'You'll do what you're bloody well told. We have to get these kids out of here in case Bishop comes back. I don't know what the hell we were thinking staying here in the first place. It's bloody lucky we weren't all burnt to death.'

Larissa looked to Watson, who nodded his agreement. 'It's for the best,' he said. 'You'll be safe there. We can't just sit back and wait for him to try again. I'm sorry.'

Their combined arguments took the fight out of her. Her head went down; she wasn't happy, but she would go.

'Okay, you two, let's get going,' she said to Tayla and Shaun.

Watson and Ellie helped, carrying so many blankets and cushions out to the car it was difficult to close the doors.

Ellie had a quiet word with Larissa before they took off. When she stepped back, Larissa smiled at him over Ellie's shoulder. It made him feel just a little bit better about himself.

Ellie and Watson stood there in the dark until the sound of the car heading down towards the Surfside with its lights off became indistinguishable from the hissing of the waves.

'Shit, I should have taken one of Larissa's magazines,' Ellie said. They were only issued two magazines each for their service pistols, holding twenty-six rounds total. Ellie only had five left.

'Yeah, I think I might be able to help with that,' Watson said as they set off towards Caroline Harper's house.

Both Larissa and Ellie had visited her home before. It was on the very western edge of Gloster, overlooking the river, with a scenic country view out to the mountains beyond. It was a good twenty-minute walk at least.

Nefarian's house was more or less on their way. As they drew near, he led Ellie down a side street, inspecting each of the larger gum trees on the side of the road halfway down. When he found the one scarred with an array of shotgun pellets in its trunk, he knew he was in the neighbourhood.

'Here,' he said, flashing his torch towards the gutter, 'in one of these big puddles.'

They didn't have to look far. The shotgun he had dropped was half submerged in the puddle he had rolled into when Bishop had opened fire on him in the street. Ellie grabbed it and partially opened the slide, letting the water drain out of the barrel and the chamber of the gun.

'Here, give me a hand with this,' she said, kneeling under the tree with her torch muffled under her jacket. She quietly racked the pump action backwards and forwards six times, ejecting the six cartridges. 'Just give them a quick wipe over,' she said.

He picked up each of the stubby shells and wiped them on the inside of his jumper, then watched on as Ellie expertly reloaded them back into the weapon.

'What?' she asked, looking into his grinning face before they headed off again.

'Nothing,' he said.

————

The rain had stopped and there was a faint moon occasionally breaking through the heavy drifting cloud cover. They crouched at the corner of the street. Caroline Harper's house was on the high side, third along on the other side of the quiet cul-de-sac. It was a reasonably large house on a steep block with a pebble-crete driveway leading up to a double garage.

'What do you think?' Ellie asked, pointing out the house.

'Well, we're not going straight up the front. If they're watching, they'll see us a mile off.'

'The back?'

'Let's go.' He led off across the road and into the backyard of the house two up from Caroline's. They jumped over the fence into the neighbouring yard. From there they could look down onto the back of Caroline's house. It was dark and completely quiet, and from what they could see there was no way they were going to get in that way either. Every door and window was covered in security bars.

'Shit,' he whispered, 'what is it with you people and security grilles?'

'There's a lot of crime out here, bud,' Ellie whispered in his ear. 'Criminals with big guns.'

They both slid down with their backs to the fence. Ellie puffed out her cheeks and slowly exhaled. Watson had a bright idea.

'The car,' he said.

'What about it?'

'It's not on the driveway; it must be in the garage.'

'Yeah, it could be,' she said, not following.

'Well, there's no electricity, so what're the chances they just drove it in there and didn't lock the door?'

They jumped the fence down closer to the front of the house, Watson leading. He crept up to the corner of the garage. Ellie was right on his tail, carrying the shotgun across her chest. He crouched down on his haunches and felt along the bottom of the closest of the two garage doors until he could jam his finger-tips in under the rubber seal at its base. It wouldn't budge. He turned, looked up at Ellie and shook his head.

They crept along to the second door. Watson got down on his knees; the bottom of the door was a centimetre from the ground. He turned, nodded and pointed. Ellie squatted down beside him, their faces nearly touching.

'We'll go in quiet,' he whispered.

Ellie nodded. 'I'm not here to arrest anyone,' she said softly.

He stared into her eyes. They were cold, rock solid.

'First sign of them, we put 'em down,' she said.

Ellie then reached out and slowly, silently, raised the garage door another thirty centimetres.

They slid under it into inky blackness. It was warm and smelt of burnt rubber. They waited just inside the door until their eyes had adjusted to the dark. The car was just visible, radiating heat and ticking as it cooled. Watson placed his hand on the warm bonnet as Ellie slid past to take the lead. She was holding the shotgun one-handed, carefully feeling her way forward with her free hand.

Watson placed his hand on her shoulder, and they moved as one. There was a doorway barely distinguishable in the back wall of the garage. They headed towards it, stopped, waited and listened, and then Ellie slowly turned the handle. It opened smoothly and quietly. They stepped up and out of the garage.

They were in a narrow hallway at the foot of a set of internal stairs. There was no light, no sound. They stepped up cautiously, still moving together. At the top of the stairs, they entered a white-tiled kitchen. Intermittent moonlight bounced off the shiny surfaces. There were rooms off to their left, and to their right was a large glass doorway leading out to the backyard. Watson felt a cold breeze on the back of his neck. He turned as a gust of wind blew in under the garage door, and the door they had left ajar at the bottom of the stairs slammed back against the wall.

Fuck.

There was a thump to their left, somewhere deeper in the house. There were quick mumbled voices, movement in the dark. Ellie spun left, aimed and fired. The room flashed, blinding white, their eardrums concussed.

More movement, shadows darting in a doorway at the far end of the kitchen.

'Get down,' Watson yelled. He grabbed Ellie's jumper and yanked her down to the floor with him.

There was a hard crack and a flash from their left and another from the doorway to their front.

'Fucking *move*!' Ellie screamed, and she fired another ear-shattering round and dived to the left behind a kitchen counter. Watson dived after her, rolling across the tiles. There was gunfire coming at them from two directions, from their front and to their left. The kitchen was flashing. Chunks of furniture, tiles and plaster splattered through the air. It was disorientating, blinding and deafeningly loud.

Watson screamed, 'They'll kill us here!' He jumped to a knee and unloaded six or seven rounds into the doorway to their front, then dived over the counter to the other side. Ellie followed and charged forward, firing and racking the shotgun. Illuminated by the strobe light of the flashing weaponry, she charged on into the next room. Watson followed. It was smoke-filled and empty. There was an archway into a large open room full of heavy bulky furniture, squatting in the dark.

Watson sucked in a breath, his heart pounding, his mouth parched.

There was movement over near the stairs, the way they had come in. A flash and a crack, a shot fired from the other end of the open room. More movement in the dark. Ellie fired the shotgun; a figure was caught in the flash running down a hallway at the end of the room.

There was a rumbling, then an eruption of sound from the bottom of the stairs.

'The car,' Watson yelled.

Ellie fired again and went bounding through the room towards the figure moving in the darkness down the hallway. Watson followed as the sound of the garage door being ripped off its hinges shook the house to its foundations.

Ellie took up a position behind a leather armchair, the shotgun pointed down the hallway. Watson chanced a quick peek out the front window. A car careened backwards down the drive, screeched to a halt and then tore off up the road.

'Drop the gun and come out now!' Ellie roared.

There was low moaning from the end of the hall.

'Drop the weapon and come out into the hallway NOW!' Ellie repeated, louder this time.

There was a thump as something heavy hit the carpet in the dark at the end of the hall. More moaning. They waited, straining to hear.

There was a thump, then another.

'Okay, I'm coming out.' It was a woman's voice, weak.

Ellie stood up, the shotgun ramrod-straight, unwavering.

'Come out into the hallway,' she ordered.

There was a shifting in the darkness. A figure emerged no more than five metres away.

'Hands!' Watson yelled.

The figure moved towards them out of the shadows, into the moonlight streaming in through a shattered window.

'Ellie? Is that you?' Caroline said. She was dressed in jeans and a t-shirt, no shoes. She was holding her stomach, crouching over in pain. She kept shuffling forward.

'Ellie?' she said again, hopefully.

'Yes, it's me,' Ellie said flatly, then she pulled the trigger.

36

Whoa!

Ellie had hit Caroline in the middle of the chest with a full load of twelve-gauge buckshot. Watson didn't bother feeling for a pulse; even in the pitch-dark it was obvious she was stone dead.

He turned; Ellie hadn't moved except to lower the shotgun just slightly from her shoulder. She held it mid-chest, the business end still pointing forward to where he knelt beside Caroline's shattered body.

His heart jumped with a quick rush of adrenaline.

'You good?' he asked.

Ellie didn't move immediately; the barrel wavered, and then slowly lowered.

'Yeah, we better get going,' she said. 'Make sure Larissa's all right.'

———

They went out the way they came in. The garage door, which had been completely trashed, lay in the driveway, rocking in the breeze.

Ellie took the lead, covering the dark, rain-slick streets and back fences at a steady hop. Watson did his best to keep up, but after five minutes his chest was heaving and his breath burning in his throat. He made it halfway over a wooden paling fence before he ran out of steam and went straight down on his back.

Ellie wasn't happy.

'For Christ's sake, Craig.' She stood over him, her own chest hardly registering exertion. 'What's the matter with you?'

'I'm just . . . a bit . . .' he gasped.

'Just get up,' she said, not bothering to let him finish. 'We've got to get back to Larissa and the kids before that arsehole finds them.'

Ellie dragged him up by his arm and hounded him the last kilometre back to the barracks. She had his keys off him and the motor running before he slid, panting, into the passenger seat of his own car.

———

They came up on the Surfside car park quietly, lights off. There had been no sign of Bishop or his car on their way over. Larissa had parked at the furthest, darkest corner of the car park, hardly visible from the road.

Ellie pulled in and cruised up beside the other vehicle. It was quiet; no noise other than the wind rushing through the trees on the headland and the waves crashing onto the beach. There was no movement; the windows were dark in the other car.

Ellie got out fast and had pulled the passenger door of the other car open before Watson had managed to get out. She gasped. He could sense it was empty well before he got there.

Watson heard it first. Ellie was frozen with the rigor of wide-eyed panic. It could have been a gull, but not this late at night.

He heard it again, clearer this time, from the beach, the dunes across the road, a snatch of sound on the wind.

Ellie heard it the third time around. She moved fast to the back of the car, her head cocked.

'Tayla,' she yelled back into the wind and took off at a full sprint.

They both heard it clearly as they hit the road between the pub car park and the beach.

'Help us! Here! Help!'

It was Tayla's voice, shunted on the wind powering off the ocean through the dunes.

Ellie was well ahead by the time they hit the other side of the road. She didn't see the top of the wire fence, usually at waist level but now mostly buried under the shifting sand. She went arse over head and thumped heavily into the loosely packed sand.

Watson assumed the worst, pulled his pistol as he sprinted across the road and went to a knee, scanning the closest dunes for movement.

A dark shape suddenly stood in silhouette against the top of the dunes to his immediate front. He shifted his arms, aimed the pistol at the moving shape, took up the slightest slack on the trigger.

'Help me, please,' Tayla begged, sobbing.

Ellie climbed unsteadily to her feet.

254

'Tayla,' she called.

Watson dropped the pistol down between his knees.

Ellie and Tayla met halfway down the small mountain of soft sand. Tayla threw herself into Ellie's arms, incoherent.

'Quickly,' she managed to gasp as Watson joined them. He kept the pistol drawn, down by his side.

'Tayla, what is it?' Ellie asked urgently. 'What's happened?'

'It's Shaun,' the girl cried. 'He's over there with Larissa.'

As soon as the words left Tayla's mouth a snatch of sound carried to them above the wind from the beach on the other side of the dunes.

'Larissa!' Watson screamed.

The three of them turned and heaved themselves up the steep slippery surface of the dune, sliding back down one step for every three or four they made to the top.

'Larissa!' Ellie called again.

She made it to the top of the dune first and went careening down the other side, arms flailing in a semi-controlled, flat-out stumble-run to the bottom.

She called again and again and was answered from a point somewhere in the darkness not far along the debris-strewn beach.

Watson and Tayla ran together, stumbling down the dunes and across the sand to where Ellie had pulled up and dropped to her knees close to the crashing waves.

The fight had gone out of Shaun by the time they arrived.

He was face down on the wet sand, with Larissa sitting on his back. The boy's left wrist was handcuffed to hers.

'Bishop's car went past us,' Larissa explained.

'Shaun just freaked,' Tayla interjected.

'He jumped out, went after him, we chased him out here. Luckily, he ran out of puff.'

'But you're all okay?' Ellie asked.

'Yeah, we're all good,' Larissa replied, and Watson caught her eyes and a snatch of a tired smile in the shifting moonlight.

———

Shaun wanted to be alone. He didn't want to talk. Watson grabbed a doona out of the back of Larissa's car and threw it in the back of his own. Shaun sat there by himself in the dark, his head in his hands.

'So, Bishop headed up the hill?' Watson asked when he climbed back into Larissa's car.

'Yeah, he was going flat out,' Larissa answered. 'There's no way he could have seen us.'

They were huddled together, Larissa and Ellie in the front, Watson and Tayla in the back, sharing blankets, doonas and pillows.

'What about when Shaun got out?' Ellie asked.

'Bishop was long gone, up the headland. Must have been doing eighty, with his lights off.'

Watson was keeping an eye on the darkened windows of his car. He could see the occasional flutter of movement as Shaun shuffled around in there.

'Do you think he went back to his place?' Watson asked.

'I couldn't really tell where he was headed. I mean, his lights were out and next thing Shaun was bolting across the car park after him.'

Tayla put her head down, sniffing back tears. Larissa turned and reached out to her from the front seat.

'Don't cry,' she said. 'It's all right.'

'He just wanted to help.' Tayla started sobbing again. 'He just wanted to help me. I think he blames himself.' She sniffed. 'When our dad left, Shaun wanted to be the man, you know. He thought he could look after everything and'—she paused, wiped her nose with the back of her hand—'and look after me, but then all this fucking shit happened and, yeah: he blames himself.'

Larissa squeezed Tayla's hands. Watson felt his eyes burning. His pills were back at the house, but he knew they weren't the reason he was having trouble breathing.

It was a one-sided conversation, as usual.

'Meet me at the lookout. Ten o'clock tonight. Don't keep me waiting, Craig.'

When she'd hung up on him without waiting for an answer, he held the phone as far from him as he could. Like the memory stick that Alison had given him, which now lay untouched, unwatched, quarantined in a drawer, it had been defiled by her.

Her car was still warm, but she wasn't in it when he got to the car park lookout at twenty past ten. It was another new Mercedes; Andrea was moving up in the world. The whispering campaign, the subtle sabotage of political back-biting was well underway. Andrea had twice publicly thrown her support behind the embattled state premier. There was no surer way to confirm a coup was in play.

Craig waited for five minutes, leaning on her car for support, off his face. At ten thirty it came to him. He knew where she was waiting for him—the sick bitch!

He swallowed his third Oxy in an hour and headed out to the cliff top. Their place: the only place he and Alison had left.

He had to get out of the car.

'Just gotta get some air,' Watson said.

It had starting raining again, cold and misty, swirling in the wind. His cheeks felt raw and chafed. There was a flash of movement in the back of his own vehicle. He could sense the three pale faces peering out at him from Larissa's car, rubbed his hands together, blew on them, stamped his feet.

Fuck it.

He climbed into the front seat of his own car. No idea what to say. No idea what to do. They sat there in silence for twenty minutes. Occasional wind gusts flurried up against the sides of the car, spattering a fresh coat of dewy streaks across the windows. The hissing roar of the surf was relentless.

'He's probably up there laughing at us,' Shaun said eventually.

'No, mate, I don't think so,' Watson said, unsure how to play it. 'I think he's finished.'

'Bullshit. He'll get away. We'll get out of here in the morning, and he'll get away, and Tayla and Mum and everyone will be looking out for him and I'll be just like'—he swallowed back a sob—'fucking useless.'

Watson felt like the middle of his chest had been sand-papered out.

'Don't think that, mate,' he said, swallowing hard. 'You've already done more than a lot of other blokes would have. You stuck by your sister. Bloody hell, you've put your life on the line for her. What more could you do?'

'I could have stopped it. I should've known. When I found out, I just should have fucking killed him there and then.'

'You're a kid, Shaun,' Watson said, turning around in his seat to face Shaun, for the first time feeling confident in what he was saying. 'I know it's hard for you to accept it just at the moment, but you are a child and he's a fucking adult.'

He hadn't planned the words, they just appeared out of nowhere.

'There's some bad, bad people out there, Shaun. People who are so fucked up they don't know the damage they do, and if they do know, they don't care. Parents who treat their kids like garbage. People full of hate and rage. They think they're getting some sort of revenge, some sort of payback for the shit that might have happened to them. Or they just get some sort of kick out of making other people feel worse than they do about themselves. It's all about them, mate, not you. Not us. They're the ones who cause all the pain and all the shit. There's no need for you to feel guilty about anything. Anything at all.'

As soon as he'd finished speaking, Watson felt a deep resolve settle itself within him.

'And I'll tell you something right now, Shaun: you'll never have to worry about that abusing piece of shit again.'

And just for a second, he wasn't completely sure who he was referring to.

37

Watson was too edgy to doze, let alone sleep. He started the motor a couple of times and gave the heater a blast, on full, just to take the chill out of the air. There was no movement from Larissa's car, parked just far enough away to allow the doors to open.

His eyes were pulsing with pain, his stomach felt like he had swallowed a bag of broken glass. He was fighting a losing battle not to drive back to the house and pick up some pills. Twice his hand had gone to the keys in the ignition and twice he had resisted. He knew he wouldn't back off a third time. He was sweating, twitchy and anxious.

The two-way crackled, just faintly, as dawn broke, a deep purple smudge on the horizon behind the dunes. He sensed movement in the other car, then the radio crackled to life.

'Police call sign two-one-eleven, this is Air Force two-two-alpha. Over.' A broad Australian accent shuddering under a whooping rotor blade.

He grabbed at the handset, but Ellie was already a step ahead. Her voice came booming through the in-car speaker system.

'This is Police two-one-eleven, we hear you loud and clear. Over.'

'This is Air Force two-two-alpha we are ETA fifteen minutes. Confirm your location. Over.'

The thought struck Ellie and Watson at the same moment. There was ample room for the chopper to land right there in the pub car park, however if Bishop was listening in on his own police radio, he could be on them in a matter of minutes. There was no way the chopper would land if there was an active shooter on the scene. They needed to get Tayla and Shaun out of harm's way at all costs.

'The oval, the high school oval. Over,' Ellie responded, eye-balling Watson for confirmation.

Smart, Watson thought. He nodded. It would take them the best part of ten minutes to drive from the car park to the school oval. Watson could hang back, intercept Bishop if required, allow Ellie and Larissa to get the children to safety.

'The oval. Confirmed, two-one-eleven. We have a busy day scheduled so be ready for pick-up in one-three minutes. Over and out.'

'We'll be there,' Ellie shouted into the handset, dispensing with the formal radio procedures. Watson heard Larissa laughing, and her car starting in the background of the transmission.

He buzzed his window down halfway, letting in a stream of freezing morning air, but the three beaming faces grinning at him from the other car were almost enough to warm his bones.

———

Ellie and Larissa took off immediately for Gloster High School, Shaun reluctantly taking a back seat in their car. Watson followed close behind but stopped right outside the hotel, engine running, blocking both lanes of the road. He got out and stood with the vehicle between him and Bishop's place up on the headland, oblivious to the chill wind, his pistol sweating in his palm. After five minutes and with no apparent movement from up the road, he holstered his weapon and climbed back in the car.

He made the ten-minute drive to Gloster High School in five. Ellie and Larissa were waiting for him at the front gate. They drove in through the teacher's car park and then down a spongy, waterlogged path out onto an oval the size of two football fields.

The first weak rays of light had only just revealed another drizzling grey day when a thudding speck became apparent, coming in over the river from the south.

They parked side by side, close to the middle of the oval, as the massive green camouflaged beast made a thumping low-level pass above them. Watson had retrieved the shotgun from the boot of his car and attempted to keep his eyes on the access path as mud and loose, wet grass spattered all around in the thunderous downdraft.

The chopper did a lap of the area before coming in fast, flaring up at the last moment and then descending onto the oval in a raucous, green tornado.

A helmeted crew member crouching in an open cargo door on the side of the helicopter motioned for them to head towards him once the chopper had settled on the muddy grass, its rotor still turning. They huddled together and ran the gauntlet of showering mud up to the open door.

Watson hefted Tayla up onto the cabin floor; the crewman

grabbed hold of Larissa's arms and then Ellie's and dragged them onboard too. Watson grabbed Shaun's hand and looked firmly into his eyes before shoving him up onto the cabin floor. Then he stepped back, two, three, four steps away from the cabin of the chopper.

Larissa yelled something but her words were lost in the down-draft, her eyes registering panic. Ellie stood, but the crewman placed his hand on her shoulder, forcing her down into a seat. The crewman lifted his helmet visor and motioned for Watson to move quickly to get on.

Watson gave him a thumbs-up, then he turned and ran back to the car as the chopper became airborne.

38

The third Oxy caught up with Craig before he hit the gravel path at the end of the car park at the lookout. There is no euphoria or buzz attached to what is close to an opiate overdose. His brain felt like a wet sponge, the blue-metalled path felt like thirty centimetres of glutinous quicksand.

He lost his way twice in the darkness before he worked out where to turn off the path and head out to the cliff tops. He held on to the gnarled tree trunks, his thighs turning to jelly on the uneven ground between the thick bushes.

Andrea was standing there out in the open, on the bare narrow rock shelf, right on the cliff edge. Her hair ruffling slightly in the breeze coming up over the side of the cliff, her right fist resting hard up against her hip, her arm cocked, her black suit immaculate. She sneered at him, contemptuous.

'Glad to see you could make it, Craig,' she said, casually brushing a stray strand of hair off her lips.

He moved out onto the ledge towards her, concentrating on putting one foot in front of the other. He stopped, swaying, meeting her gaze. He said nothing, felt nothing.

Andrea tilted her head, waiting for something. He thought he caught a quick twitch of unease on her face, but he was unsure; he was struggling to remain conscious.

'You're such a weak fucking coward,' she said, resigned.

He nodded, expressionless.

'You know why we're here, don't you, Craig?' she asked, stepping towards him.

He just stared at her.

'Because this is the last place you have left, isn't it?' She reached out and drew her fingertips across his chin.

'Because this is where you and my little girl like to come and spend your sad little moments together, isn't it?' Her lips curved into a smile that went nowhere near her eyes.

Andrea was right: he knew why she was there; he knew why he was there. She needed to take everything from him, to strip him bare, to punish him for his weakness.

He caught another quick flash of tension across her brow and saw Andrea's eyes dart over his shoulder to the bush behind him.

'Do you think I don't know where you are every minute of every day, Craig? Do you know how much power I have over you?' She caressed his cheek with her fingertips but he saw her eyes dart back over his shoulder again.

'Do you think you can play me, Craig? Do you think you can treat me like a fool?'

She ran her fingertips down his throat, his chest, his belly to his crotch. She looked down and cupped his balls in her hand.

'I know everything,' she said, stepping in closer, squeezing him between her fingers, 'and I always have.'

A white flash went off in the deepest recesses of his mind. A snapshot from the past.

Her nose was almost touching his; he could taste her sour cigarette breath in his mouth. She squeezed harder and he became conscious of the pain. He watched her eyes, focused over his shoulder.

She stiffened suddenly, and her expression changed. He couldn't read it.

Andrea pulled away, her eyes gleaming, triumphant, as Alison stepped out of the bush onto the cliff top.

39

Watson jogged back to his car, sitting with the doors still open in the middle of the school oval. He stowed the shotgun in the passenger footwell and headed back to Ellie and Larissa's house, full throttle.

The place was a mess; they hadn't even bothered closing the front door behind them when they left. He found his pills on the kitchen floor, where he had left them when Larissa threw them at him.

I'm a fucking drug addict.

It wasn't the first time he had come to the realisation, but it was the first time it had really stung. It was the first time in a long, long while that he thought he might have something, or someone, to lose.

He pushed the thought back, storing it away for now; he knew he wouldn't be able to function in his current state. And he had things to do.

He took an Oxy and half a Xanax, just enough to take the edge off, to make him feel normal. He kept the leftover half-Xanax in his pocket. Just in case.

Then he pulled the last few silver blister packs out of the remaining boxes, snapped out each individual capsule and tablet into the sink, and ran the tap, washing the pills down the drain. He swallowed hard, turned and left the house.

———

Watson eased the car into the same driveway they had parked in when they last made their way up to Bishop's house through the bush at the end of the beach. His head was clearer now the Oxy and Xanax had kicked in; he knew he had about a three-hour window before the fug set in again.

He had to think it through.

This is fucking madness. I don't want to get in a gunfight.

He touched the cool metal of the shotgun and remembered Shaun's devastated face in his rear-view mirror. He saw the blank expression of a teenage girl photographed and corrupted by an uncaring, sociopathic adult, and he saw the desperate pleading face of another girl, betrayed by everyone who should have loved her.

Alison's hand went to her mouth, her eyes shining in the moonlight.

'Mum, what are you doing?' she pleaded.

Andrea stood back, folded her arms.

'Enough with the histrionics, Alison. I told you what he was like.'

'Alison, I . . .' Craig started, but words failed him. He had never been confronted by such utter devastation.

'Mum, you can't!'

'Shut up, Alison,' Andrea spat. The words stung Craig like a smack across the face. 'If you hadn't kept coming here, seeing him, none of this would have been necessary.'

'Do you think I'm stupid?' Alison screamed. 'Do you think I don't know what you're like? This is all your fault, you fucking bitch.'

Andrea stared at her daughter coldly.

'What? This?' she said, regarding Craig like he was something that needed wiping off her shoe. 'You think this is all my doing? Have a look at the pathetic waste of space. He's garbage.'

'You! You did this to him,' Alison sobbed.

'You stupid little whore,' Andrea snapped.

Craig grabbed her by the throat.

Watson wiped at his eyes. His hands were freezing.

'Enough,' he told himself. 'Think.'

He gazed out at the headland, jutting into the wild ocean. A squall of gusting wind and rain splattered across the windscreen.

'Fuck this,' he said, threw open his door and climbed out.

There was a small garden shed at the rear of the house backing onto the dunes. There was a rusted padlock on its door that didn't withstand a couple of vigorous kicks. Inside were a lawnmower, some old garden tools and a quarter-litre of mower fuel in a dented tin.

Not enough.

He broke into another four garden sheds and a garage before he found the mother lode. Ten litres of fuel in a big plastic jerry can. He carried it back to his car, reversed out into the street and hit the gas.

He was doing a hundred and twenty when he hit the bottom of the headland road, the engine racing, his hands moist on the wheel. He could see it from fifty metres away: the red car sitting in Bishop's driveway, close up against the garage door.

He hit the car doing fifty; poleaxed it, smashed it through the garage doors. His airbags exploded in his face, smacking him back into his seat. But he was prepared for the collision. It took him only moments to recover from the shock of the impact.

He had to shoulder his door open. The front of his car was totalled, the engine destroyed, smoking and gushing steam from a cracked radiator. He dragged the shotgun and the fuel out of the passenger-side footwell. Did a quick check of his surroundings.

Bishop was nowhere to be seen. If he was inside, he wouldn't be for long. And with the garage blocked and Watson's car hard up against Bishop's little red number, the arsehole wouldn't be getting away in a hurry.

He walked fast to the front door, shotgun in his right hand, finger on the trigger, jerry can of fuel in his left. He placed the fuel on the ground at his feet, no more than two metres from the front door. He aimed the shotgun and fired twice into the locking mechanism. The doorhandle, the lock and fifteen centimetres of wooden surrounds exploded into shrapnel. The door swung free.

Watson hefted the plastic fuel can under his arm and heaved it through the doorway. It landed with a heavy slap, slid across the tiles and came to rest on its side three metres away. He fired again, shredding the plastic can, sending a geyser of fuel splattering throughout the room.

From his pocket, he took a box of matches he had found in his search for fuel, opened it, took a single match, struck it and ignited the lot.

The fuel vapour erupted almost as soon as the flaming box entered the house. A burning whoosh of hot air smacked

Watson in the face, singeing his eyebrows. The entire bottom floor erupted in flames.

He didn't stop to admire his handiwork. With the front of the house now effectively blocked, he legged it around the side to cover the only remaining exit.

He caught a flash of movement inside the sliding glass doors at the back. The house was filling with smoke, and there were cracking, smashing noises coming from inside as the flames took hold.

He moved sideways at a crouch, the barrel of the shotgun trained on the doors. He quickly scanned the upper windows. Nothing.

A crunch of broken glass. It took a second. Didn't seem right. Movement to his left. Bishop's bald head, through the gap in the fence, emerging from the shattered glass doors of the next-door neighbour's house.

He couldn't swing the barrel quick enough.

Crack. Crack. Crack.

Bishop was firing.

Watson felt a stinging sensation through the back of his thigh as he dived sideways. He lay on his side, extended the shotgun, and fired through the fence. Once. Racked it. Twice. A little further along. Racked it a third time. Put a load of twelve-gauge buckshot through the fence.

A loud yelp from the other side of the fence. Watson climbed to his feet, jogged to the side of the house.

A flash. Bishop ran across the other end of the path out the front of the house.

Watson fired, caught fresh air, went to move. His leg wouldn't work properly.

Fuck.

He kept going, half jogging, half hopping down the path. Not a good place to be caught if Bishop stuck his pistol back around the corner and opened up on him. He could hardly miss.

Movement further up the street. Bishop, going at full pace. Running towards the headland.

40

There was a first-aid kit in the back of his car. His left thigh was numb; the rest of his leg was aching. He sat down on the driveway, his car between him and the top of the headland. He could hear the interior of the house crackling and popping. Smoke was streaking out the downstairs windows and the door.

Watson dragged down his trousers and inspected the damage. There was a neat puncture in the outside of his thigh, about halfway between his knee and the top of his leg. It was slick and meaty, deep red, but there wasn't a lot of blood. There was a slightly larger hole, about the size of a twenty-cent piece, on the inside of his thigh. Jagged flesh protruded from the wound and what looked like tiny globules of yellow fat. He heaved into his mouth, felt faint, the world went grey.

He took a moment to steady himself and to take a quick glance up to the top of the road.

No sign of Bishop.

He squeezed a tube of antiseptic gel over the entry and exit wounds. It was cold and it reduced slightly the sharp, stinging pain arcing across his thigh. He broke open a bandage. Wound it tight around his leg. He rummaged through the kit, just to confirm there were no painkillers. An excellent day to have just flushed fifty of the best pain relievers on the planet. He shook his head and spat evil-tasting bile onto the grass.

He stood, gasped as a current of pain sparked up his thigh, his back, into his head. He fished the half-tablet of Xanax out of his pocket and swallowed it dry.

There was blood on the driveway. Not his own; he was hardly bleeding at all. Groupings of dark red droplets starting to smudge on the rain-slicked surface. He checked the shotgun. One shell left. *Fuck it.* He dropped the shottie beside the car, pulled his pistol and headed up the road.

It was blowing hard, but the rain had stopped. High grey cloud scudded on the wind above the cliff top. Heavy surf roared into the rocks below. He walked on the road, couldn't do uneven surfaces. He struggled to focus on anything other than the screeching, tearing pain ripping through the top of his thigh.

She was strong. He had both hands wrapped tight around Andrea's throat but she simply shoved him back, ramming both hands into his chest. He stumbled slightly, and when she pushed him again he went down hard on his arse.

She stood over him; he could see gleaming teeth, shining eyes, disgust.

'Leave him,' he heard Alison shriek, and then felt a hand on his shoulder. 'Just leave him alone, you fucking bitch.'

Andrea took a step back towards the cliff edge, arms folded.

'I should have known,' she said dismissively. 'I should have known that you'd both be the same.'

Even through the opiate haze, he could tell that there was a problem with his back. There was a hot pain shooting up his spine, into his neck.

'Why can't you just leave us alone?' Alison cried.

'Because I can't have a pathetic, weak drug addict hanging around if I'm going for the top job, Alison.' She spat her daughter's name. 'Do you know how many times I've had to intervene already to save his useless fucking hide?'

Watson leant forward, trying to get up.

'We can go somewhere,' Alison said. 'We can go away. We don't have to have any part of you and your . . . job.'

'Ha.' Andrea shook her head. 'You have absolutely no idea.' *She turned slightly, silhouetted against the moonlit sky, the breeze ruffling her hair. She tucked a strand neatly back behind her ear.*

'It's time you knew anyway,' she said.

The blood trail didn't lessen. If anything, it was getting thicker. Random dots and splashes interspersed with thick little puddles. It gave Watson a spurt of energy.

He's hit bad. I hope the motherfucker's suffering.

His leg was going numb, seizing up, he was having to drag it along.

The headland road ended in a wide turning circle at the top. A small, grassed public reserve backed onto the thick bush leading out to the cliff top. There was no sign of Bishop. Slick red dots led the way into the reserve.

The wind had picked up, scattering the clouds. Watson heard a chopper thumping away in the distance. Maybe a rescue on the other side of the river or out to sea.

There was a muddy path leading into the almost impenetrable bush. Watson propped, scared, peering into the green.

A drop of blood had left a crimson smear spreading across the surface of a water-filled pothole on the path.

He could just sit tight. Wait him out. Bishop was bleeding bad, out there on the cliff top.

'Did you ever wonder where your father went, Craig? Why he took off?'

'Oh, Mum,' Alison moaned.

Craig started to shake.

'Watto. Legend. King of the kids. Oh, but not for you, was he, Craig? No, he was too busy for that. He was a ladies' man.'

'Mum, stop it, you're being ridiculous,' Alison yelled, gripping his shoulders hard.

Craig's heart was pounding against his ribs; he was having trouble breathing.

'He had women everywhere. He looked so good in a uniform. So tanned, so fit, so . . . so fucking hot. At least, that's what this stupid little sixteen-year-old thought.'

'No!' Craig raged.

He stepped onto the path. He could only see five metres ahead before the trail twisted to the left. He hugged that side of the track, concentrating on taking one step at a time. Freezing droplets fell down his neck, running icicles down his spine. He eased his way around the curve, the Glock leading.

A big splash of blood and a broken branch lying in the middle of the path.

A crack of light through the green. Crashing surf, the thick smell of salt.

What was that?

Whimpering. Not far away.

Crack! A single shot.

Watson threw himself sideways into the bush at the side of the track.

'Don't come any closer.' The voice was high-pitched, phlegmy. 'I don't want to shoot a cop. I never wanted to shoot a cop.'

Watson was in the mud, his leg scorching. Black-and-white bolts of pain shooting through his brain pan. He blacked out momentarily, came back.

There was shuffling at the end of the track. He pulled the trigger. The bullet zinged off the surface of the track and vaporised the limb of a small tree on the other side of the path.

'What are you doing?' The voice had a panicky edge to it. 'I never meant to hurt anybody.'

Watson pulled his face out of the mud. Shook his head.

'And he fucking used me.' Andrea's eyes were blazing. 'Strung me along for months. Told me all sorts of lies. Even shared me with a couple of his mates. And then, when he realised what had happened, what he had done, he dropped me, like a sack of garbage.'

'No!' Alison screamed. Craig felt her hands leave his shoulders. 'No!' she screamed again. She climbed to her feet, facing her mother.

'Yes,' Andrea said, almost triumphant. 'I was pregnant with you, Alison.'

Watson couldn't stand up. He needed a distraction.

'What about the car, Bishop? What about Laura Sweeney and her father? You hurt them.'

'That was an accident. I never meant to hurt them. I just needed to stop them. Talk to them.' Watson heard him spit. 'It's not like you think. It was different with Laura—and her old man, he was bent. I was just going to pull them over, talk to them, do a deal. But they wouldn't stop.'

Watson dragged himself another metre along the path. He could see daylight, a patch of blue through the trees.

'The girls,' Watson yelled. 'What the fuck were you thinking?'

Alison took a step past him, towards her mother. He tried to rise. A deep spasm hit him in the small of his back.

'That's right, Alison—he's your half-fucking-brother.'

'The girls. They were fucking into it. Don't let 'em tell you any different.'

Watson climbed to his knees. He saw movement through the bush. He tried to stand, but years of opiate abuse had diminished his natural ability to control pain. His vision swam; a dark figure filled his vision at the end of the path.

Andrea unfolded her arms as her daughter silently approached, but Alison simply brushed her mother's side and kept walking. Straight off the edge of the cliff.

41

His vision cleared, just enough. Bishop was there at the end of the path, squat, muscular, shiny bald, the pistol in his right hand pointed at Watson's head. His left hand, wrapped in a blood-soaked bandage, held his left cheek where a shotgun pellet had opened him up from the corner of his mouth to the base of his ear, like an axe wound.

'You shouldn't have come here,' Bishop said. He squeezed the trigger.

The explosion was ear-shattering. The bush and the left side of Bishop's chest erupted in slow motion. Watson watched him spin, his pistol turning somersaults in the air as he went around.

Watson turned. Larissa stood at the corner of the track, panting. She grunted in satisfaction, racked the shotgun, expended the empty shell case. Ellie elbowed her out of the way, strode forward fast, firing.

Bishop doubled over, kept spinning, slow-mo. Ellie fired again, stepped forward, fired again, again, again, out onto the cliff top. Her last round exploded the top of Bishop's shiny dome, leaving a faint pink mist hovering over the cliff top until it was snatched away by the wind.

Andrea didn't even call her daughter's name. She stood frozen, silent.

Craig had no recollection of her leaving the cliff top, no recollection of anything until he woke up in the back of an ambulance, sirens screaming, panicked voices, paramedics reviving him with a shot of Narcan.

'We're not here to judge,' they said. They had seen a thousand overdoses. 'No one needs to know.'

He just didn't have the words.

'Oh shit, Craig.' Larissa jammed the shotgun up against a small bush and knelt down at his side. 'What's happened? Are you shot?'

It took a moment. 'No. Yes. Just a little bit,' he said. 'My leg.'

'Where're your pills?' she asked.

'I dumped 'em. Flushed 'em down the drain.'

Ellie walked slowly back towards him, holstering her pistol. Serious eyes.

'I can get up,' Watson said. 'Just give me an arm.'

They huddled together, the three of them, down on the track.

'You scared the shit out of us, you selfish prick,' Ellie said, gently placing both arms under his shoulders, helping him to his feet.

He gasped, tried to put some weight on his left leg. No go.

'Can you walk?' Ellie asked.

'Just hold me up,' he said.

Larissa wiped her face on his shoulder, sniffed.

'That was you on the chopper,' he said.

'We just dropped Tayla and Shaun off and came straight back,' Larissa told him.

Putting any weight on his left leg was excruciating, but Watson felt an urgent need to get out to the cliff top. To make sure it was over.

'What?' Ellie said.

'Just . . . take me out there,' he said. 'I need to go out onto the cliff.'

With Ellie and Larissa taking his weight, one on each side, he hopped out onto the narrow rock platform. The heavy grey clouds were breaking up and being carried south by the wind. There was a long, clear streak of bright, blue sky where the white-flecked ocean met the horizon.

There was a heavy squawk of static. Larissa grabbed at a walkie-talkie clipped to her belt. She pressed the receiver and spoke but was met with garbled words and rushing static.

She walked a circle around the platform, sending but not receiving. She got a weak signal as she backed onto the path. 'I'd better see what this is about,' she said. She continued further down the track to where the reception was clearer.

Ellie eased out from under his arm, still holding on to him but standing where she could look into his face.

'The memory drives you took from Bishop's house,' she said quickly.

'What?'

'The two memory sticks you took out of the shoebox with the photos.'

'Yeah, what about them?' he said. A spurt of acid hit his guts.

'There's some photos on them. Me and Caroline. It was a one-off. He was there.'

Watson got a flash. Two dead. Executed. He looked into Ellie's eyes.

Her face softened. 'You'll just have to trust me.'

He didn't move. He could hear Larissa finishing up on the radio somewhere down the track behind them, making arrangements with the chopper.

He fished into his pocket, found the two flash drives and handed them over.

They glittered momentarily in the pale sunlight as they sailed out over the cliff.

42

Larissa and Ellie had a car parked at the top of the headland road. Watson crawled into the back and stretched out full length with the doors open, trying to keep his leg as straight as possible. Larissa sat in the front passenger seat while Ellie walked in circles around the headland, talking the chopper into landing up there on the small grassy reserve.

Larissa turned, reached over from the front seat and took Watson's hand. He held it gratefully in both his hands and tried a smile. She looked at him seriously and said, 'I meant what I said back there, you know?'

He pretended to know what she was talking about but not convincingly enough, it seemed.

'You don't know what I'm talking about, do you?'

He shook his head.

'On the beach last night. With Shaun?'

His face brightened. His colour returned with the memory.

'We're all good?' he said, hardly daring to hope.

She nodded. 'I think so,' she said, squeezing his hand, smiling.

———

The chopper was a blur of pain and noise and IV lines. The impact of the bullet had liquified some of the muscle in the back of his thigh, snapped his hamstring. The paramedics couldn't quite believe he had managed to walk the two hundred or so metres to the top of the headland.

It was two weeks and two operations before he regained any sense of clarity. He was back home, on crutches. He was having trouble sleeping, but they told him that was to be expected.

The text messages had stopped the day after his return. He was in the process of deleting them. Maybe it was the fact that he was completely drug-free except for a course of antibiotics. Maybe it was the first time he had spent the time reading all the messages in succession.

There was a familiar ring to them.

You can't hide, maggot.

Watch your back, faggot.

Roper, his boss from Central. The bane of his existence. The man who had sworn he was going to make Watson's life a living hell. That he was going to do everything within his power to force Watson to quit the force. Maggot. Faggot. Every second word that left the man's mouth was like that. Who the fuck spoke like that anymore? And what the fuck was his problem?

He didn't bother asking.

He had become something of a minor celebrity since returning to civilisation. The Hero Cop who had rescued a fellow officer from the clutches of a depraved abuser. The Man of the Moment who had solved the baffling riddle of the murdered councillor and his daughter on a country road. The Brave Officer who had survived a shootout with a crazed, corrupt fellow policeman.

Serious questions were being asked in the back rooms of state parliament about the botched and aborted flood mitigation program. There had been a catastrophic failure in oversight.

Watson was summoned to a meeting in a government high-rise with glorious views out over the harbour. He was commended. He was applauded. He was told that the evidence pointing to the rorting and theft involved in the Gloster Region Flood Mitigation Plan could not be located. That it would not be located. Ever. And that if, and only if, he kept the matter under wraps, so to speak, then the locals and the farmers negatively impacted by the recent floods would be compensated. Generously.

He agreed to the terms on one condition: *There is a certain Detective Sergeant Roper . . .*

———

He was detoxing, purging. He had plenty of time on his hands. A month's leave. Psychological counselling. He had been pumped full of morphine on the chopper out of Gloster. The drug tests taken as a matter of routine after a police-involved shooting were therefore inconclusive.

He had been back to Gloster once. Ellie knew the score; after a happy half-hour catch-up she left him and Larissa alone. They spent a quiet afternoon together, talking and walking. Since his return to Sydney they texted, emailed, chatted on the phone. Larissa was coming down to visit him the following weekend.

———

He found it in a desk drawer: the memory stick Andrea had given to Alison. The one Alison had handed to him the night when she called it quits.

He hadn't looked at it. He remembered Alison told him the videos were of him and her mother's 'friends'. Andrea had been careful to make sure she couldn't be identified or implicated, he supposed.

He was on the mend physically. The operations on his leg had been declared a complete success. Mentally he was coping, just. But he knew that if he really wanted to start afresh, with a clean slate, he would have to face his past.

He plugged the memory stick into his laptop. There were three files. Videos.

The first was just him, naked on a nondescript motel bed. Strapped down. Being abused. It was only ninety seconds, enough. He was sweating by the end of it, heart rate up a bit, nothing to worry about.

The second video was only sixty seconds. The camera was angled over his shoulder. Andrea's friend Cynthia, supine, eyes closed, mouth agape, heaving while he thrust into her furiously. The camera moving forward, closer to the back of his head. A sudden jerking motion, out of focus momentarily as a hand covered his mouth, and then Andrea, unseen behind the camera, went to work.

He was flushed, hollow. He wiped his eyes, walked to the kitchen and poured himself a glass of water. Hesitated over whether to watch the third one.

He took a moment. Staring down into the water-filled tumbler sitting under the tap in the kitchen sink. Watching his rippling reflection.

What?

He played the second video again. Cynthia's head rocking back, her hands clawing at the lounge, her neck straining, her skinny tits bouncing. The camera moving, descending close up behind him and then—*there*—the mirror on the wall above Cynthia's head. Andrea standing behind him, snarling, barebreasted with a massive, strap-on dildo swinging from her lower waist. Andrea shaking a pill from a small prescription pill bottle, the camera descending further. Andrea, forcing his head back and shoving the pill into his mouth. Andrea, her pink tongue touching her top lip as she leant in and rammed home the dildo from behind.

43

It came as a surprise to no one. The press conference was called for 11 a.m. in the press centre at Parliament House. Full capacity, all the news channels represented. There'd been a meeting of the party caucus that morning. The challenge was on. There'd been a leadership spill. Rumours about a cover-up had been circulating for weeks. Andrea had capitalised on her daughter's death, garnered long-term public sympathy as the brave grieving mother, and put her hand up for the top job.

Craig flashed his police ID at the door. Showed security his thick A4 envelope containing nothing but papers. A thick wad of colour prints. He limped to a seat in the second row.

The place went nuts when Andrea led an entourage of serious suits towards the microphone-sprouting lectern at the front of the room. Cameras snapped, whirred, clicked. Shouted questions. Harsh white light. The crowd heaved forward.

Andrea, immaculate, waited for silence. Confidently read a brief prepared statement.

Fifty-seven to fifty-four. She had won the day. Humble. Proud. Moving forward.

He wasn't sure whether she caught a flash of him there, relaxed behind the blinding intensity. Maybe. He saw a brief flicker.

He waited until the end.

'Just one more,' the bespectacled press secretary said. 'Yes, you.' He pointed at Craig, who'd had his hand up as soon as the floor was opened to questions.

He caught a quick nervous tic at the corner of her mouth. The flash of a golden teardrop at her ear.

'I have some snapshots, some prints, I'd like to hand around first,' he began. 'Then I want to talk about Alison.'

About the author

Born in Sydney, John Byrnes moved to the Mid North Coast of New South Wales in 2012. He has a broad range of employment and life experience having spent time in the Australian Army, worked fishing trawlers out of Darwin, worked bars and doors in pubs and clubs all over Australia, and somehow ended up with an Economics Degree. When he is not writing or pondering the darkness within men's souls he works part-time in financial services.